THE GREAT DAYS

Eli Brown lives and writes
in Oakland, California. He
received his M.F.A. in Fiction
Writing from Mills College.
His poetry has appeared in
The Cortland Review and
*Homewrecker: An Adultery
Reader*. *The Great Days* is
his first novel.

THE GREAT DAYS

A NOVEL

ELI BROWN

BOAZ PUBLISHING COMPANY
Albany, California

Boaz Publishing Company
968 Ordway Street
Albany, CA 94706.
For more information: www.boazpublishing.com

Library of Congress Cataloging-in-Publication Data

Brown, Eli, 1975-
  The great days : a novel / Eli Brown.
  p. cm.
  ISBN 978-1-893448-05-6 (alk. paper)
1. Future life--Fiction. 2. Religious fiction. I. Title.

PS3602.R697G74 2008
813'.6--dc22

                                          2008016274

Printed in the United States of America
Designed by Elizabeth Vahlsing

For my parents, who have never stopped giving.

Acknowledgements

I owe my health and happiness to my family and friends. Thanks to the following people who were instrumental to the completion of this book: Sarah Steinberg, David Goldstone, Elmaz Abinader, Anna Mantzaris, Michael Gross, Mia Bray, Laurel Goldman, Bruce McAllister, Students and Faculty of Mills College, WitchCreek Arts, Shannon Klohr, Judy Bloch, and Katie Faulkner. I'm especially indebted to Julie Bennett, Tonya Hersch, Leonard Chang and Laurie Fox.

Jesse,

I can't tell you what it's like to be near him. Do you remember feeling safe? Papa gives us shelter while the rest of the world runs around setting things on fire.

We're simple people growing chard in the desert, but we will change the world. This will be the last letter I send. Keep your eye out for the signs, they will start soon. The next time you hear from me, war will be a thing of the past, greed and illness will have disappeared, the whole world will be speaking a new, unified language. World peace is just the beginning. Every thought, sensation, action will bring pleasure, not on some cloud somewhere, but here, on this earth, in this body. You'll be able to govern your own genetic triggers, play them like a keyboard just by thinking about it. That's what the other 85 percent of the brain was designed to do. No more unconscious living. A new language designed not to bind thought but to free it, without rules of grammar. A palette for innovation. Real freedom of the mind. The entire globe will combine their efforts—free, clean energy, eradication of the last of the diseases. I know it's hard to imagine. That's part of why it has taken so long to get this close, a failure of human imagination. But we are close. I'm writing to tell you we're close. It will happen in our lifetimes. But there is a lot of work to do before then, many hurdles. No one escapes the cycle of birth and death until Eden is restored. That's the scope of our effort.

You're probably still angry with me, and I know

you still feel guilty about the dog. What you can't see is that everything has already been forgiven. It's all going to be bright. What you have wanted all your life, what every person in the history of the world has felt missing is right around the corner.

Please don't worry about me. I'm surrounded by love. This is the best decision I've ever made. Tell Mom I love her. She'll see soon. You both will.

Love,
August

Standing in the darkness with the others, August touched his face to be sure his eyes were open. There was a steady current against him, the ocean of night air receding from the coming sun. Something dry and frantic scrambled over his sandal—a cockroach, a lizard. He could see the others now, like gray pillars around him. It was the beginning of the world; everything was ash and paper.

The sun split the clay line of the horizon and rose, a bubble of lava. They knelt, lowering their heads. *Blessed is the Eye of the Lord, which sees all. Blessed is the Breath of the Lord, which nourishes the world. Blessed is Papa Kurma Narshima, the Voice of the Lord. May we be granted true-sight, true-voice, true-heart, and true-mind that we might serve the will of the Lord. They bowed. Blessed is the Eye of the Lord...*

Their tongues and chapped lips caught tiny sweepings: desiccated sage seed, the almost-nothing carapace of a gnat, long dead, still floating along. They bowed, row after row, curling into themselves, clenching their bodies like fists, their shaved heads brown as knuckles. The world was already bright. The desert tightened, offering up the last molecules of the night dew.

Twenty cycles of chanting, then silent meditation for forty minutes, the coasting silence carrying them. August loved the finality of it, the decision they all made at the same time to stop the noise and have peace. In the silence, a hawk made a sound like a fingernail scraping the enamel of the sky. They were supposed to consider the end of all suffering.

The early morning air beginning to hum from the horizon filled August with blooming energy; he was in love with all of them, their doughy, half-awake faces. Their bodies perfumed the air; their soft, sour breath mixed with the breeze coming off the desert and the smell of oats cooking in the main-hall.

The tiny bell was struck and the chanting swirled around them again:... *serve the will of the Lord*. It echoed off the distant mountains: the earth singing with them. The others would continue the morning mutter for another twenty cycles, but it was time for August to go meet Papa.

When he stood, his unfurling back ached. For a moment he was dizzy. He stepped away from the group, a match fallen from the box. As he walked toward Papa's trailers half asleep, the river of chanting lifted and carried him. There was something he was supposed to do today, something important. The sun was like a sweaty hand on his neck. His right sandal was loose so he shuffled every few steps to keep it from falling off. The sand sifted in under his toes. He remembered: he had to greet the NewFaces.

The compound was eighteen acres of fields and a scattering of buildings surrounded by a wide necklace of chain-link fencing to keep coyotes and hares out. As he walked through it, he slipped into the baked paths that spiraled through the compound.

It was summer and already the day had become viscous with heat. The same sun that haunted Solomon sent its fury down on the crazed sand between the warehouses and trailers. It would hammer on the shaved heads of the initiates, bleaching the straw hats that snagged on the stubble of their scalps. The flagpole at the entrance gate was rigid as a fork upright in a bowl of thick gruel, but the flag itself sagged, the blue Center spiral hidden in drapes of breathless canvas.

August trudged past the crops: tomatoes, cucumbers, peppers, kale, chard, basil. Every day the plants threatened to die, drooping their parched leaves near the ground, only to rally at night, lifting themselves again toward the east. The monstrous tendrils of the melon patch had outgrown their grids and now offered watermelons and cantaloupes side by side like undetonated artillery. On the northern perimeter, he passed the pile of stones that had been pulled from the fields, now home to chola lizards that swelled like corpses in the heat.

Summer kept everyone in a reverent silence. After six years August was still surprised by the heat's presence, so merciless it seemed almost deliberate. The air became a heavy drape pierced only by the siren of the cicadas, smothering any excessive movement or bodily urge. Metal objects became rabid: the blades on the hoes and shovels; the latch on the door of the generator shed where the engine and its can of gasoline slept; the brass faucet glinting behind the main-hall that seared any fingertips that grazed it. The chain-link perimeter bit like an electric fence. The oxygen seemed to flee to the upper atmosphere, leaving the initiates to gasp like fish in the heavier gases. At the toilet sheds the flies seemed drugged, pinned against the wood, unwilling to move unless touched, then bumbling slowly through the syrupy air. Reality warped, assuming a pliable sheen.

Near the middle of the compound, past the modified

warehouse where the initiates slept, past the crooked boards of the toilet sheds, past the old well and the main-hall, there were eight white trailers arranged in a tight cluster: Papa's quarters.

In the middle of that octagon, Papa was bathing. The tub was an old one, big as a cow with a great rusted patch on one corner where the enamel was knocked away. The claw feet had sunk into the sand. When August came forward, kneeling to bow, Papa was completely submerged, except for his knees pushing out of the water, stubborn and white as icebergs. August rested his forehead on the sand, waiting, trying not to doze. He heard the water bursting as Papa came up. "Namaste, August."

"Namaste, Papa."

August looked up to see Papa smiling down on him, wet as a newborn with an ancient face. Papa's hair grew so quickly! Already there was a thick silver fuzz bristling over the splendid magnet of his skull. August rubbed the base of his own skull where the dull angle of bone lifted the hairs to scratch reassuringly against his palm. Papa's blue eyes didn't waiver, and again August had the feeling of being discovered, as if everyone else in his life had been looking just past his shoulder.

Once, as a child, he had hidden in the cabinet under the sink while his mother and sister called for him, listening to their desperate phone conversations with his father, with the police: *I don't know, he was outside, I don't know*. His memory of it was slightly artificial, like black-and-white films that have been retouched with anemic pastels, because it was a story his mother had told and retold during holidays; his Mull mother whom he had not seen for six years, who suffered, brought him into the world of suffering, fed him Mull food and clothed his body, but did not know how to give him peace. Papa knew exactly where he was hiding, and was asking him to come out. It was an honor to be receiving that gaze from the most important spiritual figure since Christ, the cultural catalyst who would bring real lasting change to the entire planet. The Founder. August could feel himself being exposed as Papa's true-sight lit his every cell.

August knew that there were people who had met Papa, yet were not impressed, who had explained the miracles in terms of sleight of hand or science, who called the revelations mass hysteria. He also knew that those people had not allowed themselves to be looked at in this way. They had not been vulnerable or brave enough to be *seen*. They thought Papa was merely a charismatic man. They were like children covering their own eyes to disappear.

"Do you have a response?" Papa's body glowed with health, the silver hair that sprouted from his arms, the red folds of skin where his elbows bent. His thick wrists were evidence of an enormous vent of energy inside him, an eternally flowing spring of vitality. His wet fingers rested on the edge of the tub. August saw again that his fingernails were broad and flat as coins.

"Yes, Papa."

Papa brought a sagging yellow sponge up to his neck and scrubbed under his jaw.

August said, "Krishna's skin was the color of water."

Papa smiled, wringing the sponge out slowly. "This color?"

"Yes, Papa."

"Really?"

"Yes."

"How old are you, August?"

"Twenty-five."

"A quarter century of struggle. Keep working on it. This is an important koan for you."

"Yes, Papa." August sighed with relief; this was a talking day. In the last year Papa's voice had begun to evaporate. It came in waves, each silence a little longer, a little more profound than the last. It was a part of Papa's final evolution. Still it made August uneasy.

Sometimes when Papa wanted to tell him something but didn't have the words, his eyes became terrible to look at, like the fluttering of an insect still alive in solid amber. It was August's job to look into those eyes and interpret. August read to Papa, interpreted his orders, gave lectures when necessary, and acted as intermediary. He oversaw the initiation of NewFaces and managed Center business in dozens of miscellaneous ways, but his interpreting duties were most important. Papa must be understood.

As Papa's silences became more frequent, August learned to watch his body. He doted on him, pouring water or tea as soon as it was needed, rubbing Papa's feet, and watching for signs of impatience or anger: held breath, or the eyelids closed a little too long when he blinked.

Today, it was clear, Papa wouldn't need interpretation. He stood suddenly and was, for a second, a waterfall, then a sixty-two-year-old naked man, slick and gleaming in the sun. Before lowering his head, August was eye level with the gingerroot of Papa's penis. Papa kicked at the water, found the bone of soap he was looking for, and lowered himself again, sinking back into the tub until August could see only his ruddy feet pressed flat against the white.

Papa said, "I want to continue with the Gita. But first we should have a chapter from *Berkman's*." August rose, heading for the screen door that hung crookedly between two sun-bleached paper lanterns covered with fading Sanskrit: the study-trailer. He could smell Papa's breakfast. He knew Mother Jessica would be in the tiny kitchenette of a nearby trailer cooking miso soup, fried potatoes, and tortillas.

The other Mothers would be waking up soon, each in her own trailer, looking out to see their bathing husband. August leaned into the shade of the trailer—already the temperature difference was enough to give his neck goose bumps—and grabbed two books from the shelf near the door. When first chosen as a Center initiate, August had been given a small list of things to bring. *Only the following necessary personal items: tooth brush, pillow, eyeglasses, one pair of tennis shoes or hiking boots.* Books had not been on the list, so when August became Papa's reader he was surprised to find that Papa had a library that took up an entire trailer. Most of the collection consisted of sacred texts from various religions. There were also shelves of Mull knowledge, including two sets of encyclopedias.

Before an irrigation specialist was initiated, the crops had been watered by a system of channels extrapolated from diagrams in books like *Water Garden, Backyard Fountains*, which Papa provided. There were no novels, no fiction of any kind. It occurred to August for the first time that no fiction meant no lies; it was a library of Truth.

As August shut the door he said, "True-books." He was grateful to be on the inside, past the sparkling charm of the Monterey Chapter crowd, past the initiation, close to Papa, orbiting him like a moon.

The Physics volume of *Berkman's Encyclopedia of Scientific Understanding* was a thick book with a tooled-leather binding and thin gold script on the cover. August rested it on an upturned bucket and began to read where they had left off: "'Uncertainty is a measure of—'"

"Skip ahead." Papa was ringing the sponge around each of his fingers.

"'The ramifications of this principle puts limits on what we can hope to understand through observation. The very act of seeing spoils the veracity of the phenomenon.'"

By the height of the sun, it was approaching six o'clock. They were running late. The others would be finishing morning meal, usually a bowl of soaked oats with pickled daikon. They would wait until Papa addressed them before beginning work-practice. Some would spend the day building a shed over the new well; a handful would stay in the kitchen or wander the compound on miscellaneous tasks. Most would head out to the fields. Prior to his appointment as reader, August had worked the crops. It had been difficult; even with a hat the sun bounced off the streams of water, burning his face from below. By evening meal his back was usually bent, numb and rigid as a cane.

As he read, he felt himself blush with humility and gratitude to have been selected for this special position. Seattle Chapter had published one of August's poems in its monthly publication, *True-Mind*:

> No *wings, no feathers, no song,*
> *no nest, no color*
> *what a beautiful bird.*

before Papa, flavor
after Papa, nourishment.

Papa must have read it, because a week later he told August to report directly to him in the mornings. That had been nearly three years ago. August felt he had shed a heavy skin. He was strong and clean and good at these duties; he had been built for them, his heart led him through each day like a dog pulling on a leash. All of the trouble in high school and college, the suspensions, the disappointed professors— *You have so much promise. One of the sharpest students I've had and yet*—all of that was washed away by this appointment. It made sense; something intuitive in him had been resisting the smoke and mirrors of the Mull world, then Papa illuminated his path, leading him to his true task.

"'… Even under the most rigorous scrutiny, particles and events yield a limited set of information. Additional details aren't hidden, they simply aren't there.'"

Mother Jessica came out of the trailer holding a plate of food. Behind her, Mother Star brought towels and Papa's sky-blue vestment. August continued to read while they wrapped Papa in towels and kissed his hands, their white robes glaring around the edges of the page. Papa stepped from the tub and the parched soil around his feet darkened with water.

"That's enough Mull science—now the Gita, 11:12."

They rubbed Papa's body vigorously while August opened the smaller book and read: "'Seeing thus Your terrifying teeth and faces like the fire of the end of time, I lose my sense of direction and find myself nailed to the ground. Have mercy, I am lost in this vision. I see the myriad hoards rushing into Your mouth with crushed skulls caught between the tusks. As the streams toward the ocean, as moths for the candle, all people also full-speed enter Your mouth to find destruction. I cannot open my eyes, I cannot close them.'"

When Papa was dressed, August kissed each of his feet once and followed him toward the main-hall. Walking a few steps behind Papa, August remembered the haze of the morning mutter then realized with surprise that there had been no dark visions. "Most mornings," he said, "I'm still flooded with fear and nausea. They're more vivid: screaming, demonic animals."

Papa didn't slow his pace. "I know you think the LSD you took in college ruined your mind. In fact, you are just gaining true-sight. You mind is opening to hidden things."

"There is a dog that circles around me. It has a long head like an alligator skull. Hollow eyes. Its teeth spiral together, tangled in knots. It can't open its mouth—"

Papa cut him off. "The creature is a messenger from Ego. It was sent to spy and to scare you from the path. As an initiate approaches the light, Ego becomes more and more ferocious, like a cornered animal. Ignore it, it cannot hurt you. Papa will protect you. But don't feed it. It eats fear, attachment, little worries, selfish thoughts. That is why it can't open its mouth—it only eats Ego-food."

They heard singing, hundreds of voices floating into the dry air. August couldn't help but smile: this joyous music, this community of hardworking people, this magnificent man who would lead them all to perfect understanding, this strange paradise in the desert. They were almost an hour late when they stepped into the main-hall: a large warehouse that held the kitchen, twenty-four tables where the initiates ate, and the dais and podium where Papa delivered the addresses. It was still cool inside. The tables had already been cleared. Sister Melinda was standing on the stage leading the singing. She stepped down, then two hundred and fourteen initiates bowed as Papa took his place.

His voice was full today; he wouldn't need interpretation. August joined the forest of initiates gathered near the platform. As Papa raised the wide stars of his hands, there was a hush. His body was a shaft of sky blue.

"We eat just enough to sustain the body—not to feed our gluttonous appetites. When your stomach is light, your soul is having a feast! Completely satiated! That is why our simple food tastes so good!" Papa enunciated each word as if English wasn't his first language. His voice could still take August by surprise, rising up his legs, filling him with warmth and longing.

Papa pointed at Sister Rachel. "Daughter, how was the food?"

"Delicious, Papa!"

"But it's just wheat and water. Just a lump of corn muffin!"

"It was like manna, Papa."

"Papa nourishes you! If you work hard the soul becomes limber. Keep the stomach light and the soul becomes strong. This is how we practice true-joy. Today if Ego gives you trouble, ask your Brothers and Sisters for help. Say, 'I am thinking little thoughts.' There's no shame in this if you admit it, but you must ask for help. The ocean of true-mind is in community!"

August let the words peel back until they were nothing but the polished stone of Papa's voice. With the others

around him and the voice lifting him he felt his little self dissolving. Pain and worry bled out into the others. There was
nothing to think of next. He had suffered; they had all suffered so much. August raised his hands high in the air, letting
the tears come down his face. The others pressed him close
and held him up as Papa spoke. He wept so easily; a kind
smile, a single true statement could open the waters in him.

Brother Matheson was standing to his right, an enormous
man, the pumpkin of his face high above August's. He had
been a bodyguard in Hollywood before finding Papa. Now
he served as security for the Center, escorting Papa on occasional tours of the other Chapters, "greeting" uninvited visitors, and conducting redirection. He rarely spoke. When he
did he always seemed a little angry. But now, as the crowd
pressed tightly together, August felt Brother Matheson's
arms lifting high, then settling behind him, reaching out to
gather people into a communal hug. With Papa's help everyone would find serenity.

Papa was talking about the Great Days again. They were
near; patience was the key. Violence and disease would be
swept up in a sudden, greedy wind—like the gasp after a
dream of drowning. Governments would evaporate. Then
the true history of the world would begin; people would
devote themselves to the community of the earth.

Amid the frenzy of change and growing joy, August
would find his Mull mother and sister. They would jump up
when they saw him, their eyes shining the same color. He had
seen it in his mind so often it felt more like a memory than a
fantasy. Jesse and Mom. Maybe they would surprise him,
appearing out of some celebratory crowd to embrace him.
Maybe he would be a little famous, because of his role in the

transformations: Papa's right-hand man. They would have caught his face on television, though when they hugged him, they would see that it was good old August—nothing overblown—just August back from a long holy war, victorious. His father's absence would have become a forgiveness.

In this fantasy, Jesse would be weeping a little, but her subtle smile would shine from August to their mother and back again like a lighthouse beam. His mother, rubbing her eyes with the backs of her hands, would look at him fascinated, adoring. The room would be very quiet. All of them breathing and full. Maybe August would be crying too? Finally his mother would open her mouth.

"August, honey—"

"No, Mom, please, you don't need to say anything. Now that you see, now that everyone sees what we have been trying to do—"

"I had no idea. I thought I had lost you. First your father, then you. I couldn't forgive it. I was angry with God." He would go to her then, wrap his arms around her, show her that he and Papa and God had been following a plan, butterfly wings finally unfurling from the cramped, grotesque chrysalis.

Maybe he and Jessee would wander into the kitchen to make a meal together, knocking each other aside with their hips like they used to. She would tell him everything she had been doing: school, boyfriends. Then he would tell her about life in the desert—about the sand in everything, the black widows, the heat. She would shake her head. He would wave her awe away. It had been nothing, he'd say.

There was a surge of yelling and laughter, everyone was cheering. August opened his eyes. Papa couldn't be seen; the initiates had pressed forward, enveloping him. August turned to Sister Rebecca, yelling into her ear, "What did he say? I didn't hear—"

She hugged him. "Papa is taking another Mother! He's going to pick the final Mother!"

2

August woke from a nightmare of broken glass and stared into the darkness of his trailer. Trying to summon reassuring images, he found the well-worn memory of when Papa had first asked him to interpret. August had been reading to Papa for months already when he approached one morning and heard a commotion in the book trailer: a crash, Papa's voice: "No, no. No!" Then soft voices. August couldn't hear what the Mothers were saying but their tones were soothing, as if they were comforting a child.

Then another crash. When August knocked on the door there was an embarrassed silence. Then Mother Li said from inside, "Come back later." But Papa opened the door glaring. He looked like he had been in a fight: there was a welt on the side of his head near his eye and he was breathing hard. His eyes were riveted on August but seemed to move with an invisible motion like dark moons, seen from the poles, spinning furiously through their cold seasons. Mother Li's face appeared pale behind Papa's. Even as she said, "Not now, child," Papa reached down, grabbed August's shoulder and pulled him through the door. His knuckles were bleeding. The trailer was a mess; books littered the floor and the desk chair lay on its side, one leg broken cleanly off. There was a fist-sized hole in the wall near the door; pink insulation sagged out of it like flesh. On the desk were the letters

August had scrawled two weeks earlier when Papa had asked him to write the word *DESK* directly on the surface of the wood in thick black ink. August had thought it was some sort of koan.

Mother Monica was in the corner with her hands pressed tightly over her face. She removed them, shook her hair back to compose herself, then covered her face again. August had never seen a Mother cry before.

Papa gave August a book as Mother Li pushed him toward the door. "August, you need to come back later."

Papa turned on her like an animal about to bite and she stepped back with Mother Monica. He tapped the book in August's hands, watching him as if August knew what to do. August glanced over his shoulder, but Mother Li only shook her head.

August said, "Papa, I don't understand—"

"No!" Papa's fist came down like a meteor, slamming the book to the ground. August felt the wall against his back.

"Mother?" August said. Their faces were stony. Papa bent down, picked up the book, and spread it like a gutted fowl in front of August's face: the Bible.

Mother Monica's voice cracked, "This is the worst it's gotten…" Mother Li touched her arm to silence her, then all of them watched August. As August held the book, Papa flipped to the first pages, which were covered with handwritten notes. Papa pointed to a set of numbers crammed near the bottom in red ink. August recognized one of them right away, and recited it from memory. "And Moses said unto Jehovah, 'O, my Lord, I am not a man of words, for I am heavy of mouth, and slow of tongue.'"

Papa's face lit up. He turned, beaming at the Mothers

before tapping the notes again. His smile was like a fissure threatening to crack the room in half. August turned to the correct page and finished the passage: "'And the anger of Jehovah burned against Moses, and He said, "Is not Aaron the Levite thy brother? I have known that he speaketh well, I am with thy mouth and with his mouth, he is to thee for a mouth, and thou art to him for God."'"

Papa had closed his eyes, nodding, and August rushed to find the next passage. "'...thy tongue I cause to cleave unto thy palate...'" The Mothers were hugging each other. August continued to read, something gathering in his chest like a thundercloud: "'...thou shalt be silent and not able to speak... And he was making signs to them, and continued dumb.'" August flipped the pages. "'...And I lifted up mine eyes and looked, and behold, his body was like a chrysolite, and his face as the appearance of lightning, and his eyes as torches of fire.... And as he was speaking I set my face toward the ground, and I became dumb.'"

When August finished his face was hot. Papa was looking in his direction, though his eyes were glazed. The Mothers stared coldly. Hadn't they heard? Papa had spoken through the texts: the revelation was rendering him speechless. August would have to rise to speak for him. The cloud in his chest glittered with lightning as he closed the Bible softly.

Papa blinked, looking around as if he had fallen asleep on his feet. He swayed and said, "Okay? Yes, then." The Mothers yelped, rushing to him. He leaned hard against Mother Li.

She said, "He's coming out of it," and waved August away. August looked for Papa's permission to go, but Papa had turned, the back of his neck shiny with sweat.

Now it was just the way things were. When Papa couldn't talk, August spoke for him.

Soothed by that memory, August had started to fall asleep again when he heard the distant hum. It was just a rattle coming from the mountains and he hoped it was a commercial plane. When it clawed closer, he knew that in a few moments the entire compound would be awake, shouting and grabbing at one another in the dark. It came every few months to take photos and to harass them, a mechanical tornado sending sand into their eyes, blowing the windows open. The Mothers would shepherd the initiates into the main-hall like a hoard of refugees until the hellish thing disappeared again. August stood up. It had never come at night before.

By the time he had pulled his clothes on, it was near enough to rock his trailer. The door tore from his grip and swung open. The helicopter was directly above him. The men inside were invisible behind the light. Were they looking at him through the scopes of their weapons? August jumped to the ground, running for the main-hall with the machine rearing and swiveling above him. Sand bit against his skin and he covered his face with his hands.

The wind sucked him back, then threw him forward. As he fell, something bit him hard beneath the shoulder blade, a cracking pain. He couldn't breathe. Why had they shot him? Would it be a massacre? He rolled to a stop and tried to get back on his feet but immediately he was lost in the vortex. He couldn't figure out which way to run. The pain spread into his ribs. *Please, Papa.* Would he die in that unbearable lens of light and dust, the Movement's first martyr? He made a blind lurch in one direction, then another, ridiculous, rodent-like, trying to make himself difficult to track.

Please, please. He caught a shadow, the memory of a shape in the corner of his vision. He went for it headlong.

Eyes pinched shut, he heard the tones of the chanting before he could really make out the hall. Their hopeful voices grew against the horror of noise above him. He touched the wall, found the door, and fell inside in a flurry of sand. Immediately, the initiates guided him; they had been waiting. As his eyes adjusted to the dimmer light, he saw, in the middle of the hall, an enormous nest of people holding hands and chanting. Papa was somewhere in the middle: their collective heart.

Reaching behind to feel his wound he smiled when he felt not a hole but a welt. It must have been a rock cast by the wind. Ignoring the pain, he filled his lungs and sang as loudly as he could. Their voices filled the shelter until the storm outside was broken by the power of their prayer; at dawn the helicopter puttered away and the initiates collapsed in a heap, praising Papa.

At lunch the curtain bisecting the main-hall had been drawn aside to allow the air to circulate. The tables were crowded. August recognized the scene from elementary school: all of the children sitting at their meals behaving well, spooning the food from identical plates. Then, too, it was the same cafeteria as juvenile hall, and the same pool of whispers that floated above the dining tent at the SunRise retreat after his breakdown in college. Only these weren't children, they weren't criminals or depressed lost souls; these were his Brothers and Sisters, two hundred and fourteen fighters, creators of the future.

Most of the initiates talked softly over their bowls of oats, though one table rocked with squeals of laughter. Brother Monkey was entertaining the children again. He had pulled his shirt up over his big mouth like a turtle and covered his eyes with spoons. The boys, Tad and Hunter, both about five, yelped and writhed every time Brother Monkey leered at them. Little Sister Melody was ten, and pretended to be too old for his clowning; nevertheless she watched him out of the corner of her eye as she ate. Then she giggled, a chunk of food launching from her mouth. Brother Monkey occasionally made even Papa laugh. He had managed now to hide himself entirely under his shirt. The spoons came up like antennae, twitching and scanning the children's faces.

August was usually annoyed by Brother Monkey's antics but he didn't want to hear more speculation about who the next Mother would be. *Did Papa tell you? Who would you guess?* Brother Monkey, at least, didn't gossip. The final Mother, the final revelation—things were moving so quickly! It meant the Great Days were even closer than he had hoped.

August acknowledged Brother Monkey as an elder by greeting him before sitting down with his bowl: "Namaste, Brother." Brother Monkey didn't return the greeting. Instead the silver antennae popped up startled, then receded like a snail's. August sat and smiled at the children. "Namaste, little ones."

"Namaste, Brother August," they cooed in unison. Their bowls were dotted with the muddy remains of oats,

cinnamon, and raisins. As the only children they were allot-
ted more luxuries than the other initiates. They could help
with work-practice if they wanted to. Otherwise they tended
to wander the Center amusing themselves. The boys threw
rocks and tasted different kinds of dirt while Melody usually
followed the Mothers around.

From beneath his shirt, Brother Monkey began to hum a
hypnotic tune, which August recognized but couldn't place.
The two antennae clicked together, swaying like dance part-
ners. August had begun to think that Brother Monkey might
be a little too cracked to survive on the outside. Here, under
Papa's guidance, he was able to work toward the Great Days
with the rest of them. When the first well began to fail and
Papa was urging them to conserve even more water, Brother
Monkey had raised his hand and asked, "But without water,
how am I gonna get rid of this stubborn ring-around-the-col-
lar?" It had gotten him a stern warning from Brother
Matheson, though August saw that Brother Monkey's gift
was to put things in perspective, turning a difficult matter on
its head. Though he was tangled up inside with old television
jingles and prone to mischief, he was fiercely devoted to
Papa. Brother Monkey was always the first to pick up a hoe
and the last to put it down.

August now touched him lightly on his lower back. "How
are you Brother?"

Brother Monkey whistled the tune louder and August recognized it: "Peter and the Wolf." Was that his answer?

Maybe Brother Monkey was mocking him. People
thought August had no sense of humor; it went along with
his reputation for being intelligent. August felt like he knew
the secret passages that led him to a conclusion before other

people, though he tended to miss important things. When others laughed, August was usually still waiting for the punch line.

He did laugh when things worked themselves out in perfect ways. When God's hand was so clearly guiding things that he could just let go, letting life bubble up and out. He laughed at birds and children, no, not *at* them, but because of them. He cried for the same reasons. He sat next to Brother Monkey sometimes to balance himself, knowing that the others would see two ciphers: one too sober, the other a clown.

As August began to eat, his body leaned hard toward the food. This was part of the training: to eat what was put in front of him without wanting something different. There was a pricking under his tongue as the saliva found its way into his mouth. He liked the plainness of the oats. He savored the lucidity of hunger, and enjoyed turning Ego away with just enough to keep the body moving: *This is all you get—just this watery mush—I can live on this forever, how long will you last?*

Addressing the kids, August lifted his spoon and said, "There's a whole spectrum of tastes humming just beneath the old Mull palate. They used to be drowned out by the four brutes of the tongue: salt, sour, sweet, bitter. But Papa shows us how a simple diet cleans you out. Then we really start smelling the world, like a tea around us: steeping sage, cactus flowers, little birds, lizards, the chalk and iron of the sand. These oats, for example, are passive, cooling, slightly woody like moss on your tongue."

Melody wrinkled her nose and said, "Where did your scar come from?" She watched August's cheek as if she expected the scar itself to answer.

"I already told you about that, remember?"

She shoved her bowl away and crossed her arms. "Tell me again," she said. The fuzz on her skull was so thin and blonde it was almost invisible. August knew she wished she could grow her hair out like the Mothers.

"It was a dog, little Sister."

"A big dog?"

"Yes. A big red dog."

She touched her own cheek. "I don't want to get old."

"Get old? This isn't old, honey, this was just something that happened. You're going to get more and more beautiful. Besides…" He reached over the table and tapped her sternum lightly. "The only thing that matters is true-heart, right? Do you practice your mutters every day?"

She was smiling at the idea of getting more beautiful and looked out the wide doors where the sun had fallen from its zenith. Each piece of sand scattered in the doorway had its own tiny shadow. She had grown into a lanky girl already, long thin arms, awkward legs. Her slanted cheekbones and dark eyes looked like her mother's.

"There aren't any dogs here," she said, scratching the back of her ruddy neck. "What does Papa mean, 'Don't wink at the bears'?"

August smiled and replied, "No it's 'Don't *feed* the bears' and 'Don't *flirt* with Ego.'"

"Oh, I see."

"Do you?"

"Well…" she said, "what bears?"

"The bears in your mind, they get habituated quickly. They get dangerous. He means don't tempt yourself. But

your advice is good too. 'Don't wink at the bears.' I like it."
She was looking outside again. August continued, "When I
first met you, you were just a plop of dough in pigtails. You
used to whisper things to your mom and she would speak for
you. Very shy. Do you remember that? Your mom used to
say, 'Melody wants me to tell you that she doesn't like
spaghetti or frogs.'"

August turned to look for her mother and found
Meredith sitting at the other end of the hall, smiling at something someone had said. Her head was as square and sturdy
as a block of freckled pine. Her face was broad and her features sat simply on her face, not stunningly beautiful but
with a refined power, the kind of beauty that Ego could not
reproduce—unique, incorruptible. As he watched, her grin
spread, laughter opening her body until he could see the
crooked fence of her teeth and the darkness behind them.
Had he ever, even in his happiest moments, looked so
unguarded? He could stare at her for hours, though he was-
n't sure if other men felt the same. Maybe his attraction to
her was a peculiarity, a taste he had acquired.

Before they had been accepted as Center initiates August
and Meredith had become friends while cataloguing
donated items in the basement of the Monterey Chapter
building. Wading waist-deep in antique chairs, televisions,
and broken lawnmowers he'd listened to the course of her
life. She was able to recount the tiniest details of distant
anecdotes as easily as what she had eaten that morning. Her
life seemed composed of an endless series of distressing situ-
ations. She didn't ask too much about him. Instead she
talked about her disapproving parents, her divorce, and
Melody. What did he think about homeschooling? How

long should she wait before calling the county agency again? What kind of cereal was most nutritious? He'd try to come up with commonsense responses and she would nod as if he had dispensed great wisdom, then move on to another story. He often thought his company could have been exchanged for any quiet, intelligent man who listened to her; but he enjoyed the distraction of her voice, the honey of her smiles, and sometimes, when they crouched together to move a filing cabinet, he was sure that she loved him. He remembered being ashamed of the scar that branched brightly down the side of his face, even though she never seemed to notice it.

Now he was staring at her again, the muscles on the side of her head dancing as she chewed. The woman he had known before the Center was so different than the woman he was watching. She was worn now, fitting looser around her soul. Before she had been nervous, and overprotective of Melody. Outside, he had seen her kick a dog hard when it came snuffing too eagerly toward her child. Now she let Melody wander around the compound unsupervised.

He had once craved her black hair, but now with her head shaved, her eyelashes and eyebrows stood out more, marking the surface of her skin like sources of a rich, dark mineral. And her rawness was hypnotic: she was less and less Mull every day, less and less able to make small talk. She had been accepted as an initiate two years after him, a rarity because she brought a child with her. Now she was being polished, always exhausted, a little confused. It meant she was incorporating Truth quickly. It meant she was going to have great understanding. Sometimes, when her hair grew out a little, he could see gray hairs above her ears.

She had let him kiss her once. It was the night she had

accidentally spilled hot tea on Melody. The child's arms reached out, petrified by the heat. Meredith snatched her up and rushed her behind the cafe counter, under the faucet, dousing her with cold water.

When the clerk approached her, she glared at him with such fire that he simply asked what the next person in line wanted. Melody hadn't really been hurt, her arms just reddened for awhile, but it was Meredith who couldn't stop crying. That night—he was embarrassed to remember it—standing just inside the door of her apartment she was weeping a little. He had hugged her in the darkness and let his face drift into hers. He had wanted to comfort her, and yes, he could admit it now, he had hoped for something more. He knew it looked like he was trying to take advantage of her. Maybe, unconsciously, he was. After all, he was still a little Mull then, still being played by Ego. He had pressed his lips against hers and felt her mouth moving. Was she returning the kiss or trying to tell him something? Then she'd opened the door and he had gone back out into the night to the tiny, cramped room he shared with three other Chapter volunteers in a dingy Movement apartment.

If she thought about that night, she was kind enough not to bring it up. It was such a long time ago, outside. Now, she took another bite and he thought he could taste the food as if her mouth and his were the same.

Sometimes, in August's fantasies about the Great Days, he and Meredith were married. Of the two hundred and fourteen initiates there were only two married couples. They slept in the communal hall and were allowed only three hours a week in b-trailer for "private time." Papa said that the Great Days would revolutionize marriage along with everything else. It was better to wait for it.

There were occasional romances at the Center. They caused trouble, arguments developed, tasks had to be reassigned. In the worst cases they led to washouts. He didn't think it was Ego-feeding to appreciate Meredith's beauty, but he found himself disappointed if he didn't see her at meals. His fascination with her was an unproductive kind of attachment, like craving salt or sugar.

He had asked Papa about it before they began reading one morning. Other initiates had to make special appointments to receive from Papa, but as interpreter August could ask for his wisdom every day. "Papa, I find myself watching another initiate, a woman, during meals," he'd said.

"Are you in love with her?" Papa asked.

"I'm not sure, Papa. I mean I feel in love with everyone sometimes. My heart has opened so much since I got here—sometimes it's hard to understand what I'm feeling."

"Do you have sexual feelings for her?"

"Sometimes. We knew each other before the Center—we studied at Monterey Chapter."

"There is nothing wrong with your feelings, but be very careful not to let them get out of control. Let them on the bus but don't let them steer. If they begin to make trouble, throw them out!"

"What kind of trouble?" August asked.

"Don't let your attraction make an idol out of her. Sometimes we think: 'I want her to want me.' That is Ego-food. You are trying to make a puppet out of someone else's soul. It will end in trouble. No attachment. Let your feelings change. In Mull society my relationship with the Mothers would cause great suffering from jealousy and misunderstanding. Here at the Center there is no problem because Papa's heart is perfectly clear—the light shines bright enough for all of them. They are all happy. No need for little lies. No attachment. Just love. Remember Jim and Patty?"

"Of course, Papa. They asked you to marry them. When you refused, they washed out. Then they tried to come back—"

"Ego had already consumed them," Papa said, shaking his head. "Jim and Patty were already dead. Ego was using their bodies. They may have looked like your friends but they were Ego-puppets. Papa could see through their disguise. Ego is the poison precipitate of genesis. It has a special hatred for initiates. It crouches like a wolf just beyond the perimeter to pounce on defectors. Outside, Jim and Patty were completely vulnerable to its obscene power, and it destroyed their minds. When they came back they were smiling, still in their Center uniforms as if nothing had happened: Trojan horses with bellyfuls of maggots waiting to burst forth and corrupt the Center. It can happen to anyone who turns from Truth, anyone who willingly shuns the light. If you see a washout smiling, you are seeing Ego's teeth."

In his more perverse moments, August tried to imagine what it must have felt like to have Ego chewing inside like that, scraping along his bones until they were completely hollow. How long did their agony last?

Someone touched August on the shoulder, waking him from his daydream: the man with the round nose—what was his name? Tall and though much older than August, always showing him deference: "Brother, I don't mean to intrude," the man said.

"Of course, sit down," August replied. He was grateful to think about something else and slid toward Brother Monkey to make room on the end of the bench.

"I'm confused about Papa's... about how he's losing his—"

"Papa isn't losing his speech. He's trading it for something truer." The man wanted more. "I know it's hard to understand sometimes," August continued. "Papa is operating on a different level. It's like when Jesus scolded his disciples because they didn't understand that he was speaking in parables. When Papa says that Ego has ten thousand heads he doesn't mean it exactly like that. Ego could take that form if he wished and probably does, but it's his *intention* that has ten thousand heads."

August was getting off track. This man's worries made them all vulnerable. Small misunderstandings could fester, spreading in the fields. Still, August couldn't give him all of Papa's Truth in one conversation. He needed to touch the man where he was hurting, to find the crack in his dam and plug it. "We are talking about things that cannot be spoken. If you speak them they get all jumbled up. So Papa is developing a way to teach us that can't be jumbled. He's finding a language that can't be used to lie. The ancient tongue of the Brahma Yuga, the language we spoke before Babylon."

The man was still nodding, watching August's lips. His head rocked slowly up and down. He said, "So he's not sick?"

"Sick? No! No, who said that?" August felt himself blinking quickly, flustered as if the man had thrown a handful of dirt in his face.

"No one. I mean... no one."

"If you hear people saying that, tell them to talk to me.

Papa's actions can't be interpreted with Mull paradigms. It's very, *very* important that you don't think of him that way. You'll get confused. You'll get so lost. You will make *yourself* deeply ill if you begin to think that way."

His head bobbed faster. "Of course. I understand. I mean. The only reason... my uncle had a stroke when I was little. He couldn't say a lot of words. It just reminded me of that."

"It's not the same at—"

"Not the same at all. I understand. Papa is doing this on purpose."

"Brother, there are levels of understanding," August lifted his hands in the air like little platforms, "it can be frustrating to be on one level, trying to understand another. The only way to move up is to let go of all of your Mull thinking. You saw Papa's wisdom and Ego made you think of your sick uncle, of illness. You see how twisted that is? You have to trust Papa more than you trust yourself because Ego is riding you. What Papa is doing has *never* been done."

The man took a deep breath and held it for a moment. "Thank you, Brother. I knew Ego had me; I just couldn't see how."

When the man left August turned toward Brother Monkey and the kids, but they were gone. The initiates had begun to stack their bowls in orderly rows on the counter for the kitchen crew to wash. Mother Li was helping with the dishes, radiant and smiling.

The initiates were now standing in small groups, talking. After about ten minutes of socializing and stretching they would head out into the fields, where they would work until the sun set and the generator lights kicked on to watch them. August loved the way the community moved with one mind, like a migration of kind birds. Seeing them gathering by the door, still muddy from their work that morning, August remembered with a jolt that the NewFaces were scheduled to arrive today. He hurried to finish his food. A few initiates bowed as they passed him; he smiled and said "Namaste!" to each of them. Initially, August had tried to continue labor-practice. He had headed out to the fields for at least a few hours every day until Papa scolded him, ordering him to focus on interpreting and transcribing the lectures. Most of the notes would end up in pamphlets or the *True-Mind* journal.

August rubbed his palm against the back of his head and let his hand slide down his neck and under his shirt, where it came to rest above his shoulder blade. Labor had been such a great tool against Ego; now he felt trapped in the same room with his Mull memories and fantasies, with no weapons against idleness, no way to wear Ego out. His Mull family flapped around him like vultures trying to find a place to land. His Mull father, half alive, half dead, strong and smiling in olive-green khakis, watering the lawn; yet also pressed under the glass and metal in pooling blood and gasoline. His sister saying: "You know yourself better than this, August." His mother crying in her bed.

He left a spoonful in the bottom of the bowl to spite Ego, then stood to carry the bowl to the counter. Mother Li intercepted him, perfect timing as always, taking the dirty bowl and smiling so warmly that his fretting melted away.

Of course, here was his true Mother, his true family. He had never seen her eat. Her hands were dark, square, and strong; they cupped his bowl like it was precious. The skin around her eyes made tiny deltas: wrinkles from the sun and smiling. Papa's first wife. When she turned, heading toward the kitchen, even the thick braid that hung down her back radiated with beauty and power, not unlike the king snake August had found as a child. The bully next door had crushed its head with a stone and left it in the street. Even dead, even with the pod of its skull broken open, it was magnificent.

All of the Mothers had rivers of straight hair. It marked them. Initiates anywhere on the compound could see it from far away and compose themselves. The hair glinted in the sun and framed their faces, moving over their shoulders like a gift to whoever saw it. Their beauty wasn't Mull vanity; it was a physical manifestation of the power of true-heart. Papa's wives were allowed to shine, as Jesus' feet were allowed to be soothed with expensive balms. Seeing them opened the doors of appreciation.

Mother Li's robes just touched the ground. She floated so elegantly between the tables that she appeared to be coasting. August had an urge to lift her robe and learn how to walk that way, with rolling, humble royalty.

This Mother, this strong brave woman didn't try to pick him apart, didn't want him to get a job, get married, grind himself into the cannibalistic machinery of society. She wanted what was best for August. She saw him for what he was: someone who suffered, someone who wanted Truth and was willing to fight for it. Her understanding was cool water.

3

Outside the heat had warped the distances. Far beyond the quarters, the onion field was a line of green flame simmering the false mirage-water above it. Above that, the heads of the initiates bobbed together like a string of prayer beads, bodiless, their shovels and arms invisible.

A hot wind pushed against the shadow of his face and he could smell the rank onions, then the toilet shed. Then it was cleaned away by the air coming off the sand, a bright smell like the sweat that comes off old wood just before it burns.

Something skittered behind him and he turned quickly, looking for an Ego-phantom, but nothing was there. He shook his head. Things were getting out of hand; how long had he been standing there while the others worked? He pressed the heels of his hands into his eyes; fantastic blossoms of imaginary colors exploded in his head. He rubbed the back of his skull to wake himself up, then headed for the perimeter gate.

In six years August had only been outside six times. He had escorted Papa on a lecture tour two years ago and for a few months he had supervised the supply runs. That was before Phoenix Chapter had begun bringing in supplies so that none of the Center initiates would have to leave. Now, as he walked away from the main-hall toward the fields, his mind moved out faster than his body. He saw the circle of

Papa's trailers, the corrugated steel of the main-hall; then, as if from a helicopter, he saw the whole compound, a handful of children's blocks strewn across the vast desert, the crops leaching green from the ditches.

He tried to center himself, remembered his body and felt the oats stirring uneasily in his stomach. Near the perimeter he saw two figures that looked as fixed as posts hammered into the ground. As he approached he bowed to each of them, "Mother Jessica, Brother Matheson, namaste."

He stood with them waiting to welcome the NewFaces. The chain-link fence circling the compound met at a wide gate that had to be pushed open by hand. They could see the dust smudge against the base of the mountain where the Jeep had just come off the paved road.

No one spoke. Sweat made his clothes rough against his skin. In the worst heat, the initiates learned to conserve energy. Their bodies went into a kind of trance, like creatures on the bottom of the ocean letting the density of their surroundings buoy them. Brother Matheson had turned his back to the sun, looking out toward the toilets as if he expected the Jeep to come from that direction.

Mother Jessica stood in front of August, looking like a devotional statue: her straw hat was a gilded halo that obscured her from the shoulders up. The hat dipped slightly and August heard her quietly humming. She was imperturbable. She looked out toward the base of the distant mountain, the landscape studded with pillars of the saguaro, yucca, and ocotillo.

He recalled his Mull mother talking to strangers. In supermarkets or doctors' waiting rooms she struck up conversations as if mere proximity made people intimates. Once while standing in line for a ride at Disneyland a group of strangers joined her in an impromptu "I'd Like to Teach the World to Sing." That was before the accident. Barbara: it seemed to be a nonsense word. He looked at it for a moment before recognizing it as his Mull mother's name; his brain had provided it without being asked. He closed his eyes tightly, cleared his mind, then stepped closer to Mother Jessica, dipping his head into the shadow of her hat. She stopped humming in anticipation of his question.

"Mother, can I get you some water?" August asked.

She blinked. A bead of sweat that had gathered on her eyebrow darted down her cheek and was soaked into the hem of her robe. A strand of her blonde hair caught on her eyelash, and fluttered when she blinked. Maybe the heat was affecting her more than he had thought. Then she smiled, looking at him sideways without turning her head.

"Maybe you need some water yourself?" she said. She always resisted coddling, and insisted on working in the fields at least three times a week. Initiates had stopped trying to take the hoes and trowels from her, teasing her occasionally as they would any other initiate.

August said, "They're late. They shouldn't keep you waiting in the sun."

She put her hand on his shoulder and said, "Don't be gruff with the Faces. Their first months will be difficult enough. I want to ask you something. Step over here with me."

They walked closer to the gate, away from Brother Matheson who followed August with eyes squinted against the light. August understood that Brother Matheson was envious of his status. The ambiguity of their relationship was uncomfortable for both of them. *Good*, August thought, *let Ego squirm.*

When they had walked close enough to touch the chain-link gate, Mother Jessica looked directly into his eyes. "You're Papa's interpreter. You're with him almost as much as I am." She watched him carefully. Had she asked a question?

August replied, "Yes, I am deeply honored—"

She raised her hand slightly to cut him off, then waited a moment more before continuing. "You can see his... evolution."

"Yes, Mother. One more revelation."

"And one more wife, and his silences." She looked troubled. "I want to ask you, has he said anything to you about a doctor?"

"What do you mean? No, Mother, nothing like that. Who needs a doctor? Is something wrong?" The Jeep cut across the landscape, ignoring the pale grooves of the dirt road that snaked around the fence.

"No. Nothing," she said. "I just wanted to be sure. Some of us would like him to get a check-up is all. He's not young anymore. It would be good to make sure he's getting everything he needs. He's a stubborn man." The Jeep rolled to a stop near the gate, sending a storm of dust around them.

Didn't she know that Papa wasn't susceptible to illness? "Mother, I don't understand—is something wrong?"

"Of course not. Don't worry."

The dust from the Jeep surrounded them and he moved to shelter her. When it cleared, her gaze remained fixed where he had been, as if she had suddenly gone blind but wasn't yet aware of it.

"Mother, they're here."

"Of course. Thank you, August." She smiled and patted his back, pushing him toward the Jeep.

The driver got out first: the sweaty man from Phoenix Chapter who often supervised supply runs. He bowed in their direction while August and Brother Matheson opened the gates. Then the NewFaces got out, two boys and a girl. They were young, not older than nineteen or twenty, August guessed. They stood nervously by the Jeep, gripping their small duffel bags. One of the boys bowed, then the others quickly dipped their heads. The girl had rust-colored curls that nearly touched the dirt. It would be a shame to cut them but she was not a Mother; she had made a choice to work for Truth.

August stepped forward, pressing his hands together. "Welcome, friends!" he said. Then he hugged each of them hard, letting his heart open. "Ha, I can smell the Mull world on you: cheese and exhaust!"

As they followed him through the gate, August turned and winked at one of the young men. "You've made the right decision," he said. "Don't be nervous."

Before they had walked very far, August stopped and lined the NewFaces up. He watched quietly as the Faces knelt in a row with their heads bowed before Brother Monkey. They looked so solemn, it was almost grim—like a public execution. After they completed their first five months at the Center they would receive the spiral tattoo on the underside of their left wrist, a seal of their initiation, of their dedication to Papa, Truth, and God. For now it was only the shears growling over their heads. Their shadows stretched out behind them, gathering the clumps of falling hair. August saw a beetle crawling in deranged circles in the belly of one of the shadows like a worry. Recently those beetles were everywhere.

When the Faces were all shaved and bowls of water had been brought for them to splash on their glaring scalps, August handed one of the young men two mirrors so he could see the pink birthmark at the base of his skull. "Did you know that was there?" August asked.

"No. I don't think so. Maybe."

"Half of the NewFaces have this wine-colored stain. See, you're being revealed already," August said. "The sun will wash it out."

The NewFaces grinned stupidly at each other. They had reason to be nervous. Initiation was a long process; Mull habits were hard to break and Ego hated letting people go. Recently, the Chapters had been more careful, choosing followers who were really ready for desert life. There had been years when a third of all NewFaces washed out before completing initiation.

The elders led the NewFaces to the main-hall to show them where they would be eating. As they walked, Brother Monkey whispered to August, "I'd quit all of this for a cheeseburger, y'know what I'm saying?" He leaned close, speaking in hushed tones as if they were discussing serious matters. "Yeah, *you* know what I'm saying." Then he nodded as if they had just agreed on something important. August tried to elbow him, worried the Faces might hear, but Monkey had already composed himself. Behind them, Rebecca, Luke, and Chris gawked at each other and patted their heads. They were like children now, giddy, expectant. In half a year, the heat would slow them down, the training would sober them, the Center spiral would appear on their wrists, and they would begin to be called Brother and Sister.

By the time the sun was setting, August had escorted the NewFaces to the quarters. They sat on the bare, sweat-stained mattresses of their new bunk beds, holding folded sheets and looking uncomfortable.

"You know how lucky you are to be chosen," he told them. "We get over three hundred applicants from around the world every six months."

The Faces laughed, looking at each other. *We made it,* they seemed to say. *We're here. They'll tell us the truth now.* The quarters occupied an enormous metal-walled ware-house. The heavy air and rows of bunks summoned images of a guerrilla army camp. It was August's responsibility to help the NewFaces see beyond it. He handed them a large mug of water to pass around. Brother Monkey and Sister James would escort the NewFaces through their first days, but August had to supervise their assimilation of Truth and answer questions. It was an important role and August felt Ego tug at it: the seductive air of real understanding, the power of having the answers. Truth was complicated. It was difficult not to become mysterious. When the Faces inevitably asked why the doors of the main-hall were painted red, August would explain: "When we go in to eat, we remember that we are also being eaten. The red doors are a mouth." When they asked why the shutters on the windows high above the doors were blue, August would tell them that whoever made the warehouse painted them that way. He would have to keep tabs on himself in order not to be smug or satisfied with things the way they were. Being around fresh minds was a good antidote to apathy.

They sat rigid, trying not to slouch, still smiling like plastic dolls. Though it would take a while for them to adjust, he could tell already that they were good, hungry candidates. He found himself hoping that they would not have to endure redirection, though each of them would probably need it at least once. Without something hard underneath it, the seedling cannot push up toward the light. These Faces had spent at least two years at a Chapter and had signed over all of their possessions to the Movement, so there was no longer any need to coddle them.

"I know you're anxious to see Papa," August said. "You'll see him tomorrow morning during the address. From now on you'll be seeing him almost every day. Are there any questions about tomorrow? About the schedule?"

Chris raised his hand. "Do the tasks change?"

"Your task isn't just a chore," August said. He tapped his chest with his fingers, wanting to reach into his own heart as a demonstration. "Remember this: what you need will always be difficult. It's like we are jars of glass. Papa can see right through us; whatever we are carrying inside is naked to him. He knows what you need even before you do. Like when he asked Sister Coleman to organize the kitchen. She had never cooked a day in her life, she thought she didn't know how. She's been leading the kitchen crew for four years now. Papa *knows*. So if you find yourself grumbling, just wait, you'll see it's exactly right what you are doing. That's part of what makes living here different from the outside: in the Mull world you can never trust that the choices you make are the right ones. Here you don't have to worry about that." August nodded deliberately, and like magnets, the heads of the NewFaces bobbed too.

Their eyes were beginning to glaze. In a week the Faces

would be too tired to ask questions and the critical work of guiding them would really begin. When they got exhausted enough, their hearts would open. Then they would become weepy and shamelessly honest about themselves, admitting the slightest Ego-feeding thought. Like the other initiates, they would find elders during talk-time to confess selfishness, laziness, gluttony, and they would be given extra chores to help strengthen them. It was an honor to observe anyone go through such a process, to see spirits fighting so hard to be free.

"You're tired!" August shouted. "Welcome to the Center! You are surrounded by friends here, they will watch out for you. If you feel yourself getting scared or tired, talk to one of the elders. You *do* belong here—you've finally made it. Of all the places you could have ended up, you found home. Welcome."

He considered explaining redirection to them. Perhaps they would have heard something about it; no doubt there were rumors to dispel. Eventually they would find out on their own. A little anxiety about z-trailer, the little box surrounded by a bamboo screen near the eastern perimeter, was probably a good thing. It would make redirection more effective. Their smiles looked forced. They had absorbed as much as they could today. August decided to let them sleep.

"Tomorrow you begin bright and early. This is the last time you'll get to go to bed before the others unless you get sick, so enjoy it! I'll tell them to try to be quiet when they come in. The lights will stay on for awhile. If you have any questions or need anything, ask Brother Monkey or Sister James. Rest well, namaste."

Sister James came to show the NewFaces how to wash up,

and August jogged to make it to the elder council. As he crossed the distance between the buildings, he felt something chasing him. He knew that, if he turned, he would see the same skeletal dog that haunted his morning meditation. Keeping his eyes fixed on the main-hall, he ran faster and reached the door out of breath.

Brother Matheson, Brother Thomas, Sister Chavez, Sister Coleman, August, and the Mothers sat around a single table. There were only nine of them that week. Usually it was eleven, but Sister Dean was ill and resting in b-trailer. Brother Monkey, technically an elder, having been at the Center from the beginning, rarely showed up and when he did he was clearly bored and uncomfortable.

The Mothers sat next to each other in a row of lavender. Their hair sank heavily across their shoulders. August hadn't really noticed that all of the Mothers had straight hair until a visitor from Seattle had asked him if it was a sign of true-heart: "When Papa chose them, their heads were shaved, right? How could he have known that they would have straight hair? Could it be a coincidence?"

Visitors: they didn't appreciate what it took to be an initiate every day, to work in the fields and have that be enough, to wash Papa's feet and have that itself be Truth. They wanted something flashier. They snooped around asking questions as if Truth was hidden somewhere in the compound, as if true-heart was the prize at the end of a treasure hunt.

Watching the Mothers now, August knew that the visitor from Seattle was not entirely wrong. There was something about that beauty, the way healthy plants indicate rich soil.

Who had Papa chosen as the fifth?

Mother Li sat silently with her hands folded in front of her and seemed to be meditating as she did when there was a free moment. Her stillness was like her own atmosphere. No one disturbed it unless absolutely necessary.

Mother Jessica did not braid her hair; instead, she let it fall like a surge of water past her neck. August could smell her rose oil. She had an airy voice; it evaporated as she spoke, giving the impression that she couldn't count on having enough breath to finish a sentence.

Mother Monica was the most recent Mother; her hair hadn't been growing out for very long. It reached only to her jaw and looked alarmingly Mullish, bouncing as if she had spent time and money at a beauty shop. August wondered what she was thinking as she nervously rolled the jade bracelet around her wrist. The newest Mother was always quiet and awkward. August had seen it three times: Mother Jessica, Mother Star, and now Mother Monica. The jade bracelet passed from one to the other. They smiled too much, until another was chosen, until they weren't the newest. Then they seemed to relax into their power.

Mother Star looked very much like Mother Jessica. Her hair smelled slightly acrid when she passed; August imagined that she combed olive oil into it. She took long walks out beyond the perimeter, returning with sage, fiery cactus pears, or the pewter scepters of dried ocotillo branches, hollow and riddled with holes like alien flutes. She also collected shells, xeric clams, ancient fossils from when the desert had been a Precambrian ocean.

August thought they menstruated at the same time. He was sure he could smell it. Since coming to the Center he could smell when someone was afraid, or when someone was sick before they showed symptoms. Truth dissolved directly into him.

He sat in the folding chair, rubbing the back of his head. He wished Mother Li would facilitate. Instead, she had been letting him run the councils. He would have deferred to any of the Mothers or even to Brother Matheson if Papa hadn't forbidden it: "You are my interpreter. You have to be comfortable speaking with authority."

August now rapped softly on the table. "Lets get started. We need to start thinking already about the wedding ceremony. When Papa reveals his choice for final Mother we should be ready to make announcements to all the Chapters. So just keep that in the back of your minds. We'll brainstorm about good dates. Before we get to that, though, there is the foot-tub thing." August's voice sounded shaky echoing back to him from the metal walls of the empty hall. He looked around, waiting for someone to speak. Mother Li stood up and went to the back of the hall to putter in the kitchen.

Brother Thomas cleared his throat and said, "There's only one tub and one hose for all of us to wash our feet. If you're at the end of the line, the meal is over before you get to eat. We'd like the supply run to bring more tubs, and let's try to get more hoses hooked up."

Sister Chavez, who had designed the new well, said, "If you start adding new outlets the water pressure will drop out. You'd only get a trickle. The showers wouldn't work either."

Sister Coleman raised her hand. "Well, something has to happen," she said. "We can't drag all of that mud in here. At night sometimes it takes hours before all of our feet are clean enough to go to bed. It doesn't make sense to stand in the heat so long before meals."

There was a silence and August felt obligated to address her tone. "I know you are frustrated," he said. "But we have to be careful not to let Ego in, especially with NewFaces here now. Be aware of what you really need before you say it. How does what you think you need affect the Center?"

When Brother Thomas started to speak, August held his finger up while continuing to look at Sister Coleman; he wanted to give her space to find her center. She rubbed her face with her palms and nodded. After a breath, she said, "The projects would move along faster. Morale would be better."

August nodded. "Okay, so what do we do?"

Brother Thomas looked like he was about to speak, then shook his head.

Mother Li had been rearranging things in one of the refrigerators. They all turned around when they heard her approach.

"May I suggest," she said softly. "Order the tubs. The kitchen crew will fill the tubs with fresh water before you all arrive. They could fill the tubs all morning. Then the water pressure doesn't drop all at once, right? Still just one hose?"

They looked at Sister Chavez who nodded. "Yes. That should be okay."

August waited for a moment to see if anyone had something to add. "Okay with everyone? Brother Thomas, please call Phoenix and have them bring how many—four more? Five? Five more tubs and towels? Towels. Okay, anything else? Nothing? This is going to be a short meeting. Should we talk about the wedding?"

Sister Chavez squirmed.

"Sister?"

"It's not about the wedding."

"Go ahead."

"People have complained about redirection. They say it's…"

August watched her closely. "What?"

"They say it's getting rough."

"Rough? Redirection is rough. No one likes it."

Matheson cleared his throat and spoke in a monotone while looking into the empty air across the table. "Ego is working on us harder than ever. He's getting clever—so I have to change tactics sometimes."

"What do they mean rough?" August asked.

"I'm not doing anything new. Their minds are getting more stubborn. Like Ego is immune to the old treatments. So they stand longer, I have to press them harder, ask more questions before Ego gives up."

Sister Chavez was about to say something but August interrupted. "Does Papa know?" he asked.

"Of course." Matheson looked disgusted.

"As long as Papa approves," August said.

"Of course."

Sister Chavez shook her head but August felt resolute. "Sister, redirection isn't a game, it's not meant to be fun. It's deadly serious. If Ego gets a foothold here at the Center it could spread quickly." He knocked on the table with his knuckles, looking hard at her. "If people are dreading redirection they will be less likely to become lax, less likely to let Ego in, in the first place. No one likes it. I didn't like it. Unfortunately, until the Great Days come and Ego is banished completely, it's a necessary discomfort. I think you understand."

"I understand," Sister Chavez said.

"Understanding isn't enough, you have to tell the others, whoever was complaining. You have to show them where their process is weak. You have to put this fire out before it spreads. Can I count on you to do that?"

"Of course, Brother—I only brought it up because there was talk."

"I won't ask who they are—I'll let you deal with this. I'm trusting you with it. "

"Thank you, Brother August."

4

After the meeting, he headed for the showers. He tried to shower when others were asleep; it just didn't feel right doing it during the day while others who had come from the fields, exhausted and filthy, waited for him. Matheson's voice echoed in his head: *I have to press them harder*. When August was redirected it had been Brother Jacob who had conducted it in shifts with Sister Blaire. In his mind there were parts of Papa's teachings that still rang with the tin buzz of the cheap speakers used in z-trailer. He had complained to the kitchen staff that the meals needed more salt. It made him chuckle now to think of himself, freshly shaven, walking up to the elder initiates with a half-eaten bowl of lentils. Still mortifying, though it had been years ago. Elders almost never needed redirection and August felt an embarrassed sense of relief at his immunity.

August had great respect for the patience of redirectors. It was something he didn't think he could ever do. Their love was unwavering, their dedication awe inspiring. They were able to look past the suffering individual to see true-heart wanting out. There was something beautiful about the process, the mutual resolve to be intolerant to Ego. August remembered standing in z-trailer without eating, sleeping, or drinking, his feet going numb. Sometimes he was blindfolded, listening to Papa's recorded lectures playing over the speakers near his ears, sometimes a bright light was shone in his eyes while they asked him questions designed to confuse Ego: *Where is your heart? Why do you want to hurt the Movement?* As his Mull mind got tired, Ego became stupid, easy to weed out. Fatigue was the cure.

Then when he emerged twenty-four hours later, hazy and weeping, the others surrounded him with compassion, ushered him into the quarters to sleep even though it was hours before bedtime. No one ever mentioned the salt or the redirection. His slate had been wiped clean; his shame had happened in another life.

When Brother Jacob and Sister Blaire left to establish Taiwan Chapter, Brother Matheson had taken over redirection. He was able to do it alone, needing no support, and he often turned the initiate out quicker than the others. Was he getting too rough? August made a note to ask Papa about it then wiped the issue from his mind.

Coming around the quarters, he was surprised to see the three children chasing moths in the pool of green cast by the floodlight. There was a bat, clicking in the darkness above them, swooping periodically into the light like a distressing thought. Soft voices murmured in the darkened doorway, probably waiting for the kids to wear themselves out before herding them to bed. The level of energy at the Center was high and the children had picked up on it; people were excited about Papa's announcement. The final Mother meant they were that much closer to the Great Days; the twelfth revelation would be coming soon to break down the walls of consciousness.

Melody was getting taller—already two feet above the boys. He remembered his Mull sister, Jesse, when she was Melody's age, preparing all of his meals, getting him dressed for school every morning, and walking him home in the afternoons. She stood on a stool to stir macaroni while their mother sank into grief. It was too late for his Mull family. Melody was a fresh start, the first of the new generation. The entire community was taking care of her.

August knelt and gathered the children around whispering, "Okay, this game is called 'rumor.'" They jumped in the dust, excited to be playing with an adult. "I'll whisper to Tad. Tad you whisper to Hunter. Hunter, you whisper the same thing to Melody, okay? Let's try."

Hunter had to whisper twice to Melody, who wrinkled her nose: "That doesn't make any sense."

"What did he say?" August asked.

"He didn't say it right."

"What did he say?"

"He said, 'I put on a child.'"

"Close. The original message was: 'When I was a child, I understood as a child.'"

Melody was frowning. "Do it again," she said. She seemed to think they had failed the objective of the game.

Sister Meredith appeared like a ghost out of the gloom of the quarters where the others were wrapped in sweaty sheets, trying to sleep. She waved at August and called to the children softly.

When the little ones trudged off, August held on to Melody's arm. "During the Great Days, there won't be any confusion like that," he said. "God whispered something in our hearts before we were born but it's gotten all jumbled." Melody looked over his shoulder, at the moon or something in the sky. She was nodding—not listening. "We've forgotten what he said, so Papa is trying to remind us." He let her go and she ran, bowing once quickly, nearly stumbling. August shook his head, bemused. There was plenty of time for her enlightenment. She would be taking Truth in through her pores. He had never heard of a child so loved, surrounded only by Truth. No Mull school to beat her into submission. The Center's greatest potential—a child brought up almost entirely under Papa's guidance, she would be a remarkable human being, a forerunner to the new humanity. Someday children all over the world would be born into Papa's influence.

August stood straighter with the thought of it. He smiled, then laughed, turning in a circle to take in the entire compound. The Desert Center was a seed that had already germinated. It would explode outward in green light, covering the earth. He had the urge to shout. He spread his arms and turned again, wishing for someone to hug or bow to. Meredith had already disappeared in the dark doorway.

It wasn't easy to masturbate in the shower. If he could manage it, it would make him less distracted, but the shower was not a sexy place; the rough brick wall pressed too closely against his elbows, the black plastic sheet clung to his ass. Cramped and slimy. Still, August imagined everyone did it here, if they did it at all.

He didn't need to worry about anyone coming in; they were all in bed. Besides, the showers were respected space. He leaned against the wall and crouched a little, letting the water course down his chest into his crotch, aiming for the sucking drain. Rebecca, the NewFace, her back arched, her face open with pleasure—August stopped. He held himself and pushed her out of his mind. Papa warned against objectifying people. August tried to imagine anonymous bodies instead. When he resumed, he was already half-limp and his two-minute bell went off. Just enough time to rinse any soap from the corners of his body. August let his penis go and bowed to wet his face one more time. When the water clicked off, he smacked his chest like a gorilla, waited a few seconds, then slid the plastic aside and reached for the towel.

Pulling his pants on again, he heard a low growling coming from outside and froze. It was only an airplane cutting across the sky. Still, the helicopter could come back at any moment. By the grace of God and Papa's wisdom the Movement was winning the race. Ego's fury was becoming visible: the helicopters came more frequently; initiates were beset by doubt and had to be redirected more often. August could feel the escalation of the battle in himself as well; his hallucinations were more frequent and there was a fluttering sound that seemed to come from behind him.

August left his neck wet to feel the soft sighs of desert air that sometimes whisked across the Center at night. The stars were really burning. August watched them as he moved toward his trailer. No helicopter, not even a plane. Ego nowhere to be seen.

The NewFaces were separated at meal times to keep them from relying on each other. The other initiates included them, though, with smiles and pats on the back. August stood in the doorway watching them voraciously spooning their food. They had become slack with fatigue, unable to hold their grotesque Mull postures of pride. The heat and sand were wearing their sharp angles smooth. Their white manic eyes had already softened to sun-squints, honest eyes.

He had an urge to tell them to eat slower, then decided that they would learn soon enough. Their bowls would be empty and they would have to watch the others eating. When he found himself pushing them too hard, he reminded himself of the SunRise Retreat, and humility came flooding back. He had been pale, directionless, underdeveloped like a tadpole wriggling in a shrinking puddle.

It was the summer he had discovered that if he slanted his mind in the right direction, if he kept the eyes behind his eyes open, the LSD would never wear off. Between his sophomore and junior years at Berkeley he was living with a friend from school, smoking, drinking, playing his keyboard, watching television. He had eaten shrooms and called Jesse to describe something he was observing: the surface of reality peeling back as it burned, revealing the coals underneath, and the animals that lived there, salamanders wriggling with molecular motion in that inferno without being consumed— how they were under everything, his skin, the walls, the sky. He must have said something else, maybe something about death because the next day she was standing on his doorstep looking worried, her hair pulled back in a tight braid. She had driven all night, ten hours from Washington. She was holding him by the shoulders and shouting at him, "Hello, skinny! You look like hell."

Then, despite his objections, she kicked through the piles of trash on the apartment floor to call their mother on his phone. The next week the three of them were headed north. His mother drove the whole way, not a whiff of alcohol on her breath. Jesse sat in the backseat with his sleeping bag. He didn't remember any talking except the occasional apologetic attempts at normalcy from his mother: "Everyone needs a little vacation sometimes." She patted his knee like a dog, and tried to find some upbeat music on the radio.

When they arrived at the campground, Big Red shook August's hand and helped him carry his stuff to the tent. He was a jolly, bearded psychologist, hypnotherapist, grief counselor, and wilderness guide all in one. Before leaving, Jesse hugged him, kissed him on the cheek, and tied a necklace around his neck. She had found the stone on the beach and drilled a hole in it herself.

The retreat was voluntary, though once you signed in, you weren't allowed to leave until it was over. "Two months of camping, hiking, and structured community outdoor activities on the Oregon coast." It had seemed like a bad idea even at the time: a summer of campfire smoke with scores of other depressed people stumbling through the catastrophes of their lives. Even with half a dozen counselors holding crisis sessions around the clock, how would being in the wilderness with thirty-five other wrecks help? It was supposed to make him feel less isolated, less singled out by life; instead it felt like a leper colony. He made quick extrapolations, determining that America must be filled with people just like himself; it was an epidemic, and the sheer numbers meant there was no cure. He was surrounded by people whose every effort was a thinly veiled charade, an attempt to go through the motions of real life. People who worried that they would never stop worrying. People who had to be dragged like corpses in their sleeping bags to group meetings; who wore endless rigormortis grins on their faces to show how far they had come, to show that they were trying, doing their homework, fighting the good fight. The third day, during a hike, the necklace had snagged on a branch and fallen eighty feet into the surf.

He remembered trying to write a letter to Jesse, struggling to sound cheerful. He didn't want her to know how miserable he was, yet he couldn't fake feeling light. Had he actually sent any letters? The trees, the crisp salt air, the sound of the churning ocean—poor, clueless August! All he knew was that he was supposed to be happy. Nature was supposed to be beautiful to him. The swarms of stars smearing themselves in the darkness were supposed to make him gasp and sigh with pleasure. He didn't know yet that he had been lied to, that his whole life had been spent running the maze, trapped in Ego's game. He knew there was something broken inside him, because being put in charge of keeping the fire made him want to let it die; because group therapy made him want to punch people; because even in the forest, every tree looked rigid, lonely, afraid to be touched. But that was all before Papa.

It was a good batch this time; none of them would wash out. He took a bowl, smiling at the Sister as she ladled him a helping of potato-onion soup. There was a large bowl of raw oatmeal and toasted seaweed to sprinkle on the soup, but August left it as it was.

He spotted a single seat free at Meredith's table. He was headed there when he felt a tap on his shoulder. Chris, the NewFace, was looking sheepish. He whispered, "Yesterday in lecture, Papa said to let go of little things. Then, in private counsel this morning, he said my mind was like a spoiled child and that I should count every shoot in the onion fields. Which do I do?"

August felt a dollop of soup dripping onto his thumb.

"Don't ask questions," he said. "Just obey. It's easy."

"But he said to ignore little things," Chris said, "and now he wants me to count every little—"

"Center yourself!" August cut him off. "If Papa told you to count the onions it's not a little thing, you need to act like it's the most important thing you've ever done."

"Do scallions count?"

From the corner of his eye August saw another initiate take his seat. He sighed, trying to focus on Chris again. "You did what?"

"What did I do?" Chris asked, alarmed.

"Papa told you 'onions', but you counted scallions instead?"

"No, I didn't. I mean I will! I mean… *should* I?"

"Why would you?" August asked, hearing the impatience in his own voice. Chris looked like he had painful gas. August spoke slowly: "NewFace, this is Ego-fog, don't try so hard to understand, just walk through it. Papa said onions, count onions. Okay?"

Chris bowed. "Thank you, Brother."

August had spotted another seat when Papa came into the meal hall and stood behind the podium glaring. Those who were bustling about in the kitchen saw him first, stopped, and sat where they were. August couldn't help it: he loved Papa's stern face. When he saw Papa angry, it made August excited. It scared him, though it also affirmed his sense that things were serious. He recognized Papa's unclouded, emotional purity in the demons in the row. Even the fierce ones from Bali and Japan with tusks and bugging eyes were beautiful. Righteous. Papa's anger was not, at its root, actually fear. It was a good thing, a cleansing wind. A shaft of sunlight hit Papa from behind making his ears glow like red paper lanterns.

Papa spoke: "Where was the animal?" The room hushed and everyone turned toward the podium. August realized that he was giddy.

Papa said it again: "Where was the animal? Answer Papa!"

Sister Aisha emerged from the kitchen with flour on her hands. "Papa, this morning, the Sisters and me, we went to prepare morning meal and there was a raccoon in the kitchen." She waited to see if Papa wanted to hear more and pressed her hands together. "It was in the food. Eating everything. It must have gotten through the perimeter somehow. It wouldn't go."

Papa stepped down from the podium, moving between the tables to stand close to her. "What did you do?"

Aisha kneeled. "We had to use a broom to push it out. It was hissing."

"Did you hit it?"

"Yes, Papa—a little bit—it was hissing. It tried to bite Sister Jennifer. Forgive me, Papa."

Papa reached down and quickly gathered his vestment. His tan pants came into view, then his broad pale chest. There was a blue-green bruise like a rain cloud across his ribs.

There were screams. Everyone dropped to their knees and began muttering. August looked quickly to make sure the NewFaces were kneeling before he fell to his knees too. Sister Aisha collapsed, wrapping herself around Papa's feet.

"When you achieve true-heart, you feel the suffering of others—even animals."

August dropped his head to the ground in horror. Two inches from his face a black beetle had raised the cannon of its body at his cheek. The insect was bullet shaped, the kind of beetle that could be found around the well. They raised their asses in defense, releasing droplets of foul liquid that smelled like vinegar and semen. Was it a hallucination? He reached out to touch it: sturdy as a tiny elephant. It shuffled left and aimed its ass at him again.

Papa was still shouting over the rippling lake of weeping initiates: "I'm not angry! If this looks like anger it is only to teach you an important lesson." He lifted Sister Aisha to her feet and led her outside, whispering to her as the others continued to bow. August watched the beetle crawl away. Then he lurched for it to save it from being crushed by the feet of the other initiates. Unfortunately it had crawled between someone's knees so August began to bow again.

They all heard Sister Aisha cry out: a choked laugh. Perhaps Papa had told her a joke. Perhaps he had given her a glimpse of her future self in paradise. Already he had cured her misery.

As he rubbed his head on the floor, August's mind was replaying the scene: Sister Aisha's terror; Papa's skin like a map of her crime. She wouldn't need redirection. She had already learned her lesson. Papa had produced a miracle like this before. It was years ago when the chickens were alive. Because of a scheduling confusion the chickens had been overlooked for three days and Papa could not eat; food would not go down his throat. When the problem was discovered and the chickens were fed, he was able to eat again.

August now waited for one of the Mothers to enter the hall and calm them down. No Mother arrived. After a few minutes had passed, he stood and clapped his hands. "Okay! Finish your food. Then straight to work-practice! Think hard on this lesson!" People began to stand, resuming their meal with a stunned silence. Chris was still on the floor muttering. August walked over to him and put his hand on his shoulder. "It's okay. Papa isn't angry at you. You need to eat now." When Chris looked up there were tears streaming down his face.

5

During evening mutter, August dreamt that Papa was a bull. At times he had a bull's head; other times it was just Papa, naked in the grass with the Mothers. He saw the power of Papa's body, the chest like dense earth, his limbs heavy and sleek as weapons. There were no words in the dream, only the grip of fingers; the Mothers' feet, no longer bronze with the sun, were white, soft, and arcing with pleasure. Papa was talking but his voice was too deep to hear, a seismic pulse of blood beneath the surface of the dream. When August tried to focus on the mantras, shaking his head to get the images out, they turned malevolent. He saw Papa shuddering in a trench in Vietnam, the Mothers dead and bleeding between the trees. The thunder of war choked him and he jumped up, blinking awake. The initiates near him looked at him for a moment, then closed their eyes and continued the mutter. Brother Matheson's eyes remained open, glaring. August hitched up his canvas pants and settled back down.

With Brother Matheson looming like a storm behind him and images of war still flickering in his head, August felt curdled by doubts—doubts as quick and unsettling as mice darting under his feet. What if there was some impurity buried so deeply within him that even Papa hadn't sensed it? At the final crucial moments, August would be revealed as a fraud—a piece of poison in the medicine. He saw the shining future curling black, his fault.

His lips lost the mutter; he sat very still, trying to pick up the rhythm from the others around him. He could feel Ego looking for a crack to creep into. He knew he couldn't fight the visions; they would explode into a troop of baboons laughing and making obscene gestures. He could only back away from them, keep uttering the mantras. He felt his neck bobbing to the rhythm, picked up the words and pushed them through his mouth. For all its ferocity, Ego had no endurance; it couldn't compete with a trained body. It flared occasionally like this, but it was beaten, and bitter for being beaten.

August ran his hand along the back of his skull to scratch his palm on the sandpaper of his freshly shaved head. Shaping the words and letting them drop was like reverse eating: the sounds, pressed together, fell whole from his mouth. He waited until the cycle had completed, then he stood to find Papa.

On his way to Papa's trailers he felt Ego nearby and turned quickly to see the bone-dog snarling at his feet. Fur was falling off its ribs in patches, revealing yellow bone and dark scabs. What did it want from him? "You aren't real," August said and continued on, ignoring its wet growls.

The sun scraped along his scalp. He was dizzy again. He had somehow approached the circle of trailers from the wrong direction; instead of the little gate in the gap between the trailers there was a pile of white rocks. The tub was there in the middle though Papa wasn't in it. He walked around toward the other opening, a little disappointed that the dog had disappeared; he had wanted Papa to see it. Just as he was latching the gate behind him, Papa leaned out of the book trailer and jerked his head, beckoning August to come quickly.

Papa was upset. His brow had furled and his eyes had a half-closed, weary glaze. August was embarrassed by his lack of focus during mutter; perhaps Papa had witnessed it with true-sight.

"Late, Aaron."

"I'm sorry, Papa. I was having visions again."

Aaron. This meant that August would interpret today. It meant that, in the night, Papa's words had scrambled out of his head into the desert, leaving him with pure understanding, untainted by Mull language. Each time it happened Papa was closer and closer to the final revelation, the Truth that couldn't be spoken. Buddha and Christ had left the world. Papa was going to show them what it was like to stay in his body during the transformation; he would not abandon them. August was afraid he wouldn't know how to interpret when Papa lost his words completely, though perhaps interpretation wouldn't be needed: maybe Papa's radiance would be enough, a spark to light the world.

Sitting together they flipped through books until August began to understand the scope of the day's address. Papa tapped his finger on the last pages of a yellowing copy of *The Ramayana*, and August said, "Victory?" Staring at August like an old animal, Papa shook his head. When Papa entered these states his hearing was affected as well, his head cocked like he was listening to something in the distance. August wished he could join Papa in that place, with the voice of God thrumming under every utterance, the world of inanimate objects vibrating, each at its own pitch.

"Ravana? Emperor of Demons? Ego." Papa nodded—the

address would pertain to Ego somehow, possibly Ego's incarnations, Ego in the flesh.

Papa's eyes closed for a moment. August saw that he was breathing a little quicker than normal. Communicating like this, when his mind had flown above it all, was a terrific strain. When Papa reached for the heavy *Illustrated Gods and Monsters*, August saw his arm shaking and quickly took it from him.

August paged slowly through the book with Papa watching, waiting to point to the right page: a picture of the labyrinth. August had the gist of it; he had memorized hundreds of Papa's transcribed lectures. He knew this theme well enough. He tended to get nervous before speaking though the words themselves were no trouble; he felt Papa's voice rising up through the dry parts of himself like an oasis spring.

That night he arrived at the main-hall early and took a seat behind the podium, trying to center himself as the initiates finished their dinner. While he waited, August scanned the army of icons on the north wall. It had started as a small collection—Buddha, Krishna, Jesus. Over time it had become a tradition for visitors to bring an antique or expensive icon as a gift to Papa, and more shelves had been added until the entire wall bristled with porcelain, wood, and gold. Papa called them the row. There were over two hundred figures from around the world: a small porcelain Virgin de Guadeloupe, her robe undulating like the wings of a manta ray; the blood-red wood of Avalokitesvara, almost iridescent with dark lacquered grain and studded with tiny knobs of jewelry that August thought looked like blisters in the wood. Shiva sitting in meditation on an animal pelt, Shiva dancing in a ring of fire. An emaciated Buddha, a fat Buddha. A wooden Bodidharma. A silver Ganesha. August found his favorites: a jade Quan Yin, milky as a cloud near her feet with a wash of emerald across her chest, and on the shelf above her, a two-faced figure from Cameroon with sharp teeth and a penis like a spout of water all the way to its feet.

How much were they worth? Thousands at least. He smiled, whisking the thoughts away with a little broom in his mind. How ridiculous Ego was sometimes! How long had it been since he had handled money? Yet here he was trying to sell these gods, these symbols of hope.

Someone coughed. August looked up. There were still a few stragglers stacking their bowls.

The row was opulent, garish, a testimony to the frantic compulsion of Mull hands carving and squeezing the materials of the world into hopeful shapes. Little weapons, clubs against fear. It was a desperate display. Some might have been made by machine—the fat Buddha could have been poured into a mold like an ornate bowl. In that inversion his serene smile would be a tiny moon frown.

Papa and Mother Li came through the rear doors holding hands like adolescent sweethearts. August stood while Papa took a seat on the meditation cushion on the wooden dais near the podium. He folded his blue robe in his lap, gripping lightly a flat wooden stick a little longer than a ruler.

August waited for the initiates to quiet down; Papa didn't like interruption. Behind Papa there was a slight breeze coming in through the open door. The desert was dark. August couldn't see any stars. The ridge of the mountain was just visible against the sky. As he watched, an aluminum-colored light blinked on halfway up the mountain: the old gas station. There must have been someone there, some lone attendant like a lighthouse keeper. August wondered if that person was looking down at the small ring of Center lights. Or maybe there was no one there; the gas station light could have been on a timer, set years ago.

The row used to make August uncomfortable, so many eyes staring at him, but now he realized that they were sealed; light hit the tiny beads of metal and wood and stopped there. Yet they stood so smugly, with their costumes and articulating hands: John the Baptist raising two fingers, Durga's arms a shrapnel-burst of gestures behind her.

His mind was running on ahead, like a child in a park, and he let it go for a moment. He saw the row as chess pieces for some final apocalyptic game. He saw the entire wall as a well-organized toolshed: Shiva's arms could chisel a fan pattern into wood; Quan Yin's flowing robes could drag perfect curves into the frosting of a cake. Then they were weapons again; there was a struggle, a battlefield, someone brought the sculpted weight of a god down onto someone else and it came up messy with blood and hair.

He closed his eyes and spoke the Abhaya mutter. The room was quiet. Papa was looking at him, his face looming large and alive; his eyes were wet, flashing between the strong bone ridges of his skull. How long had they been waiting? There was no avoiding Papa's vision; he knew that August had been daydreaming. The initiates were grouped on the floor, yawning. A few of them, Brothers Eric and James and Sister Meredith, were dozing where they sat.

August stepped up to the podium.

"Blessed is the word of God and Papa's strength in bringing it to us." He closed his eyes for a few seconds, then cleared his throat.

"Today, many Mull are practicing meditation. When Papa used to visit college campuses, the students always asked him: 'How can I kill Ego?' There is a strong desire for health, but they do not understand what a deadly enemy Ego is. They think there is some easy technique. They don't realize that trying to kill Ego is like trying to fight an army of bears."

August heard Papa's stick click on the wooden platform and turned. Already he had said something wrong. Papa was gazing out at the congregation. It meant August was supposed to pause to let this point sink in.

"Papa says this is important. Ego wants terrible things for you. Without the right knowledge and practice it is very dangerous to try to be rid of Ego. Real freedom is always preceded by terror. Run as fast as you can toward Papa." The nodding rippled through the initiates.

The lights flickered and the generator on the other side of the compound hummed in a higher pitch. It was deeply satisfying to be so rooted in Truth, so saturated with understanding that he could cast it out like grain to chickens. Being Papa's interpreter was the fulfillment of every promise made to August, the recompense for every wrong.

"You know this mental prison is foolproof, you made it yourself. You designed every gate and brick wall and razor-wire fence of it specifically to keep yourself trapped! You must do something you thought was impossible. Before you experience true freedom, you will not believe it is possible. How did Daedelus get out? You must grow wings. You can't know if the wings work until you leap. Jump. Jump like your mind is a burning building. Papa will catch you."

Papa didn't click his stick again for the rest of the forty-minute lecture. August found himself making his closing bow to the congregation full of energy and love. There was a silent period, then slowly they began to stand one by one, to shuffle out toward the quarters where they would have an hour of talk-time before bed.

August missed that period of community before sleep. It had been one of his favorite parts of Center life for years: all of them wandering around chuckling, telling stories and rubbing each other's shoulders before the lights went out with a boom. Then they would crawl into their bunks for the whispering, coughing night.

As the crowd thinned, August looked for Meredith. He was intercepted by Chris, who said, "Forgive me, Brother August. Do leeks count?"

"Count?"

"13,456." Chris beamed as if he had invented a new number. "That's yellow and red onions together, not individual leaves, just one shoot per bulb."

August stared. Had they recruited a lunatic? He spotted Meredith making her way to the door and said, "This is going to have to wait. I want you to go right to bed, okay? Get some sleep, Chris."

Meredith was filthy. There was a streak of red clay against her cheek and the front of her work shirt was clotted with mud. She was shuffling with a dazed determination and didn't stop when August came near. August put his hand on her arm and she blinked at him sleepily.

"Sister, did you fall again?"

Her hands came up and held his arms. For a moment they

stood there locked like acrobats preparing for a jump. "It's stupid, this dizziness," she said. "It's just the sun. Got to wear a hat. Remind me to wear a hat, August."

She smiled and he wanted to crawl into her dark mouth. She was selfless, brave, and her determination to work for Truth pushed her along like a second, dense body just behind this exhausted one. Her asthma had disappeared completely when she came to the Desert Center, a testimony to the healing power of Papa's practices, but recently she had been having trouble getting up in the morning.

She was falling asleep as she stood there. Her weight shifted, into August's arms. She was still smiling. When her shoulder dropped against his, the smell of her neck sent a magnetic movement of blood looping down into an erection, and he let go of her arms. She sagged then stood up again. The hall was nearly empty now. Only a few initiates were left sweeping the floor and closing the high windows with long poles.

He felt the tide of true-heart pushing up under him. The debilitating, sticky Mull love he used to feel for her had been replaced by this ocean—not just August loving Meredith, but everyone loving everyone like the cells of the body pressing close together with familiarity and hope. "*Sister.*" August spoke close to her face, "Sister, where is your daughter?"

Meredith's chin kicked forward and her eyes opened, afraid, sweeping around the hall for Melody. Then she remembered: "Already asleep. Mother Li put her to bed."

"Take my shower," August said. He touched her shoulder, shaking her lightly. "Sister, take my shower."

"But it's yours."

"I took one two days ago. I can wait till next week."

Her chin dimpled and she took a deep breath, too exhausted to cry. Her hands pressed together and she said, "Thank you, Papa." August jumped like a marionette, and his hand jerked off her shoulder. He looked behind him to see if anyone had heard. She was awake, her mouth and eyes open wide. "August! I mean Brother August! I'm sorry..."

"It's okay."

"I'm so tired."

"It's okay—you were right, compassion came *from* Papa *through* me."

"I'm sorry."

"Go quick. Take the shower so you can go to bed. Namaste, Sister."

"Namaste, Brother." August turned to go but her eyes held his, worried. "I'm just tired."

"It's okay—just a little mistake."

"Please don't report me." She bowed deeply. When he returned the bow she was already walking quickly toward the showers. August stood watching her as the fluorescent lights went out.

Outside he leaned against the corrugated metal walls listening to the others preparing for bed. *Report her?* Did they think he was some sort of spy for Papa? He saw that he was no longer one of them. Like the Mothers, he was floating between Papa and the initiates. An insect crawled over his toe and he kicked the sandal off. Picking it up he saw he had crushed one of those black beetles. Its remaining legs skittered and he used his sandal to grind it into the dust, holding his breath against the sour smell it made. He knelt, muttering in penance. As he stood he saw another beetle nosing at the wet remains of the first.

On his way to his own trailer, the blue smell of the cooling desert reminded him of a flower he couldn't name. In the cloud of stars above him he saw a rogue dot cutting through its neighbors: a satellite. Perhaps a government camera up there was watching as he headed for bed. He pressed his hands together toward it and closed his eyes in a greeting for whoever was watching. The motion was familiar and he remembered peering through his Mull father's microscope, seeing the galaxy of creatures in a drop of water, some of them jetting straight across like that.

Would he have found Papa if his Mull father hadn't died? Certainly Ego would have committed some other cruelty. No one escaped suffering. The world would have clouded over; somehow August would have been drawn to Papa's bright love. He felt gratitude wash over him and thought he might cry. "You're tired," he said to himself as he reached his trailer.

Inside, the little light spread a pink tint across the cramped space. It was attached to a solar panel on the roof, another luxury. The trailer was bare: a sink that didn't work, a small table near the window with a stack of books he had borrowed from Papa, and the bed. Above the bed a small photo of Papa and another of Jesse. Before turning off the light, he leaned close to her picture. She was smiling with a row of trees behind her; he thought it might have been taken in Santa Cruz. Papa had told him it was okay to have a reminder of the Mull world, just a small one, to keep their suffering in mind. He had chosen a photo she sent. It had been accompanied by pleas for him to "come home." Did she mean for him to live with their mother or to join her at college? He turned out the light and lay across the bed without getting under the sheet. He had the sensation again of being at sea, on a mission: a great raft of them, remote, adrift, seeking a new world. Pilgrims.

Jesse was smart. She had a scholarship. She would be finished with grad school soon. Or had she graduated already? Of course, she had resisted everything about his involvement with the Center. Where was she now? Out there at the whim of Ego, being battered and lied to. Imagining his sister suffering, even in small ways, felt like drowning in gasoline. Of course he had tried to bring her in. She was just stubborn and there was no way to force someone to open their eyes. Still he was sure that if she heard Papa speak even once, she would begin to understand. That was all it had taken for August.

His college roommate had had a long, lupine face. He wore tiny round sunglasses like John Lennon. He smoked constantly and had strong opinions about everything. It was his idea to go to the Tibetan Buddhist service because there was a free meal afterward: "It's vegetarian, but fuck it, it's free." That was where August had seen the poster of John Narshima on the bulletin board. He had stared at the face almost in recognition. The flyer read: "The Path to Peace: An ex-army officer speaks on Love." Then, a week later, a cute girl from art history class had said she was going to hear John speak and August said he was going too, as simple as that. He might not have gone to the Buddhist service, might not have seen the poster, might not have been talking to the girl. His life was saved by those chance events. He could have easily missed them, yet they had a sense of inevitability. He was destined to be near Papa. He had lived many lives trying to find him.

At that early lecture Papa had told the story about his troops in Vietnam. He was being honest about how ugly things were; he had seen what people could do to each other. His voice was more compelling than his words: a soft thunder, like the noise a tree would make if it spoke. There had been something he promised with the rhythm of his speech that August was desperately thirsty for. After the lecture, still weeping, August signed up for meditation workshops and began volunteering at the Monterey Chapter.

The Movement made him feel safe for the first time since the accident, surrounded by human padding, couched like a cow in the middle of the herd. When his application to live at the Desert Center was accepted he knew he would dedicate his life to the Movement. He wandered around in those early days, grinning with the helpless joy of getting to hear Papa speak every day, of getting to walk near him.

Remembering this, he now saw himself as a speck, a tiny, swimming creature among millions of others, suddenly near the warmth and light of Papa, so lucky and undeserving.

The NewFaces stayed close like a brood of baby ducks as he led them across the Center. Brother Monkey trailed fifty yards behind them, whistling. August had volunteered to show the NewFaces how to clean the toilets, wanting them to see that, as an elder, he was not above getting on his hands and knees in the stink. He paused at the generator shed to demonstrate how to lift the heavy gas can without straining his back. Then they cut across the compound near Papa's trailers and Rebecca whispered, "Which one does he sleep in?"

August understood: even for Movement volunteers,

Papa's wives were a curiosity. Occasionally in the mornings August heard moaning and would wait at a discreet distance until Papa came out for his bath. It had startled him last year when Papa, Mother Jessica, and Mother Star all emerged from the same trailer laughing and flushed. Fortunately, Papa knew August's mind better than August did himself. He let August struggle with the information for two days; then, on the third, he asked August to read to him about Krishna and the gopis. In that scripture, Krishna multiplied himself, so that all of the cow-herding girls who loved him could dance and make love with his clones without jealousy. Understanding came as such a relief that August had begun weeping as he read while Papa touched his shoulder: *Ego has you waiting on pins and needles for something bad to happen. Nothing bad will happen. Freedom is always preceded by fear. I will pull the curtain away and you will see.*

That wasn't a revelation the NewFaces needed yet. August waited until they were some distance from the trailers, then said, "Papa rotates between the trailers. Remember, his heart is completely open so he has enough love for five marriages. If he had a hundred wives like Solomon he would still have more than enough to go around. He is like a well that never runs dry. None of the Mothers have ever been pregnant. We are Papa's children."

Papa's bruises had startled the NewFaces and now, four days later, August felt they needed a comforting force to support them. "You know, in a dream, when you realize it's a dream and you can do anything you want? Papa is free like that. He walks through the walls we keep bumping into. He can reach into your mind and move the grain of sand that was blocking you, the little pearl you've been rubbing, the scab you can't stop picking. He is floating above us, trying to lead you out of the maze. You have to trust him more than you trust yourself."

They were nodding; they even had a kind of sober squint, which looked like understanding, though it wasn't. Not yet. All August could do was be a signpost, a landmark to guide them as they made their way down the path. Chris pointed across the distance where Mother Jessica was escorting a thin gray figure toward Papa's trailers.

"Who is that?" he asked.

"The lawyer. He works for Papa."

It was a necessary evil for Papa, because there was money to be managed, a lot of it. All of the pledges in eighty-two Chapters around the world made monthly donations, and all of the Center initiates had given everything they could, their properties and life savings. More money meant more Chapters, pushing them towards the critical mass of understanding that would prepare the world for the Great Days. August had no idea how much money was accruing and didn't want to know, it was like a hoard of rats breeding somewhere. Still, they would need it. Just before the Great Days the world would shudder like an addict's body when the toxins began to leave. People would need to see Papa's face; they would need a beacon to find their way. The money would be spent on advertising as well as to provide food, medicine, and shelter for an increasingly confused and desperate world.

This last thought made August breathe a little faster, and he looked around to see if there was anything to be done right now, even the smallest thing to bring the Great Days sooner. All he saw were the NewFaces waiting for him to say more.

The desolate chicken coop sagged. As they passed it August said, "All of the chickens except one died two years ago. Pepper is the only one left."

Rebecca asked, "Was it an Ego attack?"

"Maybe. Or maybe the desert is just too hostile for them."

Pepper, scrawny and balding, peered at them from the shadow of her coop like an aging widow in a mansion. August continued: "She doesn't lay eggs anymore. She just loses feathers and comes out at dusk to peck around. We love Pepper. She has endurance. You have to understand Papa's wisdom. Why would he locate the hub of the Movement here? Mohamed, John the Baptist, Jesus, Moses—they were all xeric creatures. The desert pounds the selfishness out of us. It's a blank slate. The desert is the perfect place to start over."

When they reached the toilet shed, August opened one of eight doors to reveal a white seat and the dark hole fifteen feet above the heap of human waste. A dozen flies startled into the air. The smell was a little sour and August made a mental note to talk to Brother Jeff about adjusting the pH.

"You know these are self-composting toilets. No water. They smell. If the smell is really bad, then probably something is wrong and you should tell Brother Jeff or me." As he talked, Brother Monkey stepped down to the third door and went inside, still whistling.

August opened the bucket next to the seat, lifting the scoop. "This powder helps the decomposition and keeps the smell down. If you only urinate don't use it, but if you defecate—" The Faces shuffled impatiently. The flies danced about their glazed eyes, like the birds that circle a cartoon character after a blow to the head. Or maybe the NewFaces were fantasizing about chocolate chips, seeing the thick black chunks floating there in front of them. August smiled. "You have to go fill the bucket at the main-hall. Use the outside hoses. Just a little soap, one squirt is plenty. If you use too much soap the seats get sticky..."

In the next stall Brother Monkey stopped whistling, then they heard him banging against the wall. He shouted, "Holy shit!"

The Faces looked at August. He lowered his voice, "You'll get used to him. You can learn a lot from Brother Monkey, he has deep understanding."

Brother Monkey exploded from the stall and stood staring into it, still pulling his pants up. "Holy shit," he said again.

August tried to ignore him. "Scrub the walls first, then the seats," he instructed. "Check the floor to be sure to get any scraps of toilet paper—" The Faces had stopped paying attention. They watched Brother Monkey, whose jaw had gone slack. His hands had turned to fists on the drawstring of his pants.

August cleared his throat loudly and said, "Then when you're done, be sure to toss a little extra enzyme in. Just use half a scoop or so. Kind of sprinkle it around." He tossed the powder into the hole and there was a rustling sound from inside. August froze. Something came out of the hole, a surge of black spilling over the lip of the toilet. August's arm flew up, pushing the NewFaces back. Hundreds of beetles washed down onto the ground. Chris was moaning, "Oh God, oh God..." Brother Monkey jumped and whooped like a cowboy.

August blinked, holding the scrub brush like a weapon. The others must be seeing what he was seeing: the beetles made a perfectly straight rank, lined up like an army bristling for combat. No, of course, not lined up, but trying to stay out of the bright light, spread out along the line of shade under the shed.

They must have been clustered inside the lip of the toilet, sleeping in the cool stench. How many times had August shat with them shimmering near his genitals? Rebecca covered her mouth, turning white. August pushed the Faces back toward the main-hall. "No, don't worry. This isn't right. It isn't this. Don't worry."

6

The next day, everything about Papa seemed slightly larger than normal. His hands, his head, the egg domes of his eyes flashing to catch every initiate's face. His mouth was like a hole dug with a shovel, the voice that came from it like the ground itself speaking. "This is dark mischief," he said. "There is no karma accrued by killing these demons! This is proof that Ego is terrified by our power—he has sent these minions to frighten us, to keep us from forwarding. The Great Days." He struck the podium and the wall shuddered behind him as a small avalanche of beetles fell to the ground like a cluster of grapes.

It was a blessing that Papa's voice was strong, as August wouldn't have known what to say. He could imagine the eggs lying dormant in the soil that had been trucked in last year from Phoenix. They had been growing under the surface of awareness, bursting weeks ago, releasing the rice-larvae that twitched and swelled underground. On the surface the crops looked healthy, but the cauliflower, cabbage, and broccoli were already ruined under the tender green domes. The roots were gone, devoured.

"There is nothing wrong with the fields—these creatures came from the soil of the mind. Ego is trying all of his tricks! We confounded the helicopters so Ego has sent these. They are not natural creatures. They are demons. Killing them is like putting out a fire. No karma."

They had not slept through the night, and the crowd of initiates sighed and fidgeted. Despite the teams of initiates stationed outside the quarters with brooms and flashlights, the beetles had found their way in, scaling the walls like a curtain of obsidian beads, rolling across the floor in a surge. Though the initiates soaked sponges with ammonia and taped them to the legs of the beds, the beetles still fell from the ceiling in a slow, blind hail. At dawn Brothers Mark and Acosta led a team that dug a shallow moat around the main-hall and quarters, lined it with tarp, and filled it with gasoline, but the drowned beetles made bridges for the live ones to cross. Eggs and larvae were found in the storeroom supplies. The smell was dizzying. The yellow liquid that the beetles secreted from their tapered abdomens was nothing compared to the stench that came from them when crushed. Fires were kept raging in trashcans on the perimeter of the Center and buckets of the writhing beetles were dumped into these blazes. The soot that resulted coated everything with an oily gray film.

After his speech, Papa went to consult with the Chapters on the phone and August helped the Mothers organize the initiates. A crew was sent to the fields to determine what crops could be salvaged. The other initiates were spread throughout the compound sweeping up beetles. August found masses of the creatures in the sink in his trailer, squirming in a foam of their own spittle. Trapped by the smooth enamel sides, they collapsed onto each other, wrestling in slow motion over the mouth of the drain. Or were they copulating? Looking closely, August could see that their wingless backs were slightly textured, like the soft dimpling of hammered metal. As he watched he saw one take another's leg in its wire-cutter mandibles. The leg popped off, snipped to a clean stump, and they continued to wrestle. There was no cry of pain, no spasm. August wondered if he could get close enough to distinguish any feeling there at all.

That night, he sat in Papa's study trailer looking for information to use against the beetles. Usually he had to contain himself when he was in Papa's studio. It was always such a heady rush of anticipation and humility. There was a map of the world with pins where the Chapters were located. Stacks of papers and books on the floor. There was a coyote skull, an antique model of the solar system with a light bulb where the sun should be; though mostly it was papers, yellow slips of annotations, books bulging with hastily scribbled notes. Papa wasn't looking for the answer; it had already been given to him in a burst of light. Now he was trying to find ways to communicate it.

Papa's message wasn't always sweet. He never said life was supposed to be easy, he didn't tell them to wait for the afterlife, didn't pretend that God was only merciful, kind, or compassionate. After all, Papa had commanded men in Vietnam. He had seen the blood and cruelty up close, witnessed God's complicity. It had occurred to August that Papa might be unable to lie; perhaps it had been forbidden him, like God's hand touching his throat. August tried to imagine Papa as a younger man, before the revelations, with his war gear, his face in the emerald forest surrounded by danger.

Now, sitting at Papa's desk, August saw where he had written the word *DESK* on the wood. His eyes caught a piece of paper taped on the bookshelf. On it was written the word *bookshelf*. It wasn't Papa's handwriting; one of the Mothers must have done it for him.

In college, August's roommate, who had been trying to learn French, taped little scraps of paper on every surface in the room. *Horloge, coucher, chaise, mur.* August had once poured a cup of coffee only to find a piece of paper with the word *café* floating in it.

He rolled his pants tightly around his ankles to keep the insects from crawling up his legs and folded an old copy of *True-Mind* to swat away any that scuttled across the books he had pulled from the shelves: *Farmer's Almanac, Desert Insects, Organic Gardens*, and a four-book set called *The Agricultural History of the Southwest*. Inside the latter two beetles looked very similar to the Ego-beetles, *Coleoptera Carabidae* and *Coleoptera Tenebrionidae*, but there was no information on eradicating them. He found accounts from 1860 of grasshopper plagues that had devastated the entire Midwest as well as references to white-fly trouble in the Imperial Valley.

Sitting there exhausted, he drank a bitter tea to stay awake. Occasionally his mind wandered to his Mull family. It was near sunrise when Mother Li came in with more tea. August was ashamed that he hadn't found anything worth reporting. Mother Li touched his shoulder and said, "Don't worry. He's feeling good this morning and he still has his voice. He has news. It'll cheer everyone up."

August stumbled out of the trailer. In the east he could see a glowing wire of green and orange like corroded copper warping along the horizon. No use trying to sleep. He took a short thick-handled broom from the dreaming hands of an initiate slumped outside the doors of the quarters, and hurried to the main-hall. The lights were on inside; a small group of Sisters sat on one of the dining tables near the back, salvaging grain from a sack into enormous bowls. They were whispering quietly while they picked, trying to glean enough for breakfast. Another Sister walked around and around the table, kicking away any beetles that tried to approach. They nodded at him, grimacing as if to say: *It's pretty bad, isn't it?*

Melody was curled up, dozing with her head in the lap of one of the Sisters, probably too scared to sleep in quarters with the beetles skittering around. He imagined her mother's chest rising and falling in the darkness and had a fierce urge to go join her, sliding himself between the sheet and Meredith's warm sleeping body, burying his face into her neck to smell the clay scent of sleep. It was a fatigue-lust, not for sex or even another body snuggled against his, but for quiet, for rest, a kind of death wish. He shook his head at Ego, whispering, "Not today, fiend."

He crouched, studying the insects with a hypnotized fascination. The needles of their limbs seemed too narrow to be animated from the inside. Could there be muscles that small? Gripping the broom, he was unable for a moment to find a place to start sweeping. The beetles littered the floor of the hall, sleeping or stunned by the lights. Some crept toward the walls or moved in slow tight circles. He began in the western corner, trying to clear the area near the kitchen so the Sisters would have a place to cook. The beetles clung stubbornly to the concrete; it was almost impossible to sweep them along without crushing them and releasing their foul viscera. The smell was ruining the morning air, making the walls dance away from him. Even though Papa had condoned it August didn't want to kill them. The stench stuck to him, making him want to run. Kneeling, he swung the broom handle slowly above the ground, trying to encourage them to the door; even so he ended up smearing several into long yellow tracks. Every single beetle was a dilemma and he was surrounded, exhausted. If he had a fire hose he could wash them out in one huge gush. He resigned himself to a delicate sweeping of one after the other, trying to roll them along instead of crushing them. It was ridiculous. He could see that he would not accomplish much before the morning meal. "C'mon, demons. Go. Move. *Please.*" He tried to imagine himself as Shiva, crushing the world, the blackened bodies scattering before him.

"They can't understand you."

August turned and saw Melody watching him with puffy eyes, half-asleep. She seemed undisturbed by the insects around her. August tried to absorb her ease, her child's faith. "I know," he said.

"Then why are you saying 'please'?" She was a little like a bug herself, thin limbs, rounded head, dazed. August wanted to lift her above the contaminated ground and carry her on his shoulders.

"I don't know," he said. She was blinking at him, more asleep than awake. "Where is your mom?" But the girl had turned back toward the group of Sisters.

When the others came in for morning meal, August patted them on the back and offered greetings. They looked miserable; August was grateful to have been awake all night instead of tossing and turning with them.

While they ate, he stood near the door to let the morning air move against the back of his neck. Sister Meredith was sitting with Melody on her lap near the back tables, both of them trying to catch a few more moments of sleep.

Papa walked up to the podium, raised his hands, and the hall grew quiet.

"Ego has interrupted our work-practice but Ego cannot postpone Joy. We will go ahead with the wedding!" He beamed, waiting until the initiates understood what they were about to be told. There was a ripple of voices. Several of them who had been dozing opened their eyes. To August, the scene looked like one of those time-lapse films that show a field of flowers opening shakily toward morning.

"I have chosen her. She will be the last Mother. Our wedding will bring the Great Days within our reach!" The room exploded with clapping; the initiates sang the celebration songs in snippets. August was suddenly deeply exhausted. He was trying to take in what Papa was saying but he couldn't take his eyes off the crowd. They were laughing and leaning into each other. It was as if the sun had risen in the hall itself: a little world with a tiny population, a new humanity, all standing there celebrating their small good fortune.

August shook his head, pressing his hands to his eyes. He was dirty with the stink of the beetles, and the bitter tea had coated his teeth with a sour fuzz. He could smell, suddenly, his own body, not just the sweat, but a dark smoke that seemed to come from inside him. The Great Days. August didn't feel ready. He needed a shower. What was Papa saying? He tried to find the root of his fear, but he was too tired to chase his mind around. Instead he watched Papa's mouth and tried to let the words work their way in.

"You have been very patient! Things will begin to move very quickly now. Remember, in the beginning, the Great Days will be even harder than before. Ego is very aware of our plans. He has rallied the world against us. We cannot be stopped now. The last Mother will complete our family. The channel of light will begin opening. Are you ready?"

"Yes, Papa!" The roar was deafening. August tried to yell his answer but the air felt dead in his lungs.

"Are you prepared to give yourselves to the fight?"

"Yes, Papa!"

"We will continue with our practice! We will not stop now! You will know the final Mother!" For a moment, the cheering drowned Papa out. He smiled at the crowd as if he had created them himself from scraps of knotted cloth. They pressed forward and August lost sight of him. He tried to find the NewFaces but they were lost among the others. He was looking for someone else for a second without knowing whom; then he realized he was looking for Sister Meredith. How was she faring?

"Are you ready to meet your new Mother?" August stood on his toes, trying to catch a glimpse of Papa's face.

"You will call her Mother Melody!"

August felt himself unraveling; he found his hands covering his groin in a primal gesture. He needed to sit down but the crowd was pushing too close. Was there more than one Melody in the Center? He looked toward the back but still couldn't find her.

The hall quieted as the words sank in. The initiates looked at one another. They were clapping though clearly they were confused by the name. Had he chosen someone from another Chapter? Mother Li and Mother Jessica rose and walked through the initiates who parted before them. They stopped in front of Sister Meredith, who held her ten-year-old daughter in front of her by the shoulders. Did he mean Meredith? She looked past the Mothers, past the initiates, directly at Papa. Melody looked at the Mothers, then craned her neck to look up at her mother's face.

"Me?" She shook her mother's hand. "Mom, me?"

Meredith's face dipped and rose again, her eyes fixed on Papa's. She was nodding. Her fingers dug into her daughter's shoulders. Melody squirmed out from her mother's grasp. August saw understanding spreading like warmth across her small face. The hall was very quiet as the little girl blinked at the faces watching her. In a heartbeat she had become a princess—of course it was her—who else? Meredith's mouth opened; no sound came out.

Mother Li looked back at Papa, who shouted, "Sister Meredith is stunned! 'How could the final Mother come from my womb? How could I deserve such an honor?'" The sound of his laughter was like a sheet of metal falling to the floor. "Sister doesn't trust her own joy. She thinks 'I'm not worthy.' But she is! Her hard work, her faith have made her a flash of lightning—" Papa clapped his hands and all the initiates jumped. "—in a cloud of water." The Mothers were leading Melody up toward the podium. Meredith had turned slightly; some invisible supporting strut had snapped and her body was listing. Her chest leaned toward the door but her eyes were riveted on Papa, who had taken Melody's hand and now kneeled in front of her. He whispered something in Melody's ear that made her giggle, then shouted, "Mother Melody! You will change the world!" There was cheering again and August lost sight of Meredith.

Melody was laughing at the crowd. Her happiness pushed through her little body, pouring from her face. August could not remember seeing anyone so happy. She was not afraid. She had no mechanism for deception; she had not learned how to smother her emotions. Her chin rose and her eyes blazed in victory. She beamed around the room, over the heads of the initiates. August felt eyes on him; many of the initiates were looking to him to help them understand. He didn't know how to interpret this.

There was a shout. Meredith had collapsed near the door.

7

Two days after the announcement the plague began to taper off and they focused on the wedding preparations. Papa retreated into his trailers, refusing to see anyone, leaving August to give the addresses by himself.

Meredith had lapsed into a drowsy illness and was allowed to convalesce in the quarters with one of the Sisters checking on her frequently. Apparently Ego had found a window into her when Papa made his announcement. August checked on her every day, though she resisted conversation and seemed barely awake. Even so, the desperate tension around her eyes never melted. She complained of exhaustion and neck pain. Once or twice a day she would get up from her bed to walk aimlessly around the compound, sometimes making it as far as the perimeter before someone spotted her and guided her back to bed. She didn't ask about Melody, who had begun sleeping in the Mothers' trailers.

Behind those closed doors, Melody was learning to refine herself as all the Mothers had before her. None of the initiates were allowed to see her in this crucial period. She was being taught to keep her body purified, practicing tea ceremonies and posture. She was learning how to accept adoration, the loving, hungry gaze; how to embody the infinite source of divine love without being overwhelmed.

August spent his days with the NewFaces or fighting the remaining beetles. He left the wedding organization to oth-

ers as much as possible, wanting to be free to go to Papa's
side as soon as he was called. He had been having trouble
sleeping again; a sour anxiety had settled into him and he
longed to sit near Papa's serenity.

August gave brief improvisational addresses in the mornings, accentuating Papa's unwavering wisdom. "Of course
the final Mother has to be young. 'A child shall lead them.'
A true innocent is the only one to bear the scrutiny of the
coming Great Days. Soon the eyes of the world will be upon
us. They will see in Mother Melody a being of unclouded
purity. Think of the Christ child, the Krishna child. Ego has
lost strength. We all felt the crisis, but now, trusting Papa, we
are carried by his guidance even closer to the Great Days."

He began to carry the beetle broom around with him regularly, sweeping the corpses during the day, leaning it next
to his bed at night. Though dealing with the beetles was still
disconcerting, there was a mindless rhythm in sweeping that
reminded him of work-practice in the fields. Holding the
flaking broom took him out of himself and made him feel
productive. He found he could sweep the bone-dog and
other visions away with it as well.

He had been keeping his spirits high for the sake of the
initiates, but the lectures were beginning to feel halfhearted.
He needed to talk with Papa.

A week before the wedding, August wandered the compound after breakfast, looking for the NewFaces. They had
been in the fields pulling yams and pumpkins for the wedding ceremony soups and August wanted their help sweeping; with luck the Center would be beetle-free for the

wedding. After the wedding, when the schedule returned to normal, the Faces would probably be completely broken in.

A group of initiates now gathered in front of the shelves of buckets near the well, the NewFaces among them. At first August thought something had gone wrong; then he recognized Brother Monkey's voice as he made little grunts and whistles behind the buckets. An onion popped up over the top shelf and did an uncanny jig on its green shoots, then a carrot joined it. The onion bowed and said "Namaste!" in a squeaky-mouse voice and the carrot returned the greeting. Then they were collected in one hand while the other brought up a large gourd. The onion and carrot bowed so low that August understood the gourd was supposed to be Papa. It approached the other vegetables in a slow, deliberate pace. The rhythm was perfect. August had never noticed how unique Papa's walk was, yet there it was, perfectly replicated by a gourd. He thought Brother Monkey had gone too far again, but the gourd just passed them with a small bow, then the onion and carrot began to bow and mutter. The food sped through the chants like a tape on fast-forward and everyone laughed.

With the handle of the broom August tapped the NewFaces on the shoulders, ordering them to sweep around the main-hall first. Then he went to check on Meredith. She was sleeping restlessly when he sat down on an adjacent bed to watch her. Though her neck was wet with sweat, the gray blanket was pulled tightly up around her. Her head rolled back and forth on the pillow making him want to hold it still. What a fight she was giving Ego! Just below her brown skin there was a ferocious battle taking place. He wondered if he should suggest redirection; it might give her the edge she needed to come back to herself, making her body inhospitable to Ego. He didn't like the thought of her standing, sweating long hours in z-trailer without eating or sleeping. Still, as uncomfortable as it would be for her, it would be worse for Ego—a fever to break the illness. She would come out feeling exhausted and clean. The Mothers would offer her soup and make jokes until she was back on her feet again. He decided to talk to Brother Matheson; perhaps he could go easy on her, maybe twelve hours—with bathroom breaks—instead of the full twenty-four?

He touched her cheek, feeling a love like a wreath of blossoms around his head. She just needed a little backup, a little support and she would feel better. They would all be feeling better soon.

Five days before the wedding he was trying to find the right words to finish the morning address when Brother Matheson spoke to someone loudly in the rear of the hall. Matheson stood with his arms crossed and his back to the podium, his voice buzzing like a fly against the metal walls. Someone said "Shhh!" and he was quiet.

The air in the hall seemed hazy and August thought he could smell the walls oxidizing. Dust had gathered on the shoulders of the row like the first breath of mold. The broom leaned against the podium; August had an impulse to lift it like a scepter to help him generate majestic words. He said, "Brothers and Sisters, keep at it. Breathe. Lift each other through these long days. Papa is counting on you." He clapped twice, bowed, and absorbed the brief rush of warm energy as everyone in the hall returned the bow in unison.

Mother Li caught his eye and he raised his hands again. "Hold on, stay where you are. Mother Li has an announcement." As she approached the podium she whispered, "Papa has his voice. He wants you in the trailer."

As she began assigning duties for the wedding, August pulled Brother Matheson outside. Had he always been this big? August craned his neck to look him in the eye. "Brother, your chatter was distracting."

Matheson wagged a phone in front of August's face. "It's Seattle," he said. "They say they won't be able to send their visitors until the morning of the wedding. You know how they are."

"You could have taken it outside."

"Also Phoenix is here tomorrow. I can't manage them. You'll have to do it, or get one of the Mothers to babysit them."

The anger rising in August's throat bloomed bright yellow behind his tongue. He tried to imagine water sluicing down through the top of his head. "The wedding is in five days— the visitors are already on their way. You can't request another assignment now."

"This isn't a request. Something came up. Can you do it or not?"

"How could I? I'm interpreting. What came up?"

Brother Matheson shook his head. "We just need to get someone to chaperone Phoenix."

"I guess we can get Sister Acosta to do it. What about you?"

"Good," Brother Matheson said and turned to walk away. His back was broad as a brick wall, his shaved head like a boulder balanced between his shoulders.

August jogged to place himself in Matheson's path but instead found himself stumbling backwards as the man trudged ahead.

"Brother, what's your task?" August said.

"Meredith."

"What do you mean? Redirection?"

"Ego has her."

"But did she do something?" August felt himself blushing with guilt. Days ago he had thought redirection was exactly what she needed. Now, facing Matheson, he was sure she just needed rest.

"NeverMind."

"Brother, as long as I'm speaking for Papa, everything that happens here concerns me. Tell me what happened." Matheson stopped. Their ranks were finally colliding.

Matheson studied August's face before he spoke. "She was holding on to the new Mother."

"What do you mean holding on?"

"Melody was in the kitchen for some reason. Meredith found her there and just grabbed her. She wouldn't let her go. Ego is all over her. It will use her to get to Melody." His eyes seemed too bright, enjoying August's reaction.

"Where is she now?"

"Already in z-trailer."

August wanted to talk to her himself—Meredith's behavior was indeed strange—but he had no time, Papa had called. "Brother, you have to go easy on her. She's been sick—she faints."

Matheson shook his head again. "You don't tell *me* how to redirect. I don't care how many speeches you give, you have no business telling me how to burn Ego." He leaned close, his shoulders rocking toward August like the first stages of an avalanche. "That's *my* task, you don't know anything about it. You stand up there, talking, making them clap. But when they fall apart who puts them back together? When the enemy gets in, who kicks him out?"

"I'm just telling you, she's been sick."

"That's my task."

"She's been weak for a long time."

"This conversation is over." Matheson moved forward again; August bounced off his hip and watched him stride toward z-trailer.

When August arrived at the circle of Papa's trailers, Mother Li was coming out of Papa's bedroom. Her braid hung heavily between her breasts. "Child, what's the matter?" she said. "Look at your face!"

"What happened with Meredith last night?"

"Oh." She touched August's arm. "She'll be all right. Matheson is on it."

"I just talked to Matheson. I don't know if redirection is exactly what she needs right now."

"Listen to you!" She beamed at him as she would at a toddler doing something silly. "May I suggest, don't worry about Meredith, she's stronger than you think. What's going on inside you, child? Papa needs you, this is no time to be losing your center."

"I'm just concerned, Mother." The braid looked wet with oil. August thought it would be warm to the touch. He had an urge to grab on to it and hang on.

"Well, cheer up. Papa's got his voice. Plus he's in a good mood, so go in there and talk to him. He asked for you. But—" She tapped his chest with her finger, making a hollow thump. "Center yourself. I know it's a stressful time. Don't start thinking with your meat-mind." August felt himself recoil. No one had spoken that word to him since he became an elder. It was ugly, an insult used to distract NewFaces from their Mull thinking. Why did she think he deserved that?

She walked across the circle, stepping into the shadow of another trailer. When she opened the door August heard laughter and remembered a wedding shower he had seen as a child with his Mull mother: a roomful of women getting their nails done, while listening to country music. He knocked on Papa's door.

Inside, Papa was applying powder to his naked body, sitting on the edge of his bed with one leg over the other, working the powder between his toes. Folded next to him was a bundle of blue cloth: his wedding garment. It was like the one he wore every day except that it had golden filigree around its openings, at the neck, the sleeves, and the bottom; the Mothers must have been refitting it. Papa grinned. "Namaste, August!" He was serene, no evidence of any struggle with words. August sat on the floor next to a long, white silk sash that would be wrapped around Mother Melody during the ceremony.

"Papa, I am not worthy of you," August announced. "I'm falling apart. I am so relieved to hear your voice."

"Learn to rejoice in the Truth of my silences as well," Papa said, his feet marbled with talcum. "The revelations are not just ways of thinking, August. They are ways of being. It might be a little messy at first, but things are really rolling now. You are not falling apart—you are finally coming together."

August rubbed his eyes. "Yes, Papa, but it's hard when…

it feels like you are taking yourself away from us."

Papa nodded to the bookshelf. "What language are those written in?"

"Mostly English, Papa."

"Whose language is English?"

"Mull. Mull language."

Papa stood, rubbing the powder onto his neck. "The chrysalis is an awkward time. When I emerge, my true-mind will be completely free of the shackles of Mull thought. I'll be able to guide you through the Great Days as a bright light—a new creature." His voice was like the sound of water poured into a great brass bowl.

August bowed, leaving his head resting between his hands. When would he learn? When would he trust? He had been worried that every word Papa said might be his last, trying to soak Papa's voice in, preparing for a drought. These good days were farther and farther apart. He had a surreal sensation that Papa had already passed into silence, that this dialogue was taking place in his head. The trailer rocked and he thought for a moment it might be an earthquake; then he realized that his own body was moving. His chest heaved but his eyes stayed dry. He tried to speak evenly. "Meredith's been fainting. Then Melody... I don't know, and your silences. Mother Li just spoke to me like I was a NewFace. I'm a little tired, Papa. I'm just a little tired."

Papa's hand touched the back of August's head and he wept harder, wanting to be done with it all, wanting to give over to Papa and be done.

"You were looking for Sister Meredith?"

"Yes, Papa. I guess I've been worried. She fainted when you made the announcement, as you know, and now she's in redirection."

"Now that you know where she is, are you still worried?"

"I can't lie to you, Papa. I was in redirection once—that was a long time ago. I've heard it's changed since then."

"It's more efficient now."

"When I was there, it was difficult. I had to stand a long time. She's been sick. I thought it might be good. Now I don't know if she can handle it."

"Do you trust Papa?"

August sat up, looking toward the perfect face. "Absolutely, Papa."

"Then you must trust that I would never push Sister Meredith beyond her own tolerance."

"Of course—but Brother Matheson doesn't have your compassion."

"Wake up!" Papa clapped his hands and a cloud of talcum exploded, sifting through the air around August's head. Through the cloud, Papa's face glowered like a red moon. "Don't you know that Papa is watching Sister this minute? Right now I can see her! Can *you* see her?" August's lower lip peeled back as he wept. The talcum sank through the air like dead light. *"Can you see her?"*

"No, Papa, I can't see her."

"Why do you think Ego has been attacking her so ferociously? Because she's *bright*—she is the *mother* of the Final Mother! She is strong. Ego has made you think you're feeling compassion while breeding mistrust and deception in your mind."

August dropped his head again, feeling worry slide out of him, a bloody useless organ. Papa was taking care of it. August had a sudden urge to sleep, to slip into a deathlike slumber there on the floor. "Forgive me, forgive me," he whispered.

A minute passed and Papa's voice was soft again: "The devil never leaves me, August. The Genius Evil is here in this room. We're old enemies—old friends. He's waiting for me to get tired, waiting for me to slip up. The Mull world will never understand me. Even the initiates don't understand. Every word I say, every move is strategy. I'm playing chess. Ego can cheat and Ego doesn't sleep. If I lose, the world burns. You have to be willing to die every second. You have to throw yourself at death because the minute you're afraid, checkmate! He wins; you are just a person and he is a god."

August had never heard this tone in Papa's voice before; it sounded as if he were speaking to himself. The glorious eyes had focused somewhere beyond August. Papa moved slowly, applying balm to his elbows and hands from a small turquoise box. The hands slid against each other like sea creatures mating.

"I can't tell *them* this, August. I'm counting on you to understand. I know that they're confused and scared. They're worried that Melody is too young. They're still wrapped up in Mull prejudices." Papa laughed softly. The sound moved down August's back like warm water. "They come here with nothing but a toothbrush and they carry the entire Mull world in their heads, most of them are still watching television behind their eyes. They're waiting for the eleven o'clock news to tell them what to think. It takes years for the baggage to rot away by itself. It has to be burned away. That's the real reason behind work-practice.

"All of them out there setting up chairs, making tea, if they knew what Ego was really like, if they saw what kind of monster moved in and out of the doors of their minds, they would be paralyzed with fear. They wouldn't be able to do any work, wouldn't make any progress. Ego would turn them into rats.

"This is bigger than any of them imagine. They can't understand my strategy. They don't need to. To shut Ego out for good we have to lead people through a very dark hallway before they see the light."

Something was coming.

"August, when I look at them, I see *him*. Crouching inside their skulls watching me, staring back at me, waiting. Waiting for *one second* when he can turn them all against me. I also see brave souls struggling toward the light, like sick children taking their medicine with total faith. They give me the courage to keep fighting.

"But *you*, my child. You have ears to hear. When the rest of them get scared, you begin to really understand. Your desire for Truth is bigger than your fear. You're like me. You aren't afraid to look hard at the darkness. Even when your heart tries to run away you bring it back.

"I need you. Ego knows I'm losing my voice. I don't know when it will go for good. He'll begin to sow confusion and distrust. You must be strong. I'm counting on you to understand me. Quickly. Fundamentally. That's why I chose you to be reader. Did you think I just liked to be read to? I needed you to see the battleground. You're my general. The Mothers can't do this work. They're caretakers, their gift is kindness. They nurse the wounded. Matheson is good but he doesn't understand like you, he doesn't have the drive to really understand. Look at me, August."

Papa's eyes were like mouths opening.

"Soon Papa won't have any words at all. I can feel it—it's close. Maybe these are the last until I find the new words. I need to be able to trust you with *everything*. We need to break one final barrier between us. Ego still has a hook in you. Can you feel it?"

"I can feel it, Papa."

"Are you ready to be free? Are you ready to break all ties with Ego; are you ready to join me?"

August felt himself without gravity, floating up into Papa's eyes, racing through space at ecstatic speeds. He was the nectar moving into the bee. He was the swollen bud, one second before bursting into bloom. "*Please*, Papa," he said.

"You have to let go. Allow this wisdom to pass from me to you without trying to understand."

"I'm ready." August had the urge to grab on to Papa's feet and press his head against them.

"You were with your Mull father when he died."

"Yes."

"Did you know that you were going to die?"

"I thought I was dying."

"No, I mean, was that the first time you understood that, no matter what, you were going to die?"

"I think so, Papa."

"How old were you?"

"I was nine." August knew Papa knew these things.

"Nine! You really knew you were going to die?" Papa stood, lifting his vestment from the bed and holding it in front of himself. "For most people it takes a long time, they're much older when they realize the inevitability, the certainty. Some people never come to terms with their own death, and almost never so young."

"It was the car accident, Papa. He was right there next to me."

"And you watched him leave his body?"

August felt his shoulders shaking. The tears slid down his nose. "My ribs were broken, my leg was broken—I couldn't breathe and he was right there, he was covered in blood and he wasn't breathing. I knew he couldn't help me."

Papa stood very still. August watched Papa's forehead. The eyes were too much.

"At the time it was a great trauma, August. Now you see it was a gift. That is why you understand the teachings so much quicker than the others: because you understood the fragility of life so early. We don't recognize gifts right away. We think: This is the worst thing that could have happened to me."

Papa was smiling, pleased with how things had worked out so far—August's life, the Movement, the whole of history.

"When the asteroid that killed the dinosaurs filled the sky there was fear, but without wiping that slate clean we could not be here. When you pull the beets from the ground they feel fear. Not like our fear but it is *fear*—their roots, their cells know something is wrong. Fundamentally. We turn that grief into food. We eat it. God eats it." He touched August's cheek, his wide thumb riding down the scar. "This..."

"From a dog, Papa. That was different."

"Not so different. Your father couldn't help you then, either."

"No, Papa." August lowered his eyes. He could not seem to remember how to hold his head on his neck without shaking. Papa stepped forward and August turned his body so

Papa could walk past him; but Papa stayed there, close, his thigh touching August's shoulder.

"Who will help you?"

"*You* help me, Papa. You help everyone." Tears rolled into the cup of skin behind August's collarbone. His body was an empty bowl, his whole being dumb with pain and hunger.

"You have been so brave. So patient. So very patient," Papa said.

It was coming. Papa leaned forward, crushing the space between them, lifting August's chin. The robe dropped and August saw his reddening body.

This, then.

"There can't be any hesitation. There can't be a single second of doubt between us. You're the one. I need you."

This was what he had been waiting for.

Papa's penis fit into him like a thumb in a fist, the head of it on the back of his tongue like a swallowed star, burning him from the inside, turning everything into rivulets of molten gold. His nose touched the silvered curls.

It was breaking through him, pushing him inside himself. He was afraid for his little mind, his child mind. *I don't want to know this.* Yet his body was doing it, eagerly, hungrily, he wanted it more than anything. If Papa had come at him with a knife he would have lifted his neck to be cut. No one would deny him this last push, this final unveiling. He would break through this door or die.

He knew how to do it, like a caterpillar knows how to curl and twist about its tail with its own mouth. The small coward part of him was trying to pull away, so August leaned into Papa's hips. Of course it would be something like this, something he would never have expected. There was no running away. He could feel it was killing him. Not killing him, but killing Ego. The liquid running down his throat was poison. He wept at how simple it was. He was afraid and glad to be afraid; glad to have the cowering parts of himself extinguished. There would be no scar this time; there would be no body to hold the pain. After this, no doubt or hesitation, ever again. Everything was wet and there was a smell like boiled seaweed. He moved like a machine built to make itself. Papa's hands wrapped behind his ears, holding him by the scruff of the scalp, sculpting him, making him. And the savage noise inside, the volcanic roar of August's life came up and out of Papa in a groan.

8

The Center bustled with preparations. A low wooden platform was built. Four hundred folding chairs were trucked in from Phoenix and arranged under a bright blue tent whose sides had been rolled up to allow air to pass through. The smells from the kitchen began to overwhelm the beetle smell. Fresh baked bread, potato leek soup, and smoked eggplant made the initiates salivate and elbow each other nervously, their meditations dissolving into fantasies of the wedding feast. Delegates arrived from Tokyo and Berlin, clustered quietly in their white visitor shirts, hoping to catch a glimpse of Papa. Mother Star led them on tours to the fields as well as outside the perimeter to see the native plants. Initiates with brooms wandered the grounds like soldiers, alert for rogue beetles twitching in the sand. The cloud of dust on the horizon that indicated approaching delivery vehicles or Jeeps fluttered throughout the day.

August threw himself into the commotion. He stood on tables yelling orders and ran from team to team reallocating workers. More than once he found himself gripping an initiate's arm too tightly. He drove the NewFaces especially hard, and began to see traces of bitterness in their faces when he approached. Good. He was their mentor, not their playmate.

He had not truly slept for days. He went to his trailer late at night when the entire compound was completely dark and he could not imagine anything else to do. Then he lay on his dusty bed, muttering the mantras until he rose again, before the others, to check on Papa.

The soft classical music in Papa's trailer played endlessly. His voice was gone again but August and the Mothers were handling the preparations so well that Papa had no orders to give. When August poked his head into the trailer a couple of times a day, Papa was napping or holding yogic positions in a wash of violins, invulnerable to the anxious preparations around him.

August didn't think about their encounter. He felt as if he was treading water over a yawning abyss. It was supposed to have wiped him clean of Ego, but he was afraid of what would come when he let himself relax. He had no strong hallucinations, only a rustling sound that he had learned to associate with bad acid trips in college. Keeping himself in a panic pitch of activity seemed the safest thing to do. *Papa cured me. I have the cure.* He kept the mutters rolling in his head at all times to drown out the rustling. They also kept him from worrying about Meredith, who was in z-trailer for the second time.

She had emerged from the first twenty-four hours of redirection, rested in the quarters for eight hours, then joined the kitchen crew without a word. She seemed to have found her center and worked quietly for two days. Then she was found far outside the perimeter with Melody, both of them weeping, and was brought back, just before the Phoenix delegates arrived, saving the Center an embarrassment.

She was the only initiate in memory to be sent to redirection twice in one month, let alone in a single week. She would miss her daughter's wedding. August tried not to look in the direction of the yellow square of bamboo fence that surrounded z-trailer.

At two a.m. on the day of the wedding August had checked and rechecked everything, his thoughts congealing with fatigue. He found himself wandering past the gasoline smell of the generator shed toward z-trailer and stopped. It was dark; he could barely make out the bamboo partition against the sky. He knew that they would both be awake, Meredith swaying on her feet, Matheson asking her over and over again, "Where is your mind? Where is your loyalty?" A recording of Papa's voice reciting old lectures would be whispering around them.

He knew he needed sleep but it was impossible: he felt something waiting to ambush him as soon as he relaxed. How long would it take for Papa's gift to take effect? Perhaps, after the wedding, serenity would overwhelm him; his enlightenment would correspond to that auspicious event. He would be able to sleep as much as he wanted.

He heard a voice whining in the distance. A coyote? A light was on in the main-hall and he was grateful to find four bleary-eyed, cheerful Sisters making delicate pouchlike cookies with raisin centers. The ovens had heated the kitchen to a dizzy sweat that simulated noon and gave him another burst of energy. He washed his hands and helped them bake until half an hour before sunrise, when he went to check the platform one more time.

As the ceremony began August found himself with nothing to do and a tingling at the base of his neck. Though Papa was speechless, he shook his head when August offered to interpret; the Mothers were officiating the whole thing. Each of them took a turn at the microphone, welcoming delegates or praising Papa. Their voices swept over the hundreds seated under the enormous canvas tent and off into the desert. August flinched at every hard consonant or amplified sibilance. He should have slept. He tried to listen to the echo off the mountains.

Visitors wearing white T-shirts with the spiral logo over the heart sat nervously in folding chairs near the platform where great plumes of flowers arced like flames around the Mothers. A loose ring of initiates armed with brooms ambled counterclockwise around the tent as they swept away any remaining beetles. Massive bundles of incense poured white ash into the air, masking the acrid stench of the last beetles burning. The smoke bled into the sky and made the light yellow, like an old sepia photograph. The rows of potted trees behind the stage were seared golden in the light. How long had it been since he had seen real trees?

August stood near the back, trying to lean against one of the aluminum poles that held the canvas above the crowd, his ears pounding with blood. Planted in the sand behind him, a skull-sized clump of incense sent a fog around his head and he tried to let himself dissolve into it. His eyes watered. The garish scene in front of him faded from sight, then was revealed again. The colors spun, faces moved toward him, melting into each other. He felt his stomach pulsing and realized that he was laughing and choking on the smoke. His whole body was a dull ache: a beetle crushed from its shell, raw and brainless.

It was simple. It had to have been something like that, something he could never speak about, totally unforeseeable yet somehow inevitable. Still, each searing moment of his life remained with him: he was being born into the world, pale and screaming; under the red dog lurching against his face; under Papa's flesh; in the car covered with gasoline and his father's blood. When would peace come?

Leaning out of the tent and looking up he saw the sky was the wrong color: zinc, like the dissection table in biology where they peeled the baby pigs. It turned, smearing the smoke around itself. Perhaps the Great Days would destroy the earth. He saw the moon like a dent in the metal sky. It boomed with Mother Li's voice: "When Ego is afraid, that is a good sign!" The crowd cheered.

The end of the world might not be a bad idea, August decided. Maybe they had angered God, triggered some sort of karmic chain reaction that would collapse creation. The oceans would rise up, cleansing the world of all the rushing and moaning. Then maybe they would get to start again from scratch.

He squinted at Mother Melody and tried to see the ancient soul move through the child body. She was a bolt of metallic blue standing completely still behind her veil, her arms wrapped tightly with silk and flowers. Her chest was high like she was being pulled upward from the heart. Mother. Sister. Daughter. Lover. What had Meredith hoped to do with her out there beyond the perimeter?

The child approached the microphone near the edge of the platform, her white hands curled tightly around it. The jade bracelet was already hanging from her elbow. She spoke slowly, cooing like a girl teaching a doll how to behave: "Last night I dreamt the sea of creation." The crowd nodded, letting small moans of recognition and pleasure rise up toward her. They liked this story.

"I was sitting on a great raft overlooking the ocean of consciousness," she continued. "The Lord sat near me wearing Papa's face. He was feeding every creature its particular food." A ripple went through the crowd as the initiates pressed their hands together in front of them.

"I saw how tenderly Papa treated and nourished each and every living thing in the universe, and decided to play a joke on him: as he was busy I reached into the pool of consciousness and pulled up a tiny golden cricket and I put it right here near my breast." She pressed one hand against the silk near her neck as if there were a small pain there. August could see that the Mothers had demonstrated very carefully how to do this. The speech was memorized, and except for hurrying it a little, Melody spoke very well. August thought of Brother Monkey's vegetable puppet show. He had never been so exhausted; he felt his blood pouring out through the bottoms of his feet to be soaked into the sand. He was supposed to be cured.

Melody said, "I asked Papa if all the creatures had eaten and he said, 'Yes' and I said, 'Are you sure all the creatures have eaten?' and he said, 'Yes.' And then I asked a third time, 'You have not overlooked even the smallest insect?'" She cocked her head, acting it out.

"And Papa said, 'Every creature has been nourished.' So I parted my blouse and what was there?" The crowd moaned, rocking with anticipation; someone laughed and clapped. "There, between my breasts, was the tiny cricket, and it was eating a slender blade of grass that had sprouted from my skin!"

They shouted, "Mother!" clapping and raising their hands. Papa touched her shoulder and she walked back and kneeled near the other Mothers. The Founder walked slowly behind his wives, resting his hand on each of their heads. August saw, in his mind's eye, Papa's penis swaying in front of him. He shook his head and examined his own dusty toes bound in the sandals. They seemed to belong to someone else. Smoke moved in front of him. He watched his feet moving out into the bright sunlight.

A little fresh air. Just check on the perimeter. Maybe a quick nap in his own trailer. He closed his eyes, allowing his feet to take him away from the smoke and noise. Nothing had cured him. Not even Papa's perfect body. His mind hadn't made the leap, everything was still obscene. He had failed.

The clamor of the wedding shrank behind him. He found himself leaning against the bamboo screen around z-trailer, listening to soft, odd noises. How had he walked so far already? There was a cheer far off in the distance: the tent on the other side of the compound, seven-eighths of a mile away.

Maybe his body was asking for redirection. Of course, a cleansing to push him through. Afterward, Papa's gift would settle into him and he'd be free.

They were singing now at the wedding. Inside the trailer was a crackling sound under the recording of Papa's voice. The door was locked. Brother Matheson shouted, "Who is it?" Would the key for Papa's trailer work for z-trailer? As August opened the door, Brother Matheson charged at him.

Meredith was slumped on her side. Naked, blindfolded, gagged, with her hands behind her back, her legs tied with rope. Something else on the floor. A box of hissing snakes.

A hand slammed into his face and August fell off the steps. He landed on his ribs in the sand, then rolled onto his back, gasping. Brother Matheson locked the door from the outside with a large padlock. The singing was louder now. August stared up at the smoke spreading into the sky and listened to the singing. Not a box of snakes. What was Matheson saying?

August felt himself being picked up and slung over Matheson's shoulder like a child who had fallen asleep. Not a box of snakes. But it was hissing.

He kicked as hard as he could. Matheson barked, holding his gut, and August was on the ground again. As he scrambled up, his mind saw it clearly: Not snakes. Wires. A car battery, the copper jaws lying near her feet.

Matheson said, "Ego has you. You're seeing things again." August moved for the door but the lock was solid. He felt the thick hands pulling him down. His face was being pressed into the sand and he couldn't breathe. Matheson was on top of him with his arm snaked around his throat. "Don't do this on the wedding day," Matheson whispered in his ear. "Don't fall apart now. Just go to sleep." Choking, August saw a wreath of purple flowers crowding his vision, heard Matheson grunt, and felt himself sinking into the ground. *He is killing me.* The flowers bloomed in a gush, then disappeared.

Headache. Wet. Still on the ground, August had pissed himself. He woke to Papa's voice, calm, patient: "Love is the only power we have. It keeps us together on an atomic level. Science has found no explanation for gravity or the atomic forces that keep the universe from exploding outward. It is God's will. It is God's love..." Matheson was gone. August stood, nearly blacking out again, and touched the door of the trailer—was she still in there? God, what had he been doing to her? The muffled recording came through the door: "There is no other option, we've tried everything, love is it."

How much time had passed? Bile stung the back of his throat. Papa's fluid. Peering around the bamboo blind August saw Matheson's silhouette near the main-hall; it was moving quickly back toward z-trailer.

August rattled the padlock. "Meredith? Sister!" He had to tell Papa. Maybe he could outrun Matheson and make it back to the tent? He peered around the blind again and saw Matheson only a hundred meters away carrying a coil of rope. As he steeled himself to run, Papa's voice came through the door: "Nothing can be hidden from Papa because my love has no boundaries." August's mind froze. The air became a slow-motion roaring around him as he watched Matheson getting closer.

Papa had said: *Right now I can see her! Can you see her?* He could never have approved of this.

Even so it was impossible for him to be ignorant.

The paradox pushed August up out of his body and he watched himself standing there like a mannequin. Everything was completely silent, the distant singing, Papa's voice—nothing got through except a rhythmic rasping of his own breath. The bamboo had a dancing grain across its hay-colored surface, and the wire it was woven together with punctuated every four shafts, making the entire fence a visual score, the whole piece playing before his eyes. Beyond it, the searing sky and the smoke and Matheson running, holding the rope away from the pitch of his body.

There was a nauseating snap like a bone being reset, and August turned, running in the other direction, passing the trailer. Nothing now between himself and the perimeter. He listened for footsteps behind him but heard only a rustling sound, some churning machine working up a wind. *More efficient.* The noise was coming from the sky. He looked up and saw it was the pale afternoon moon, making an awful noise, coming closer to crush them all. Then he saw the black weight of the helicopter lumbering over the moon like a mosquito swollen with blood. There were distant screams from the wedding. Mother Li's voice boomed over the loud speakers, "Look how terrified Ego is! It's too late. The family is complete! Sing, let them hear us sing!" He let his body carry him, the wind from the helicopter pushing him along.

When he reached the perimeter he turned quickly but Matheson was not behind him. Z-trailer sat innocently in its frame of bamboo. Beyond that was a small apocalypse: the helicopter hunkered over the tent, pulling the smoke up around itself like a cloak and churning it through the rotors. The white dolls of the visitors were running in every direction while initiates tried to shepherd them toward the shelter of the main-hall. Half of the tent tore from its moorings and slapped at the fleeing figures. Mother Li was still screaming through the speakers, her voice breaking into clusters of noise. The smoke and dust folded up around the helicopter in an enormous lucent blossom.

Meredith. What had he seen?

Matheson came running around z-trailer pointing at August. There was another man with him. The wire fence bit into August's hands as he climbed. He landed on the other side of the perimeter with a lance of pain in his shin.

Meredith. No, the door was padlocked, he couldn't get to her. He limped backward, watching the dust from the helicopter as it engulfed z-trailer and the men chasing him. August turned away and, as he began to run, whispered: *"Don't think."*

9

When August looked back again, the Center was already a wafer against the sand. The helicopter bumbled away across the smoke-smudged sky. He kept running, the mantras wheezing between each breath, a bloody metallic taste like a row of pennies down his throat.

The terrain became rockier, pebbles becoming fist-sized stones. Thin pewter lizards dotted the rocks like exposed fossils. The ground sloped up and he was suddenly in the shade; the first low hump of the mountain rose in front of him with a crown of light behind its bald head. He was small and exposed. While he couldn't see it yet, he knew Ego was hunting him. His sandal caught a stone and he tripped, his head striking the ground. His ear rang with pain. Pressed near to the ground he could hear what he had been mumbling: "Blessed is the Eye of the Lord, which sees all…"

He saw her again, more clearly now, lying on her side with the gag pulling her lips back. He pushed himself up and leaned into his run. Already thirsty. The desert might kill him before Ego found him. Looking back again at the Center, he had a rodent urge to find some protective outcropping to huddle under. From behind the mountain, the edge of sunlight cut across the comatose blue sky. Beyond the Center the sand shimmered: a band of coyotes loping across the expanse, and, like a strip of cheap jewelry on the eastern horizon, Phoenix.

How could she answer if she was gagged? How could she say the right thing? His stomach folded and he retched. The sour fist of vomit punched up, slamming against his palate and out his nose. The rocks turned dark copper, bits of oats studding their surface. Ego would come soon, its arms spinning like helicopter rotors. He was moving again. From a ridge he could see several small hills rising into the foothills of the Harquahala Mountains. He wedged himself, wheezing, against the base of a rock and tried to catch his breath.

The stream of smoke from the Center dissipated until the moon was the only chip of smutch left. Around it, the stars appeared one by one like welts as the Center disappeared into the darkness. He was shivering now; it felt like a fever and he laid his body over the rock for warmth. Where it pressed into his belly, the rock seemed to have a pulse. By now they would know he was missing. Matheson would have told Papa. Or had Papa seen it all with his third eye? Did he know about Meredith? Did he allow it?

August's stomach made sounds like a dog—whimpering, pathetic. He tried to remember something from her face, some clue to help him understand. All he could see were her breasts, the gag, the car battery.

He woke in the middle of the night to watery light; the dead eye of moon had come close to stare at him. There was a glimmer on the floor of the desert like a star fallen to earth: Papa's trailer. Melody's honeymoon.

When the moon dropped behind the mountain August was in complete darkness, and it gave him some relief. Invisible, he eased into it, letting the shadows dissolve him. Something grazed his hand and he opened it. Maybe it was poisonous: brown recluse, vinegarroon, scorpion. He rose, trying to walk, feeling his way slowly over the rocks, then he stumbled and found himself lunging on all fours, hands raw and burning. He was going downhill now, lifting a piece of the mountain between himself and the Center. He rushed face first into a bush of thorns, then lay down again, trembling. *When will Ego come?*

The morning light found him like something disinterred, his dry tongue too big in his mouth. High near the roof of the sky a buzzard made hypnotic patterns around the floaters in his eyes. The heat came on quickly as he walked along the ridges up the mountain, picking his way between the rocks and brittle bushes. Thirst spread white as fear in his throat. Sometimes coming up over a peak he looked back, to see how far from the Center he had drifted. The heat was already searing the air into eddies, like Papa's morning bowl of miso, and the Center looked like the white squares of tofu clustered at the bottom.

There was a movie he had seen while sitting on the couch between his Mull parents. Something disastrous on a spaceship, the astronauts clambering out over the hull to fix it. One loses his grip, a tether breaks, and it is over for him. He is only a few feet from the ship, moving very slowly, yet he can't make it back. He will float gently outward until his air runs out. He can hear the others on the radio saying his name. The earth is huge behind him. Everything he knows and loves is right there for him to see. He is only a few meters away now, he can almost reach out and touch safety.

August passed through a stunted forest of chola cactus that sloped into an arroyo between two crests. Though they looked soft enough to pet, he knew that, at the gentlest caress, whole branches would jump off and cling to him. As he walked he looked for Ego. When he thought of heading back toward the Center he became nauseated, saw her bound, and felt Matheson on top of him.

A split second before stepping into it, he spotted a hole in the ground. He moved his foot mid-stride to miss it; the ground crumbled under him anyway. He sat next to the burrow he had destroyed and watched the lip of the earth where something brown had dashed into a deeper hole. It could have been a rodent, or tarantula, or one of those miniature owls with a face like a clock that sometimes sat on the perimeter fence. It might have simply been a clod of dirt rolling under. He watched for the thing to come out anyway, using it as an excuse to rest. Ignoring the headache growing like a cactus between his ears, he waited to see if the thing in the darkness would emerge again, revealing its small predator body.

He sat until the hole disappeared and he began to float over the rocks. Had he eaten before the wedding? Had he drunk any water? The stones and smoky bushes rolled past him. How long could he wander out here? What form would Ego take to destroy him? When he was little, before the accident, the devil lived in the alley, in the oily patch of soil behind the Dumpster. It was August's job to take the garbage out after dinner and he dreaded the panicked sprint out and back with the fiend right behind him.

He wasn't sure who had told him these things or if they were rules he had made up himself: he knew that the devil had to stay out of sight during the day, and that it hid behind the enormous mulberry tree in the backyard. In the safety of the pollen-filled light, August ran around that tree trying to catch a glimpse of its red tail, hoping to wear it out so it would run slower at night. After the accident, he had forgotten about the devil. The alley was vacant, the tree just a tree, and nothing hid on the other side except a void the size of a man. But the neighbor's dog was already scratching at the fence.

Still the devil was real, insidious and yearning somewhere nearby, not a flesh being, but the cumulative rot of human ignorance, millennia of perverse karma clotted into a sentience. It knew him now as one of its chief enemies and would come in a form to break his mind. Only Papa knew how to beat it. Thinking of Papa led to z-trailer and the crackle of electricity.

To distract himself, August tried to imagine his sister, Jesse. He found that he couldn't draw a recent image of her. Instead he saw the little girl playing with him in the backyard, Peter Pan–green tights and the oversized down jacket she never seemed to grow into. After the accident she kept him occupied with games and stories, while the dog growled at them through the slats in the fence. When the sun set she would pull him inside to fix him cereal or macaroni and cheese for dinner. During this time, their mother didn't leave her room in the back of the house and never turned the television off. She would weep when they came in to hug her, pushing away the boxes of crackers and Kleenex to make room on the bed for them to sit next to her and watch the sitcoms together. When she wanted to "take her medicine" from the heavy jug of cheap wine under the bed, she waved them out, eyes gluey, blowing kisses at them, dissolving in the screen's epileptic light. The phone rang occasionally, though they weren't allowed to answer it, and the mail coming in through the slot in the door made a pile like a jumble of lost teeth.

The dog wanted at him, a thick red mutt with a head like an anvil, gnawing at the weak boards in his mind. It wanted to finish these memories with its mouth. August let himself linger on things before that: his father hammering in a yellowing baseball cap; the wide, dark sweat stains spreading across his back; the impossible weight of the nail bucket; the smell of sawdust, and somewhere, far away, a barbecue. That summer, his father had replaced all of the loose boards in the fence, as if he knew he was performing his last chores, knocking and cursing around the sides of the house with his square, hairy hands while August tried to help.

Then summer was over, his father already four months dead. The dog wouldn't be refused any longer; it was scrambling over the fresh wood, its frayed rope snaking in the air. For a moment it seemed stuck, wriggling on top of the fence before it fell behind the boy who was small and stupid and didn't see it, wondering why his sister was running to the house. He could see her through the transparency of memory: she was hiding inside. She had locked the door behind her and was watching through the window blinds as the animal tore his face. It was his mother who came out in her white satin nightgown, swinging her bedside-table lamp to beat the dog off him.

After the stitches, a strange woman came to help them clean the house and his mother did not go back to bed. He remembered, too, a boardwalk somewhere, cotton candy and a Ferris wheel. Then in junior high he had killed a newt in the copse behind his house, grinding it under his tennis shoe. Papa had forgiven him for that as well.

Thirsty now.

In every direction he could see the water mirage, the crazed air bending the mercury sky back at him. He squinted his eyes tightly to make the illusion even more convincing and turned in a slow circle, water everywhere. It was a cruel trick of optics, the very thing that killed you disguised as the thing that could save you, the wolf in grandma's bedclothes, the poison in the medicine bottle.

Meredith was thirsty.

The sky was thirsty.

Everything was wet. It was raining. He opened his mouth to the sky but felt nothing. Was that a drop? He pressed his hands against his eyes. There were clouds overhead. The water was cool against his back.

It *was* raining. Was it? Was she still tied up?

The water gathered dark in the sand in front of him. The earth was stubborn; it wouldn't soak it up. The water made a little pool, then slopped down the mountain. August cupped his hands and tried to catch the rain but it had stopped. The clouds were already thin. The sun stuck a bright ray through the clouds—like the drawing on the pamphlet describing the second coming of Christ his second-grade teacher had handed him after school: "I want you to really think about what you've done wrong and then apologize to God."

What had he done? Something about food, or making a mess. What had Meredith done? Her cheek had been white, pulled back by the gag, her forehead fever-red and sweating.

The rocks around him steamed. He was huddled in the shade of a narrow crevice. A tiny spider the size of his pupil hovered in front of his face. They watched each other. The spider was thirsty. The air was a syrup asphyxiating him.

He is in the car. It hasn't happened yet. His father is driving. There is music on the radio. Jazz. A piano and a trumpet dancing.

If he gets out now.

The car is moving. He is just a little boy and he doesn't know. He is looking out the window. He should be looking at his father. If he looked he would be able to remember his face. His father is humming, tapping his fingers on the steering wheel. The round shoulder, the slab of the neck. The man and boy are fragile and alive like fruit still attached to the vine. The car glides up onto the arc of the overpass. There is no hint yet. The two of them are the same species, one larger, one smaller, hearts warm and beating in their chests. And there it is, a jolt. The father coughs, holding his chest. His face closes and hits the steering wheel, then comes up again, confused.

Then August can see it, every pore and carbon grain of stubble lifted up to him. It is a man's face, his own face, though wider, more detailed, a landscape to wander around in. It is bearing its teeth, eyes shut, serene and agonized and laughing: every god and demon in the row. The car does a little dance. There is only a moment left to look.

Another spasm. The heart stops completely this time and his father makes a whining sound like a balloon with a tiny hole in it. The car swings elegantly to the left, pushing through the guardrail, singing into the air with the bending trumpet and the piano's high notes like glass shattering.

Asphalt. He followed the road for awhile but the pavement was too hot and the pungent tar stuck to his sandals. He found a boulder beside the road and stretched on the ground behind it with his head in the shade. After sunset he heard a vehicle go by.

Morning. August felt his body dying. His mouth had been open all night and his breath was like a sour wind. Something was coming up the mountain. He stood up, blinking as indigo fireworks crowded the perimeter of his vision. He couldn't see it yet; the road crept out from behind a great slope of red rock. Maybe he could flag it down. He needed water. He needed a ride.

It swung around the corner, a great pale-green pickup coming fast. He waved and tried to shout, but his voice had withered. Did it see him? He spread his arms wide to make himself big. The windshield was an explosion of sunlight.

The pickup hit his left arm hard, spinning him around. Then August felt his body slam into it again like a rock careening down a slope. On the ground now, August looked up at the sky.

A glowing protective bubble of time spread out around him. He knew the bubble would pop in a second, perhaps it already had, because he could hear someone shouting. Everything else was inert and the rust crags around him framed the pale sky just right. A horror rose into the sky, a beast whirling like a tornado. Its limbs whipped at the air above his head and its face shuddered like coiled intestines. It was Ego. There could be no running from it, no hiding, no thought of fighting it. It twisted in the atmosphere before him like its own planet, belching poison gas.

August tried to compose himself for death. Then the beast was gone and a man was upside down in the picture, looking at him. He had a large plaid belly and a cowboy hat, sunglasses like purple sunsets over each eye. "Can you stand up?"

In the truck, looking out over the green hood, filthy with dust and grease, August couldn't lift his arm, though it didn't really hurt. His hand sat in his lap, pale and embarrassed, like it belonged to someone else. Everything was big; the dusty dashboard was space enough to make a meal. There was a faded sticker stuck to it, a grinning pig wearing a beret, being turned on a spit. On the side of the pig were the letters KQPG. The man grunted behind the wheel: a grizzled face that seemed to be exuding oil and salt, a fleshy double chin. His sunglasses pushed into the red pads of his cheeks. His graying hair was pulled back into a ponytail, though a tuft of it had escaped and hung shabbily beside his face. Mull.

They looked at each other. "Just try to stay with me, okay?" There was phlegm in the man's voice. "We'll get you there quick."

August felt like a child; the seat was too broad, and when the truck lurched forward he held on to the dash with his good arm. Under the man's brown plaid shirt, his gut pressed tightly against the bottom of the steering wheel. August's left side, from his ribs to his fingertips, began to hum; it was starting.

"Is anything broken? Your arm doesn't look so good, chief."

God help me. Between the man's legs the neck of a beer bottle reached up with a gaping mouth. August's mind swung and he looked out the window. The rolling of the truck made him sick so he tried to look straight ahead at the road.

"Where did you *come* from? I swear I didn't see you. Not *camping* out here?"

August nodded but the man wasn't looking at him so he

had to complete the lie: "Yes. Camping." His voice was like steam. He checked his clothes. They could pass for camping: canvas pants, a heavy blue shirt. But the logo on the shirt, the tight spiral with the initials TMHC, True Mind HeartCenter. And the blue tattoo on his wrist. There was blood here and there, scrapes. His shirt was torn near his waist.

The man nodded, reaching under the seat. "Hell, I didn't even see you. Can you hear me? Drink this." He brought up a plastic bottle and held it out to August, who took it, watching the neon blue fluid with awe. The text said Sport Energy. What a color! Like an alien ocean. He felt his thirst reaching out of him toward the slosh and salt of it.

"Drink it chief—you're dehydrated. It's warm but that's probably better. You could puke." He pulled the truck through the curves without shifting his hands on the wide hoop of the wheel. His brown arms fell left, then right. "Hell."

The man stank. August wanted out. Where were they going? The Mull road moved too fast and not quickly enough, wagging up the mountain. "I came out to see if the rain had left any pools," the man said. "No one is *ever* out here. *Goddamn.*"

August thought of opening the door and flinging himself out. His arm hurt now, the whole thing beginning to scream. He tried to roll it into a more comfortable place in his lap and felt something gruesome grinding in his shoulder. He tried to mutter. Nothing came out.

"Name's Robert!" He was shouting like he suspected August was deaf or foreign. August could smell Robert's insides: cigarettes and something tangy like old salsa. He wanted to see his eyes under the glazed sunglasses. The truck sloped up at a sickening angle and the engine coughed into a higher pitch. Under the dashboard something moved and August stared at a clear plastic box with lizards or snakes kicking around in it.

"August."

"So, where's your stuff?" Robert asked.

Stuff? August had no stuff. He had owned nothing for years. Maybe Robert wanted money for the ride. *Please, just leave me alone.* Then he understood: camping stuff. August had no backpack, no gear of any kind. It was a test. August wanted to sleep. He said, "My friends... have the stuff. They went on ahead." *There. The lies just come right out.* August felt himself filling with shame. He could do this; he could lie, he could run. It was clear that he had made no progress at all at the Center; he was already Mull again. He pulled the tab on the bottle with his teeth and took three large swallows. It tasted like plastic, sugar, and salt. Probably more salt and sugar than he had eaten all year. His stomach cramped and he thought he might choke it up.

"Drink that whole thing. We'll be there soon. Stay with me."

August jumped; there, in the side mirror, he saw a thin, sick man looking straight at him. The side of his face was covered with grime and he sagged with every bounce of the truck. The eyes were all wrong, a thick strip of white under each iris. Tired. He closed his eyes and lay his head against the door.

"Don't go to sleep. Hey! I mean it, wake up."

"Just resting for a minute."

"Stay with me, kid."

10

The smell of rubbing alcohol and sterile sheets. When he opens his eyes he sees an angry clown in the cork pattern on the ceiling. A scratching sound. There is an IV in his right arm, a pinching pain where the needle goes in and the bag is full of the blue sports drink. The scratching sound gets louder and he sees Jesse, his sister, on the floor drawing cats on typing paper. She is ten years old, lying on her stomach with her knees bent, her pink shoes knocking together in the air above her. His head hurts. He looks up again at the clown. Someone is weeping near the window. It is his mother looking out into the sunlight.

Mommy, I'm over here. She comes to him, hugs him. It hurts his head and she lies down on top of him. He feels his ribs on fire and he begins to cry. She is crying too. *It's going to be okay. You're okay. You're okay.*

Ouch. But she won't let go—like she is dreaming and can't wake up. He says Ouch. Ouch. Really crying now, which makes it hurt more. She won't get off.

He tries to squirm out from under her and sees Jesse sitting on the floor crying too, watching them. As she cries her hand is still drawing, the pen has gone off the paper. It makes thick black lines all over her legs. Then they are gone. The room is empty and the scratching sound is louder. He knows his leg is broken. He doesn't want to look at it, knowing the sound is coming from down there. Then he sits up and looks.

There is blood everywhere; the bone-dog has chewed through the sheet and is eating his leg. The teeth scratch against the jagged bone.

August opened his eyes. The dog was gone. His left arm was wrapped tightly against his chest. The pain was mostly in the shoulder, like a nest of termites terrorizing the joint. The rest of his body was whole under the white sheet. He stared at his knees, his feet, his stomach; the length of him looked like a pale, sand-blown mountain range.

To his left a blue curtain was drawn. He could hear someone moving and moaning. Somewhere nearby an old woman yelled: "You're hurting me. You're *hurting* me!" A boy with a bloody arm was wheeled quickly by. Emergency room. A desk with clipboards hanging behind it. A large pale woman wearing pink nurse's scrubs talking on the phone. Her hair was deep black with a streak of green over her ear. He scrambled to sit up and something bit his arm. He saw the IV dripping Mull poison into him, mind-controlling drugs, to make him confused.

Everything was a lie: the smells were artificial, the light made the air look plastic. The pink woman saw that he was awake and pressed a button on the phone. She smiled at him, a broad plastic smile. Ego knew exactly where he was. The FBI would be coming soon. Then someone was pressing his arm and talking. He heard himself say, "I don't know."

The doctor spoke again and August's mouth moved on its own: "August William Russ. I don't know. I'm not allergic to anything. No medication. Nothing. No ID."

He remembered the beast above the desert. It would find him here and begin to break him. Already he had been injured. He had no protection; their drugs were moving through his veins. "I don't know. Two days, I guess. Three days."

The light in the room changed. Everyone had disappeared except for the woman at the desk. It was quieter now. How long had it been? Was it night or day? August stood and looked down to see the IV yanked loose in a spurt of blood and clear fluid. His clothes were folded in a little stack by the bed. He pulled his pants on with one arm and was struggling to get his shirt over his wrapped torso when the woman approached. "No, honey. Sit down," she said. She was trying to push him back onto the bed.

He had to leave. Ego would send the FBI; they would force him to say what he had seen. They would make it all seem wrong. They would trick him, make him hate Papa. The woman put her hand on his good shoulder and pushed. "You need to rest," she said.

The air was being sucked out of him with a panicked, fluttering noise like birds on fire. Wide doors on the other end of the room opened and August froze. A figure came through, sucking all light into it. Ego. Its body had no features, just a hole the entire room leaned toward. Its face was an explosion of teeth combing through the air, a crown of fangs, rows of molars clogging its eyes sockets, its mouth a rotating well of bones rasping against each other. August swallowed the urge to vomit. The nurse kept pushing. August lurched against her but she was strong. Maybe she couldn't see it; it reflected no light, only those with true-sight could see it.

As it got closer, the teeth were swallowed by a disguise of

flesh—a large man dressed in blue, some sort of security. Coming closer.

The woman wouldn't let go. He tried to edge by her but she leaned into him and yelled over his shoulder at the man approaching. August heard himself say: "Please..."

"No honey," she insisted. "You need to get back in bed." Her forehead glistened.

Don't think. August punched her hard in the chest. Her face blossomed in slow motion: a clown with a red circle mouth. August ran, his shirt half on.

Outside daylight, a city. More people in blue were walking toward him from the other end of the parking lot. His mind was holding on to something as he ran. There had been a face he knew, Robert, in the lobby as he rushed through. He had been waiting. August turned and turned again, buildings everywhere. It was a maze, he was trapped. A car honked; August had already left it behind.

A door. Inside there was rank steam. Voices. He couldn't understand them. The smell rushed through him and he felt his Mull body salivating. Chinese food. He was in a restaurant. They were rancid odors, rotten oil and seared flesh, still his body pulled it in, wanting it. He shook his head. The kitchen: metal, steam, and the cooks talking loudly. Something hissed. He rushed into the bathroom, locking the door behind him.

He was crying, his arm a grotesque lump under his shirt. August leaned over the sink, retching. He turned on the water and tried to cup it in his right hand. There was a green copper stain in the sink. He scrubbed his face. In the mirror he saw a moon-shaped shadow under the skin: the bruise where Matheson had hit him. Meredith. The room swung hard and the wall rushed at him. He slumped to the floor. The tiles were cold against his feet. His mind was a smoldering coal. Ego had come for him in the flesh. How much of what he had seen was real? He was losing his mind, already corrupted. Or did seeing Ego mean he still had true-sight?

The water began to pour from the sink in a thin stream onto his leg. Someone was banging on the door. Meredith. Papa's body pressing into his. He was trapped. He opened the door and a woman waved a dirty towel at him. "You can't do that here! Go away!" August walked past her, out into the light. He was still in the city.

He saw the police coming with their hands hovering near their guns. The nurse was with them, pointing, her face swollen and red.

"Get on the wall!" they yelled.

They held him against the brick. His shoulder twisted in a plume of white pain. He let himself slump against them. How much torture could he handle before he swore allegiance to Ego? He had no real secrets to tell about the Center. He saw himself in a cell strapped to a chair, with Matheson moving toward him, his hands alive with lightning.

The cell was painted candy turquoise. Everything, the walls, the bars, the toilet, the metal bed frame, a stupefying expanse of unnatural blue. He could see, down the corridor, a piece of the main office, a corner of a desk and a cop's beige elbow resting there. Occasionally the cop would lean into the frame. Someone laughed and the sound bounced down the hall, breaking into an electric buzz.

August walked around the cell rubbing the back of his head. Now it was over. Had he thought he could leave the

Center and survive? There was nothing more to be done. He allowed himself to sit down.

His arm throbbed in the sling. A balding man with glasses entered, bringing the smell of cologne. The man took August's pulse. He pressed the ear of the stethoscope to August's heart and shined a light into his eyes.

"Are you dizzy?" he asked. "Do you feel nauseated?"

"A little," August said.

He was given a large plastic glass of water with a chalky powder floating in the bottom. When the man left, August poured it into the toilet.

He guessed from the light in the window that it was four o'clock. The initiates would still be in the fields. The visitors would have left days ago. Was Meredith working in the kitchen? How did someone recover from that? Brother Monkey would take over with the NewFaces and any elder could lead the meetings. But who would interpret for Papa? No one understood the subtleties of his mystery as well as August. That wasn't true anymore. August understood nothing.

After awhile the turquoise made August gasp for air, as if the entire room were underwater. He sat on the bed facing the wall, trying to relax. With each breath his mind tugged against itself: *Papa knew about the torture. Papa did not know.*

If Papa didn't know then Papa was just a man: no omniscience, but innocent; August had swallowed his semen for nothing. Still, they had all seen the miracles: Papa was power. If Papa knew he might as well have tied her up himself. Matheson bringing the clamps together in a crack of light, leaning toward her even though she was unconscious. Her bare feet, useless as a mermaid's tail, tied together and crumpled against the wall. The dark swatch of her pubic hair. NeverMind. NeverMind.

August found his face pressed into the corner of the cell. The wall was rough brick though the unbearable paint made it look like the surface of an ocean seen from high above. A tiny stout ship cruised over the waves; six lilliputian oars kicked back and forth from its round hull. August looked closer: not a ship. An insect. Was there ever a room without some tiny bug in it? If Ego could send beetles didn't it prove Papa's power? That the battle was real?

August had been reading to Papa about the war: Krishna blotted out the sun to fool the enemies into coming out of hiding early. The resulting slaughter made the earth a bog of blood. Papa had grown silent, his chin resting on his chest. Though he appeared to be sleeping when he did this, August knew enough to stop reading and wait. Then Papa said, "The river was full of shit and corpses, the jungle all around was full of mines and tripwires. ...These Vietnamese children found a tire from one of our Jeeps. They were floating down the river on it, laughing. We heard them from far off, shouting like regular children, like there was no war. That's when I started to see through. At the time I thought, 'These children are insane. Their minds are broken.' That was me trying to explain something I couldn't articulate. Truth was beginning to filter deep into me. I don't even tell the Mothers this: When I saw it was *God* killing them, it undid me. I saw that God was everything—the boys, the Cong, the bullets, the grass, the blood, the gut smell. Everything. I saw that he was doing all of it—that he was reveling in it." Papa pointed at August. "What does God eat?"

"I don't know, Papa."

"What is there to eat?" August shook his head and Papa leaned closer. "You must answer," he said.

"There is nothing outside of God."

"So?" Papa's face was very close to August's now, warm and smelling of soil, like a tiny planet with its own atmosphere.

"There is nothing to eat, Papa."

"God cannibalizes himself. Those boys were getting chewed: ground up and digested. I saw that it wasn't just war, it was everywhere. It was not going to stop. That's trueheart: knowing that, admitting that to yourself and still finding the way to love and peace. This is why every religion has failed to bring about real change, because they have failed to recognize divine complicity in evil, even though their scripture says it clearly: God and Satan conspiring against Job. Krishna orchestrating the massacre of the Karavas." Papa paused, head tilted: "This is not a teaching for a NewFace..."

"No, Papa," August said.

"Don't go out trying to give this to the others."

"No, Papa. I don't understand it myself."

"Why has he let Ego ravage us for so long?" Papa continued. "We must understand the mind of God, even if it makes us white with fear. Understanding cuts the strings. We stop being puppets and begin to act on our own. Still his drama, but we will surprise him. Don't look so worried!"

August tried to smile.

"Don't think too much about this. It can paralyze you. Just keep to the practices—stay on the path. I'll stay near you. Nothing to worry about." He pulled August toward the door.

"Papa—"

"Enough, August. I see lights everywhere I go."

Lying on the thin mattress August saw Melody playing in the dust with the other children in the compound, then kneeling in front of Papa, mouth open. He quickly sat up. His mind skipped like a bead of water on a hot pan. He tried to mutter but the words were thick and salty in his mouth. Shaking, he crawled under the coarse blanket and pulled it over his face. The darkness was a relief, a cover over the squawking parrot cage of his mind. Something about the blanket was familiar.

There would have been no way to carry Meredith across the sands; he almost died by himself and she had been half-dead already. They wouldn't have made it. He saw her again, like a rug rolled and bound in the corner.

Papa had once said, "Don't worry too much about it; flapping your wings won't make you fly. Flapping is a side effect of flying. Just jump. Every moment keep leaping into faith. Be brave." If it was a test, why had Matheson hit him? August scurried about the maze of his mind. He just needed a clue, some hint of which way to go.

The heavy wool over his face and the smell of his own sweat—had he had a blanket like this as a child? No, not a blanket, a costume. A bear.

August and Jesse are putting on a play for their parents: August in the same bear costume he wore the previous Halloween and Jesse as a trainer teaching him tricks. The mask is thick and difficult to breathe in; still, he loves it. The eyes let in crescents of light, little moon-shaped snippets of the living room. He sees his parents laughing, the couch, Jesse in the safari hat. He has to make wide turns to see anything whole. The series of tricks would be impressive only if a real bear were doing them: standing on one leg, rolling over. He waddles around bumping into things, making everyone laugh. The inside of the costume is rough against his naked stomach, yet he doesn't want to take it off. Jesse looks vulnerable standing there in nothing but shorts, a tank top, and the hat they found in a closet. Is it a real whip she swings at him? Maybe just a length of nylon rope? The end of the skit is a kind of disappearing act: August lunges at Jesse, pretending to gobble her up while she ducks behind a big chest and through the kitchen door. His parents clap and whistle. Probably they are a little drunk. He sleeps in the costume that night and gets a rash on his chest. It is missing one of the paws so his human hand sticks out, a little boy's fingers balled into a pale fist. It is still two years before the accident. Plenty of time. Then he is playing house with Jesse in her room. *Now we go to bed!* They lie side by side on her pink covers. She says, *Like this*, and wags her lips across his, humming, *MMMMMM. Now there's a baby!* The baby is invisible, just air rocked in her arms. She hands it to him and he doesn't know how to hold it, afraid that it is upside down or that it has fallen from his arms without his knowing. *Support its head!* she says.

When Jesse comes home from college for Christmas, she knocks on his bedroom door. She asks what the accident was like. Her hands are in her pockets, hair tucked behind her ears. Her eyes are soft and make him squirm. He sees she is trying to understand him, to offer him kindness. It nearly cracks him but he's quicker than that and answers with a cold face. He tells her every gruesome detail, how there was the smell of shit in the car: one of them shat himself. He invents details to make it worse: *Dad was begging for help*. She holds her hand over her mouth. Her face reminds him of a moth, pale and fluttering.

Papa had absolved him of that cruelty and other crimes. He had touched August's chest and said, "Until you found the HeartCenter you lived in *dis-ease*. It isn't your fault. Forgive yourself. You were sick."

Had he ever really felt at ease? Had he ever benefited from the muttering? And Papa's final gift, it was supposed to cure him of Ego yet here he was shaking in a cell, in the Mull world again. What could he do? He had no money. He could not call his mother or Jesse from a jail cell. He had to figure it out on his own.

He could kill himself. His neck relaxed at the idea, and he slumped into the mattress. Suicide was the worst crime against Truth; he would have to start over in a lower plane having lost all knowing. Anyway, he wouldn't have to think about any of this. It would be better for everyone. Maybe he would be reincarnated as a dog. Just eating, sleeping, barking. It would be simple. Dog thoughts, dog sex. Papa's red penis hovered near his face. *NeverMind*. He took the blanket off.

Turquoise.

August called down the corridor: "Can I have another glass of water, please?"

The cop at the desk, owner of the beige elbow, peered down the hall. "There's a fountain right behind you," he said.

August turned and saw it camouflaged in turquoise, floating above the toilet. What else was in here that he hadn't seen yet? Maybe there was a turquoise key for the gate, a turquoise door he could just walk through. A turquoise gun. He drank, trying to wash his thoughts down. *We don't recognize gifts right away. We think: This is the worst thing that could have happened to me.*

The teachings were not working; he could not breathe through this, could not hear a divine cooling voice underneath. He was broken at a base level, his genes misspelled.

Watching the turquoise water skitter across the shallow pan he imagined going back into the desert to let the sun finish him. Still, he needed to know what Papa knew. Could he go back and face him? Would they let him in again? Papa's sweating belly pressed against his face.

He lowered himself onto the bed and sank toward sleep. Rolling to his side, he felt his shoulder scream and rolled the other way.

The door clinked and a tall woman in a baggy green sweater stepped in with a clipboard. August was embarrassed to see one of the officers hovering close to protect her.

She watched him through a pair of delicate glasses. As August stood he wondered if he was supposed to say something. Then she cleared her throat. "My name is Mrs. Chandler," she said. "I'm from County Health. You don't have to talk to me if you don't want to, but I'm here to evaluate your condition. Do you know why you're here?"

"Yes."

"Why are you here?"

What was she asking exactly? The turquoise made giddy

swirls around him. I am here to forward the Great Days. Because God is bored and lonely. Because I washed out. "Because I struck that nurse," he replied.

"Why did you strike her?"

Possible answers crowded his head: *She was trying to poison me. Ego was in the room, coming for me.* August said, "I was dehydrated and confused." The officer shifted, crossing his arms. Was this really necessary?

She wrote on the clipboard without looking at it, her eyes making little circles around his face. "Are you confused often?"

"I was dehydrated."

"Do you ever hear voices or see things that other people don't see? Are you overwhelmed by feelings of dread or terror?"

"No." Lying again. The walls buzzed. If Papa was telling the truth, then August was one of only a handful of sane people. The rest, the other six billion, including this woman, were insane.

"Do you feel like people are out to get you? Or that there is a group scheming behind your back?"

"No."

"Do you feel your actions can have disastrous consequences?"

A trick question. August rubbed the back of his head. "Everyone's actions have consequences."

She was still expressionless. "Do you feel that your thoughts or actions carry more weight than others'?"

"Please, I'm not psychotic or whatever. ... I feel badly about hitting that woman, she was trying to help me." He checked and saw that this last part was true.

"Just a few more questions, Mr. Russ."

Maybe Papa was meditating in his trailer, watching him with true-sight. August straightened his back. *I know I'm lost, Papa. Forgive me.*

"Do you see certain important colors or patterns everywhere?"

"Turquoise."

She didn't blink, eyes like microscopes. "Does turquoise have a special meaning for you?"

"I'm kidding. The walls. Never mind." *They'll put me in a ward and keep me poisoned with drugs.* The officer stuck his pinky into his ear, jiggled it vigorously, then examined whatever he had removed.

Mrs. Chandler said, "Then there are no colors that have special meanings for you?"

"Well, colors have special meanings. Funerals are black. There are flags, team colors."

"What team? Do you mean the cult?" August swallowed. Was this how the interrogation would start? "Did they ask you to do things you weren't comfortable doing?"

Tell me where to go, Papa. August felt for the wall behind him. It was farther away than he had thought and he shuffled to regain his balance. "I'm not going to speak about my community," he said. "You can ask questions about me. I'm not in a position to speak for the Movement." Finally she was silent, scribbling on the board while the officer looked at her. August wanted to sit. "I'm going through a hard time, but I'm not crazy."

She made some more notes on the pad, clipped the pen to it and held out a card. "On your way out they'll let you use the phone in the hall. I strongly recommend that you call this number and get yourself some counseling. You need to talk to someone."

"On my way out?"

The officer finally spoke. "The nurse dropped the charges. So you go back to wherever you came from."

11

August walked out into the sun and stood for a moment on the steps of the police station, holding a white plastic bag with a bottle of aspirin for his shoulder and some papers he had signed. There was a small park across the street with a sandbox and a slide. He had been waiting for them to take him to the FBI compound, some huge nameless labyrinth underground. It had just been a tiny turquoise cell in the municipal police station.

The pain in his shoulder urged him to walk. He dropped the bag and its contents into a trash can. He slipped his arm out of the sling and tried to swing it. It protested so he pulled it tightly against him and wrapped it again. Fetal, useless as a chicken wing.

The town seemed smaller, less baffling than before. It was just a town. There was a Mexican restaurant with a picture of a mule on the window right next to the police station. A Quick-Stop oil change. Another Mexican restaurant. A warehouse. A series of small dirty homes and already the edge of town, where the asphalt took a sharp turn down the slope of the mountain. Beyond that the desert stretched out toward the east. August turned and headed back toward the center of town. A large blue sign greeted him: "Welcome to Silkweed. Home in the Hills. Pop. 2,913."

He walked down what he thought was Main Street. There was a pay phone near a gas station. He paused as he passed it. He could no more call one of the Chapters than he could call Papa, and he could not imagine what he would say to Jesse.

A post office. A stationery store that seemed to sell more candy than stationery. People passing in occasional cars stared at him and he nodded to each one, bowing to the core mind inside them. A row of empty storefronts. A roofless building with scorch marks rising like eyelashes from every window.

The Safeway sign was lit up from the inside. August wondered why they left it on during the day. The letters seemed close to evaporating into clouds of white-hot gas, seven glyphs worming under the pale sky. When he approached, the doors opened for him as if he were a prince.

Inside, the store was bigger even than the main-hall. August stared at the towers of merchandise, the endless ranks of artificial food, brightly colored, wrapped in flags, poisoned with chemicals. High on the walls, convex mirrors pointed at the aisles like the eyes of some enormous bloodless fish. Standing under one, August could see himself, tiny, surrounded by a cramped globe of festive colors. The ant people moved along their grooves, between the barricades of sugar and music. Everything was wrapped with lies, unnatural hues, promises, smiling faces. The Ego circus. The shoppers seemed drugged, unable to find their way out.

A young woman pushing a cart smiled at him and he felt disproportionately grateful. In her cart a toddler leaned sleepily to one side, mouth glazed with pink from something sugary. The child seemed oblivious to the balloon near her head but was tugging at the ribbon tied to her wrist, wanting it off. She had a stunned look, fat cheeks pulling her mouth into an open pout. Did all babies look so inane? August waved at her, and she pointed at him and everything changed, her face reddened, her eyes squinted, and she was beautiful, breathing heavily with joy.

He followed them, pretending to be looking at the shelves as they strolled in a kind of dream, a hypnotic meandering through the forest of soap and tinted liquids. They looked happy, the toddler was well fed and safe. Maybe there were some Mull who were spared real suffering, like a stand of trees which, by some trick of the wind, escapes being burned.

The woman opened a freezer door and August watched her figure through the glass until it fogged. The toddler had caught him staring and was waving at him. Her tiny wing-like hand made a terrible rustling sound in the air. Who was screaming? The freezer door closed. Ego stood where the woman had been, a pillar of fire. From the pit where her face had been August saw a canine grin growing, teeth sprouting in the darkness. As he turned to run, he saw the child's head was gone, replaced by the pink balloon spinning slowly.

Outside he leaned against the brick wall. His heart would not slow down. He tried to breathe deeply, though his lungs felt full of hot sand. Fatigue, hunger, acid flashbacks. He was no longer sure if the visions were real; he only knew that if Ego touched him it would be over. A newspaper blew open near his feet. August stared without comprehending the images: a man in a suit, a soldier, an old woman pointing at a mountain. He walked quickly, putting distance between himself and Ego.

In the parking lot of the McDonald's, a green truck pulled past the drive-through. August stared for a moment before he realized that it was the truck that had hit him. It drove down a side street and August jogged to follow it, losing it around another corner.

A residential section: green lawns, American flags, more trees. He was appalled at the spectacle, the chimes, sprinklers, and white, cement geese. Nevertheless he couldn't muster any strong feeling against these Mull. Had he done any better himself? August stopped, staring at a flowerbed with red, white, and blue flowers in a star pattern. The curtains of the house moved, someone peered out, and August walked on.

He didn't hear the squad car rolling slowly behind him until it came to a stop next to him, gravel crackling under the tires. A thin officer with shaggy blond hair cocked his head toward the backseat and said, "Give you a lift." He was chewing gum. There was a mole on his cheek like a period after the dry sentence of his lips.

"What?" August asked.

"Get in the car, son. I'll take you to the bus. There's a station in Hope."

"I'm not going to the bus station."

"We don't allow vagrants here." The officer stopped chewing and stared as if trying to hypnotize August. "Time to move on. Get in."

Hope was forty miles north on the other side of the mountains. Where would the bus take him? He was not ready to go back to the Center, though the thought of being even farther away made him panic, like a strong current pulling him toward the shark-riddled deep. Here, at least, he might be able to walk back to the Center if he carried water.

"I'm meeting someone," August said.

"Meeting someone," the officer repeated, his gum click-ing. "Who?"

August tried not to seem desperate as he looked down the street for some solution. "Friends," he said. Then he saw the green truck, parked in the driveway of a house two blocks down. August pointed. "Up the road. That truck. That's my friend. I'm staying there." The cop pushed his gum between his front teeth, then pulled forward toward the house. After a moment, August jogged behind.

The lawn beside the green truck was a great pale patch of baked dirt with a pathetic scattering of white rock. August couldn't tell if the rock had once been ground cover or if it had all fallen from the roof. There were washtubs piled near the door. All the shades were drawn. The officer had already rung the bell, calling his bluff, and August wondered where he could run. Maybe he could steal the police car. Ego was making a clown of him. Maybe he would end up in jail again.

The door opened just enough for Robert to lean his head out. August thought he looked like a monstrous Muppet peering from the edge of a stage. His hat was off, revealing the red border where it would have been, the flesh above pale and doughy. Robert looked like he had been woken from hibernation.

"Sorry to bother you, sir. I'm Officer Goff. This man says he knows you. He says he's living here?"

There was a pause as Robert blinked at August. A sour smell floated out of the house like a great vat of pickled eggs was hidden just behind the door. "He what?"

The officer chewed his gum at August. The mole crawled toward his ear, pulling his lips behind it. "That's what I thought. I just had to verify. Sorry to bother you." The officer grabbed August's good arm, pulled him from the stoop, and pushed him into the backseat while Robert watched them from the doorway.

The car rolled slowly down the mountain, making August drowsy. As they drove the officer occasionally squinted at him in the rearview mirror. Finally, he cleared his throat: "So you're from that cult, right?"

August ignored him, staring out the window at the gray weeds and stones. He caught sight of a thin rabbit with enormous ears hunkered near the edge of the road. What was it waiting for?

"Look, I just can't have you loitering around my town. It makes people nervous."

"But you'll leave me to loiter in Hope?"

"I'm putting you on a *bus* in Hope."

"A bus to where?"

"I don't care, son. Someplace you won't stand out so much. It's for your own good." His ears were freckled.

"Is this even legal, what you're doing? Can you just remove people like this?"

The officer chewed his gum for a moment and then turned on the radio. A twanging guitar filled the car. The mountain was beginning to level with the plain. August could see the scab of a town near the foothills and a freeway stretching out like a wire toward the horizon. A sweet-voiced woman was singing about love gone wrong. The officer turned the music off quickly. "You want me to take you back to your cult? Because I don't care," he said. The thought of arriving at the Center in a police vehicle sent August into a spasm of shame.

It seemed to be the effect Goff was looking for.

"Okay then," he said as he turned the music back on. The woman singing wanted them to know, really wanted them to understand, that love was just a fool's game but she was going to play it anyway.

August stepped up into the bus. It didn't feel as strange as it should have. He knew it was wrong, but he couldn't find what was right. He had no other plan. The bus would carry him deeper into the chaos of outside. Maybe Ego was guiding him now because he felt strangely committed. He had washed out; he might as well leap as far as possible.

The driver was fat and stared out the window as if the bus was already in motion.

"How long does it take to get to Overwill?" August asked.

"Depends." The driver scratched his beard, watching the hidden horizon. Did he think that was an answer? August hesitated, then felt someone waiting to get on behind him so he pushed down the throat of the bus. There were only a few people scattered here and there, looking small and childish in the padded seats. He passed a woman wearing a surgical mask, dozing with her head against the window. Was she afraid of getting sick or trying not to infect others? He chose a seat a few rows from the back, squeezing himself in near the window. The seats were striped purple and blue and had a sweet chemical smell, but they were clean. Overwill was somewhere near the border of Nevada, though August wasn't sure which side it fell on. Or was he thinking of Boulder City?

A bus, why not? There was no way to tell the difference

between dream and reality: outrageous things felt natural. Life had been a catalogue of surreal experiences: *I was in a school, a car, a pool, in the desert in some kind of compound.* ... Whole casts of people appeared, said strange things that felt right at the moment and then disappeared. He had been anxious enough, sad, blithe, ecstatic enough for it all to have been a series of intense and wholly unbelievable dreams. He had accepted the magician's logic of life without question: a planet with a little crust of plants, animals, and drama, spinning on an invisible track around a pit of unthinkable heat. August was chuckling to himself. And electricity and gravity and airplanes and the Movement—all of it was ludicrous, but why not? Make it as obscene, make it as unlikely as it could possibly be and he would still try to find his way around as if it all made sense.

If it *was* a dream, he would wake up and it wouldn't matter whether he had gotten on the bus or not. He would open his eyes in his trailer, head out to morning mutter with the others, and find Meredith smiling sleepily there, untouched. Or he would wake in his college dorm room hungover, head spinning, with his roommate sitting on the window ledge having his morning toke, the entire epic a single night of mushroom sweats. Or he would wake under the thick rainbow quilt, eight years old, hearing the jumbled honey tones of his mother and father speaking quietly in the kitchen.

Through the window he saw, crouched near the drinking fountain, a woman scolding a little boy. She shook his arm while he aimed his red blooming face over her shoulder.

If it wasn't a dream, he was way off course, making mistake after mistake. Still, what more could be expected of him? If the whole crucifying universe had actually been built and set in motion to grind him under, could anyone, even Papa, really expect him to see through it? In retrospect, nothing had made any sense. He would take the bus wherever it went.

The boy saw August and bawled harder, as if to say, *Are you seeing this?* August spoke slowly so the boy could read his lips: *You're okay. Take a deep breath.* The mother saw August staring and yanked the child away. August whispered to the heaving blue square of the boy's receding shirt, *There's more where that came from.*

A young woman with a snail shell of a backpack pressed down the aisle. She slumped into the seat across from him, took out a book, and began reading. Pretty, though costumed in Mull makeup: rust-colored lips, Egyptian black eyelashes like crow feathers above the pages of the book. A leather bracelet with brutal metal studs, a weapon on her thin wrist; her shoes had bright red flaps of fabric hanging from them like burst firecrackers. A delicate bull ring swung from the septum of her nose.

He rubbed his face. Was the oil on his palms or his forehead? The driver closed the doors though only a half dozen people had boarded. The bus rolled past the squad car and Goff raised his hand kindly, as if seeing off an old friend. August shook his head; they were insane out here. How did they manage to survive at all? They groaned out of the station and August cringed as the bus mowed through a flock of pigeons. Turning around, he saw no blood, no dead bodies.

Under the layer of artifice the girl across the aisle was simply a girl: skeleton, flesh, mouth, and eyes. Melody would be too small under Papa, covered completely by his chest, his belly, his legs like a two-headed animal.

The town scrambled by the windows and soon they were beyond its limits, passing open desert jeweled with yellow tractors and chains of fences. They'd be harvesting the onions soon. August's head dropped against the window, getting knocked at every lurch. The metal rivets along the window seemed designed to keep him uncomfortable. There was a silver button on his armrest; when he pressed it the seat lurched back two inches, then stopped. There wasn't much difference between upright and reclining. He let his head loll against his own shoulder.

The girl said something. She was nodding at him approvingly, her eyes half-closed, deeply considering her own comment. August sat up. She was attractive in an ornamental way; her lips were outlined with a darker brown and he could see the soft border where the lipstick faded into the true pink of her inner lip. Younger than he first guessed. Maybe sixteen. "What?" he asked.

"I said, I like your tattoo."

"Oh." August looked at it, a little surprised to see it there, as if it should have faded as he got farther from the compound.

"Native American symbol, right?" Something glittered and clicked in her mouth.

"Oh. Not exactly. I mean, not at all." That sounded rude so he rubbed at the tattoo. "It's a community. That I'm part of."

Her squint deepened. He could see it was a look she wore to appear thoughtful. August felt sorry for her and faked a smile that felt surprisingly real. Maybe she thought he was punk or some other kind of cool. He might pass for it: grimy, shaved head, tattoo. He needed a shower. Then she reached into her bag and began to shuffle around in it. Maybe she was done talking.

A motorcycle sidled too close to the bus, then sped past. A red and white checkered tower in a field. She was still digging in her bag. It was like rocky soil that she kept turning to break up.

"Where do you go?" She didn't look up. He wasn't sure if she was talking to him, or to the thing she was looking for.

"Like, are you a student or... ?"

"Oh. No. Not like that. I don't go to college anymore."

"A student of life," she said. She tossed her hair back over her shoulder with a movie-star flip. Flirting a little. No harm.

"I guess so," he answered. "I study with a teacher at the HeartCenter. On the other side of the mountains."

"What city?" Her hand was in the bag up to her elbow.

"It's in the desert. Just our community." Maybe he only needed space to get his head together. He could still go back and apologize.

"What kind of teacher?" she asked, looking like she had just eaten something bitter. He could hear the old recruitment script humming in his head: *It's natural to feel resistant at first. You've been living with suffering as a fact of life. When you see Papa you'll understand that he is the way.* "He's our spiritual Father. The last prophet."

Her hands stopped moving in her bag. "God talks to him?"

"His mind is completely open." She blinked and there were thick strips of white under each iris. "He isn't fogged in like the rest of us. He was in Vietnam and there was an ambush. He was the only survivor. John Narshima. We call him Papa." It felt good to be talking.

"Oh," she said. August thought he saw a flash of fear in her eyes before she started rummaging again.

"I know it sounds strange," he said. She shrugged. He wanted to shake her and make her understand the privilege of it. "My life was gone before I found him. Perfectly destroyed." If he explained it the right way she would stop peering out of the corner of her eyes like that. "He had a fever. There was shooting. Imagine war and explosions all around. He should have been killed with the rest of them. Suddenly it was completely quiet and peaceful. Then there was a shadow standing over him. *This happened.* He thought it was the enemy. First it had four arms, then eight arms, sixteen arms, wings, a crown. It saved his life." She stopped moving again as he spoke faster. "The next thing he knew he was on the helicopter. It came to him again in the hospital, then every night in prison and gave him the first revelations. It whispered to him day and night, unfolding the religions of the world, all creases on the same piece of paper. Sumeria, Aztec serpents, the split atom, the double helix, the crucifixion, Vishnu's disk, the daub of yellow pigment smeared across the stone—all letters in the same word, which Papa deciphers for us. He's the RNA. Do you know what that is? Ribonucleic acid. He puts it together. He is the Rosetta stone."

"Prison?" she asked, face tensing.

"Oh. He was court-martialed. Because of his men. It was an ambush, there was nothing he could do, but they had to punish him. Now there are over thirty thousand Movement Volunteers worldwide."

"I've never heard of you guys."

"That's okay." He resisted the urge to pat her leg. "You

will. The Great Days—" He stopped. Papa's cock, Meredith's gag, Matheson choking him, Melody.

"Are you okay?"

"Of course."

"What happened?"

"When? That's it. That's the whole story."

"No, I mean, are you going to puke?"

"No," August said as he looked out his window to hide his face. "Probably motion sickness." He felt her staring at him. Closing his eyes, he heard her stirring her backpack again. His arm began to throb like a coil of white neon.

"Try to look out the front window," she offered. "Look at the horizon in front. It helps. I don't know why, but it does."

"I just got tired," he said.

"You should take a nap." A little girl trying to be an adult. Had Papa taken her already? "So what are you doing out here?"

He continued to look out the window. A cow exposed like a piece of bone jutted from the ochre land. *Breathe.* "Taking a break," he told her.

She nodded sagely; taking a break was perfectly understandable, a good idea. August was relieved to see it. It was ridiculous; she was a stranger, a child, what could she know? Yet she approved. This Mull girl seemed to think taking a break was a great wisdom. He said it again, "Just taking a break." Maybe the girl had some sort of mental illness; she wasn't really looking for something in the bag but had a strange tick, a compulsion to dredge around in it endlessly.

Tractors, fences, and dry brush. He would just let the bus take him, plenty of time to decide what to do next. He rubbed his face again. The landscape lurched past.

Maybe there was something fundamental he didn't understand. The world wasn't so monstrously jumbled, August had just misinterpreted some important part of it. He would give himself time to figure it out. In his mind Meredith was still tied up and naked with Matheson smoldering above her, but that was days ago. She was probably released the day he left, to recuperate in b-trailer. The Mothers would have brought her some soup, smiling and laughing with her. It would have been like a cleansing illness. No matter how bad it had been, no matter how confusing or wrong, it wouldn't last. Why had he run? He could be talking with her now, asking her if she needed anything. He could have had answers by now.

In a car driving alongside the bus, a man seemed to be looking right at him. August waved though the car had already passed. The bus engine worked its sound and warmth into him. He was beginning to dream, his neck muscles letting go.

"Motherfucker, I *got* you!" The girl pulled out a little wooden box tied with a red silk ribbon and shook it in his face. "Ha!" She untied the knot, opened the box, took something out, and handed it to him. He recognized it only after he had closed his fingers around it. "Do you smoke?" she asked.

It was small and poorly rolled, the fibers nearly falling out of the brittle paper. Long ago, it would have taken five times as much pot—the good shit—to do him right, but he had been taking nothing stronger than tea for over six years. It might be just what he needed to give his panicked heart a rest. He lifted it to his nose, sniffing, and she grinned. They couldn't smoke it on the bus, and he didn't think he would survive a paranoid trip. The visions were bad enough.

"Thank you. No. I used to, though."

He placed it in her upturned palm like the wick of a candle. Suddenly without anything to do or say, she looked quietly out her own window. Maybe she would hush now. God bless her, guide her, and make her be quiet.

Night dark. He had been dreaming something; it was already evaporating. The bus seemed to be headed straight into an abyss, a submarine, power gone, sinking eagerly toward the bottom. Leaning into the aisle August saw, through the dark tunnel, the road warping and stretching out in front of them. The bus bounced and he expected to see an oncoming car or a cliff. Nothing, then a green box appeared in the distance and grew into a sign with names of cities he had never heard of: Baray 28, Penneton 39, Gila 156.

The girl was curled against her bag. Were her eyes open? Did she see him staring? He leaned to look more closely. One of her boots was near his hand, slung out into the aisle. He let his finger graze it. The bus bounced and his finger tapped the skin of her leg between her pants and boot. In the light of a passing car August saw a gem of saliva, like a dab of glycerin on her lip. Had she ever sucked someone off? Was that what the metal stud in her mouth meant? He imagined pulling her pants off and running his tongue up her thigh. His pants pinched his growing penis. Maybe he could creep to the back of the bus and jerk off quietly in the dark. Was Ego really after him? He pushed his erection down, shifting to get more comfortable, and tried to sleep again.

Of course he had wanted it, Papa had seen that. Papa knew him better than he knew himself, could smell his hunger for something desperate, something so savage, so massively unthinkable that it would tear him from himself. But it hadn't worked. Did it matter whether Papa knew about Meredith? The world would go on, no matter what anyone did or had done to them. August felt the idea of the Great Days dissolving in him like sugar under scalding water. The universe would keep churning its galaxies into a froth of light and carnage. None of it was okay, and still, he could do nothing about it. He was free. The strangling cords of hope and responsibility had frayed.

12

The morning light tongued the sky behind the apartment buildings and drugstores. A motel with a ludicrous flamingo stenciled on the white brick next to a blocky script: *Free Movies! Single $29.98.* The bus moved slowly past the gas stations, liquor stores. He was sorry to see the girl was gone; had they stopped in the night?

The bus beached itself, shuddered dead. The driver got off without a word. On the sidewalk, August stretched, yawned, and peered around. The bus station was a hushed anachronism with awnings over the streaked windows. A clock tower rose up in antiquated grandeur. Overwill. It was bigger than Hope, an actual city. He wished he could have said goodbye to the girl. Even so, as he ambled away from the bus, he felt buoyant. He had gained something in the night. Sleep or resolution. Something. The astronaut drifting out in an unending course would eventually relax into it and enjoy the view. When he was done he could rip open his suit and be still, but for now it was pleasant, the weightless motion, the universe singing its shimmering lullaby—

"Brother August."

August jumped. A short man with a face like a peeled beet was standing behind the open door of a car. He slammed the door and jogged toward August, who had an impulse to run the other way. "Who are you?" August asked.

"My name is Matt. I work for the Western Chapters." He reached for August with a thick hairy hand. August took a step back; why was he smiling like that? Had Papa sent this man to bring him back? "It's an honor to meet you, sir." Matt's hand hovered between them. "All of the work you are doing with Papa in Arizona." The smile was real; he didn't seem to know that August had washed out.

August nodded stupidly and shook his hand. "How did you find me?"

"Your bus ticket. I knew you didn't have your own vehicle. I was a private detective before I found Papa. He saved my life. Now I do errands for the Movement." It was eagerness and childlike pride boiling up that made Matt's face red.

"Errands?"

"Finding people, looking into things, doing my part." He held out a blank manila envelope.

"What is it?" August asked.

"I don't know. They told me to give it to you."

"Who is it from?"

"I don't know." Matt looked uncomfortable now; his smile sagged like a banner hung too long. Maybe he had expected a different August, one worthy of working daily with Papa. Instead he got this dirty, jumpy man who was afraid to shake hands.

August took the envelope. "Thank you," he said. Matt looked distractedly at something across the street. August followed his gaze. Nothing: pigeons, a donut shop.

Then Matt was looking at him again. "Sir, can I ask you a question?"

"Just August."

"Brother August."

"Yes?"

"May I ask you a question?"

"Yes. I said yes. If I can answer it." Here it comes.

"What is Papa really like?"

August almost laughed. He needed to relax; this man was nothing to worry about. "What do you mean?"

"I mean you're with him all the time. I've only seen him giving talks. His teachings... the teachings cured me. But I've never really been near him. Maybe it's silly to be asking. It's probably silly to you."

August felt a rush of cruel power in him. He could break this little man, here at this bus stop, bring his desperate life to a halt by saying, *I sucked Papa's dick.* Then compassion came bleeding through him, old and heavy, like fatigue. He examined the envelope. Maybe it was from Papa or one of the Mothers. Some catastrophe at the Center. Something urgent. Something he needed to fix. Or maybe a formal dismissal. It seemed surreal, a dream envelope, there would be nothing in it, a dove that would fly away as soon as he broke the seal, or a green poison gas hissing into his face. "Papa is a man," August said. "Like you and me."

Matt nodded, embarrassed. "Of course. I just thought—I guess I'd have to find out for myself. I mean the Center must be an amazing place. I can't imagine." He was looking across the street again. "I guess I have a couple of questions."

"Yes?"

"Is it true he doesn't speak anymore?"

"Less and less."

"And that he can..." Matt tapped his head with a thick finger.

"He can what?"

"Communicate—you know, with his thoughts. I mean with true-mind? They say—"

"Who said?"

"Everyone says that if you are near him you can hear him, even if he doesn't talk."

August knew he should be stern, yet he couldn't help but smile. Everything was falling apart! The Movement was a web of gossip and fantasy. The appropriate response was: *Papa's teachings live in our hearts. Everyone can hear them if they are still.* He couldn't make himself say it. He felt tears welling in his eyes.

Matt looked worried. "Brother, can I ask, what are you doing out here? There aren't any Movement houses here. I mean, none of the Chapters know where you are. I was lucky to find you."

August turned and began to walk away. He would find someplace quiet to open the letter. Over his shoulder he said, "Center business. Thank you for delivering this." He heard the man trotting after and forced himself to stop.

Matt looked embarrassed again. "Just one more thing."

"Yes?"

"How close are we?" He was begging, holding August's elbow. "How much longer?" He wanted good news. He wanted August to say, *The Great Days will come within the year.* A token to go back to his Chapter with. No doubt he deserved good news. He was as desperate as everyone else. Papa hadn't cured anything.

The laughter and tears pushed up into August's throat. He felt his face folding into a grimace. He grabbed Matt's arm and pulled his rigid body close, hugging him hard. Matt coughed as August squeezed harder. The envelope fell on the ground while Matt tried to pull away politely. His neck smelled like shampoo. A woman with a stroller eyed them as she passed. August pressed his lips against Matt's ear, feeling him flinch. He whispered as quietly as he could, "It's over."

When he let go, Matt's eyes were wide and he was staring at the ground, his face a ridiculous purple. August picked up the envelope and walked away.

He found himself standing in front of a toy store, looking in at rows of soldiers and firefighters in a mock battle. The detergent odor of a nearby laundromat swirled around him. The barrel of the tank was aimed at the apple green fire engine. A few figures on both sides, green and red, were lying facedown. One of the dead firefighters was holding a tiny axe. "Firemen are not for that." His voice startled him and he shuddered. A couple walked by, holding onto each other's waists tightly, giggling. They didn't see what he was seeing. One of the firefighters was aiming the hose at a helicopter hanging from a stretch of fishing line. He smelled fried food somewhere.

August tried to walk away from the hunger but it followed him like a beggar, foul and persistent. There was a small park across the street from the laundromat. Now he could smell bacon. He sat on a bench in the shade, looking at the envelope. It seemed mostly empty except for a thick piece of something near the bottom, another envelope? Holding it in his hands felt unsettling, like letting a phone ring. Someone wanted to talk to him but he didn't want to answer it. He folded it and slid it between his pants and his naked hip.

August watched the untouched people moving by. By noon his hunger had flared into a roaring wind; it made him dizzy, pushed him around. Someone had left a Pagoda Chinese-food box on a bench; it was full of cigarette butts floating in a brown sauce, like an alien delicacy. Had he really felt calm and relaxed on the bus? Night would come, what then? He had no money for a trip back, for food, for a motel room.

A brittle branch of French bread, still in its paper bag on top of a trash can. Eating it was a feat of disassociation. Every time he opened his mouth to take it in he saw Papa's penis instead. He chewed in a rush and the dry bread gave him such a fierce case of hiccups that he had to set off in search of a drinking fountain.

Overwill was a sprawl of shops and houses radiating around a modest downtown consisting of three skyscrapers and an outdoor mall. Rows of trees dotted the streets deliberately, like musical notation. They seemed to be thriving, fluffed by the occasional breeze. A shoe repair shop. An ice cream store. A library with concrete lions guarding the door, one of which was wearing a real beret. August tried to go inside but it was closed. What day was it? A police car hummed slowly past. A movie theater: posters of beautiful people holding guns surrounded by cars and fireballs. He tried to stick to the public spaces, avoiding the neighborhoods. He didn't want to get shipped off again.

Like the rest of the recruits, he had given everything to the Center when he was initiated: a semester's worth of college tuition, his television, his bike, his keyboard, his clothes. August felt nostalgia for those early days when he was still working in the fields and sleeping in the common quarters. He missed even the sleepless nights, when he would lie in the shuffling darkness, listening to the others coughing or muttering through their dreams. Sometimes, in the middle of the night, Papa would walk among the rows of bunks like a guardian angel, almost invisible in the darkness, letting his wide hands graze the initiates as they slept, caressing their sweating foreheads, blessing them.

Near the enormous movie theater there was a public sculpture, a teal and silver fish with a broad flat back that two people could sit on comfortably. It was made of concrete, with iridescent metal embedded under the amber of heavy shellac. The scalloped scales looked like a child's drawing of water. August sat on it thinking about Vishnu's first incarnation.

He pulled the envelope out, ready to get it over with, then touched the clasp and froze. His hands trembled and wouldn't obey him. *Stop this nonsense. Open it.* He couldn't move beyond the fear that Papa's hand would reach out of the envelope to grab him. He tried to laugh at the absurdity. Would he rather be chased around the wasteland by Ego than get a message from paradise? Nevertheless, whatever was inside would be too definite, a seal on his life, a bolt of shame for having washed out, for having left Meredith. He needed a respite. *Just taking a break.* His wandering had given him shelter from Papa's omniscience somehow, and he wanted to stay hidden just a little longer. He folded it again and slid it back into its resting place near his lower back.

A dime fell at his feet and August looked up to see a redheaded high school punk walking haughtily away. August kicked the dime, shouting after him, "Hey! I'm not... hey!" The kid didn't turn around. Did he really look so disheveled? His shoulder began to ache.

The sun sank in a dark bank of clouds and it looked like

an earnest rain was brooding. A policeman walked slowly by eyeing him. Maybe he would be passed around from city to city by these Ego-soldiers like an unlucky token. He reached for the dime and put it into the little pocket on the inside of his pants. A woman with ridiculously thick glasses was holding out more change. He opened his hand and received the insult quietly. Forty-five cents. Something cold hit his cheek. All around him the sidewalk clicked and freckled with dark wet spots.

The sun stayed hidden, going off like a wounded animal to die, and the light of the city rose into the raining sky to replace it, heating the clouds into a color that made August think of the word *penicillin*. The streets shivered into blurred photographs. The cars rushed toward August as he ducked from awning to awning. He was worried about looking like a hoodlum creeping about the darkened buildings. There was a crevice, a tiny alley between two shops that he tried to doze in but he couldn't sleep standing up and he wasn't comfortable lying down where someone might stumble on him. Time splashed past.

Down a shadowy street, through a mesh of rain, August saw a glimmer of light moving toward him. As it approached he saw Ego, flames licking up around the ember of his head like a halo of maggots. August ran the other way. Was it real? The only way to be sure was to let it catch him, and that wasn't a gamble he was prepared to make. The envelope slipped into his crotch, pinching his thigh as he ran.

He came to a bridge over a dark ravine. The rain became diamonds bouncing upon the ground. Hail. It beat against his neck and stung his ears, attacking the bridge around him in a rolling crescendo. His head burned and his back was numb from the cold percussion when he heard a crack behind him. Turning, he saw a white globe the size of a golf ball couched among the smaller rocks, itself getting hailed on.

"God help me." August cupped his hand over his ears and ran to the other side of the bridge, yelping and ducking as the big ones shot past him. He scrambled down the muddy embankment, then crawled through soot under the angle of the bridge. The cacophony made him flinch but he was safe from the comets slamming against the wood near his face.

The night shadow of the bridge was thick, an iron emptiness. The ground on either side was covered with hail. A little creek rushed madly, carrying the ice toward the shadow, then pushed out into the dim light on the other side. The ice foamed near the edges of the water. August heard the occasional splash of the frog-sized stones dropping in. Somewhere a siren wound itself into the night.

He was soaked through and shuddering. The powdery soil, still dry under the bridge, caked against his limbs, glazing him with mud. It made his clothes stiff. August touched the pocket with the forty-five cents, then the envelope. He closed his eyes. Hypothermia would be a strange way to go after so many years in the heat. Then the hail was over; the roaring became a soft hissing. The air was full of rain again. He wanted morning. Had the moon begun to shine through? Leaning out he couldn't find it. His breath hung in front of his face. Something on the other side of the river moved in the darkness. A raccoon? A dog? Maybe another stranded fool. The river was between him and whatever it was, so he let it go. He leaned back, letting his head sink into the dirt.

Beneath the hiss of rain there was a crackling sound like

tinder in fire: the ice clicking together in the water. He listened to it until the sound melted and he was listening to his memory of it.

13

By morning the rain had stopped and the river had grown to twice its size, churning along in a hurry. He could see a woman in black puttering around a shopping cart on the other bank, her head draped. A street person. August didn't want to see her face.

His limbs felt rusted. When he stood up, groaning, his sinuses were swollen and the skin on his face was still a little numb. He couldn't turn his neck to the right.

The woman was trying to push her cart through the mud and up the embankment toward the street. He felt brave though he knew that it was the result of the sunlight warming him combined with the fact that he had little left to lose; if he saw the fiend he would run again. Even if the creature chasing him was only in his mind, he doubted he could banish it. Only Papa had that power.

No matter what, he could not sleep under the bridge again. Filthy, August walked back across the bridge toward the movie theater, he saw the homeless woman still huffing up the slope, gray hair swishing where her face should be. He looked away as he passed, afraid to see Meredith's mouth gagged under a veil of hair. And what had become of Melody? Had she swallowed Papa's gifts yet? Would they all lose their minds?

August sat on the fish bench with a paper cup between his feet. It seemed people knew what this meant. Every half hour or so someone dropped something in—bills sometimes, mostly quarters. He waited like a dog for scraps; then, when the jangling metal came, he wanted to throw it back in their faces. Of course, Brahmins and monks begged; he knew there should be no shame in it. Still, how had it come to this?

By noon the street bothered him. The trees looked stunted. August missed the soft breeze that would blow down the mountains at night in the desert. Was moonlight in the desert really blue, or was it a trick of memory, some pigment in his brain tinting it? Here, everything was car exhaust. Exhausted.

There were periodic bursts of people from the theater, a human tide washing out. He would not say anything. Only what people offered of their own accord. Most people ignored him. A few scowled. How many beggars had he ignored in his life? There was a science to it. He could tell who was likely to look at him and who would speed by ignoring him. Those who looked were more likely to drop something. If he averted his own gaze people were more likely to look. He would get just enough for a motel room, a bed and shower. Clean and rested, he would know what to do next.

Dried by the sun, August spent his time scraping mud off his clothes. It made a ring of filth around the bench. Someone handed him a half-eaten sandwich and his stomach leapt up. Ham, cheese, mayonnaise squeezing like pus onto the paper. Could he eat this? Looking at it made him sick. He wrapped it again and put it under the bench. Only if he had to. He could buy some food but that would be less money for the room. He had fasted before.

By mid-afternoon he had a little under fifteen dollars; he would not have enough for the room by the end of the day.

One more night under the bridge. At least it was warm today. He began to press his hands together in namaste to those who paused in front of him. When someone held out change, he took it and bowed deeply. No doubt they thought he was crazy. One man bowed back in earnest. Where had he learned that?

When it began to get dark, a cool wind pushed down the street; he stood to try to walk some warmth into his body. He was getting sick, no doubt about it, his nose almost completely plugged.

He saw the bridge woman with her cart in the parking lot of the drugstore. The wheels were caked with mud. She was walking around it, touching her things, hunched and faceless behind the hair.

A person moved toward her with a pizza box; she barked like a dog and the person jumped back, then left the box on the curb. Maybe August could eat it? But he didn't want to go near her. He would stay on his side of the bridge and tomorrow night bathe and sleep. He knew he should be thinking about the night after that but he couldn't see past the shower and the bed—the story of his life could end there. It would be a happy ending.

As soon as the sun went down, he crawled under the bridge, wrapping himself in a frayed green tarp he had found snagged on a branch behind the drugstore. Breathing through his mouth left his tongue as numb as wadded felt. It didn't matter. Sick or healthy, it was just one more night. He closed his eyes, trying to pierce through to the dark waters of sleep.

The city was never really quiet. It emitted a low, sleepless droning. Cars rumbled overhead.

He was half-asleep, imagining opening the envelope and seeing a little diorama of the trailer, the car battery, the gag, her naked body. August sat up, trying to remember the details of the trailer exactly—had her clothes been piled in the corner or was he adding that now? Was Papa's voice playing on the speakers? He was looking for some skewed feature, a trapdoor, some hidden switch that would spin the room to reveal it as a complicated illusion, a hoax, the beautiful magician's assistant whole and untouched by the saw.

Early morning. The bridge lady was standing over him casting spells. She was wagging a stick covered in tinfoil over his head. August pushed it away. "No thank you, I don't need that, whatever it is." He couldn't see her eyes; her chin was crusted with coffee-colored scabs. He rolled to his side as she waddled away. The envelope was still against his hip, gummy with perspiration and grime. The sun rolled on the roofs of the buildings in the east, getting a running start to jump into the sky. He would beg enough money, get the room, shower, clean his clothes somehow, and call Jesse. Talking to her would clear his head. Afterward, when he was clean and had heard Jesse's voice, he would have strength to open the envelope. Bridges and begging would be behind him.

His clothes were damp. As he stood, brushing them off, he saw the woman trying to pull her cart up the embankment again, grunting as she strained, the wheels sinking into the oily soil. The cart seemed inert as a planet, crammed so tightly with things. August doubted she had seen the bottom strata for years. Was she still suffering, or had she left that behind with her sanity?

Was she Mull? It seemed Ego destroyed some so thoroughly that they were of no use, even to him. How bad would the visions have to get, how many nights under the bridge before August became like her? As soon as he had enough money he would run to the motel he had seen on his way into Overwill.

The woman's skirt lifted slightly in her efforts, revealing a pale calf, eggshell white and as thin as a child's. The person was hidden under there somewhere. She had only made it halfway up the slope when August approached to help her.

"Here," he said, positioning himself behind the cart to push. She screamed and let the cart go. It rumbled down the slope, caught a rock and landed hard on its side like a felled rhinoceros. Some of the clothing on top sagged onto the ground. The main cargo was packed so tightly into the frame that nothing else spilled out.

"I'm sorry," August said. He scrambled down to try to pick it up. Nevertheless she kept screaming: a high wavering sound getting louder. Maybe she thought he was trying to rob her.

He squatted, trying to lift the cart, but it seemed impossibly heavy, and he felt his shoulder wrenching in its socket. He let out a moan as the cart righted itself. Still screaming. Then she was on his back, clawing at his face. He tried to protect his eyes and fell forward into the cart, knocking it over again. They collapsed in a tangle, something landed hard on his shoulder and he made an animal noise. She was struggling on top of him, her smell septic in his lungs. Was she still attacking or just trying to get up? The boiled cabbage of her face swung in front of his. He screamed. Underneath it he saw Meredith, his Meredith fermented with age, filth, and madness. *God help me.* He tried to push the face away; his hand slammed hard into her cheekbone. She let out a yelp and August rolled away.

He ran a few steps up the embankment and turned to look. His right eye was blurry. The viscera of the cart had burst forth—trash, blankets, dolls with bald heads staring up at the sky, just born, regurgitated. The woman was rocking one of the dolls in her lap. Her right hand held her cheek where August had hit her, her left hand tickled the doll's stunned face. He had not meant to hit that hard. He had not meant to hit at all. "I'm sorry," he said again.

He tried to rub his eye clear but it got worse, like looking through a puddle of muddy water. His hands were filthy. August felt wetness on his cheek. Blood. Infection.

"I was trying to help!" he screamed, filling the river bottom for a moment. She didn't look up. She rocked and patted the doll. He needed to know what had become of Meredith. His mind would not survive the mystery. Couldn't he have found some way to free her? Something in the cart shifted and a wash of aluminum cans burst forth, rolling toward her on the slope. August stumbled up the embankment. Perhaps he had been living under the bridge for years and the Center was nothing but his own delusion. He needed a mirror. He needed to see himself.

In the tinted window of the drugstore, his face didn't look so bad. He could see more clearly out of his eye though it still stung. How deep were the scratches? A smaller face floated in his, someone inside the store looking out. He laughed, reaching into his pocket to feel the money. He went inside.

The cashier lifted a phone to her ear, calling for backup. August walked calmly toward the side of the store he thought would have rubbing alcohol. It was cheap, a dollar thirty. He grabbed a small bag of cotton swabs, some toothpaste. The toothbrushes were too expensive; he would use his finger. He found a disposable razor for one seventy-five. He could do his whole head. These would be his first purchases in six years. A fleshy man with a green shirt and a button that said "Harvey *Manager*" walked up to him. "Are you finding everything okay?"

"Yes. Thank you." August nodded, pretending the man was just being helpful. Harvey Manager walked slowly down the aisle, then turned to watch him. August needed to eat too. Maybe just a piece of fruit, or bread. He was salivating at the thought of it.

The cashier smiled anemically when he held out the exact change. She bagged his things and tried to hand him a receipt.

"No, thank you."

"It's your receipt."

"No, thank you," he repeated. She looked hurt and crumpled it in her hands. Harvey Manager now crossed his arms, watching him leave. August was giggling as he headed toward the grocery across the street.

After buying a small sourdough roll and an orange, he sat down to eat it on the curb. What day was it? The week spun in front of him as he searched for some reference point. The sun, the sky, the brick buildings didn't care what day it was. The idea of a calendar suddenly felt ridiculous to him. He imagined whole branches of human thought crumbling in an avalanche, leaving the fresh slate of a dayless world. Maybe during the Great Days. ... He shook his head.

The orange stopped his thinking. It was small enough that his fingers almost wrapped around it, and so bright that it seemed to be lit from inside, like a miniature paper lantern. Oil burst from the rind as he peeled it. It was the best piece of fruit he had ever eaten. When it was gone, he thought he had only eaten half of it and looked for the other half. *I like oranges.* It was a revelation and gave him a sense of self-confidence. His hunger was alive now so he ate the roll in two bites. It tasted bland and doughy, maybe a little undercooked. He wanted a whole meal, a huge bowl of soup, vegetables, a loaf of bread. But he needed to save money for the room. His eye still stung. He walked back into the grocery and asked where the bathroom was.

An old man in a purple work apron stared at his face.

"You okay?" he asked.

"I just need to wash my face," August said.

"It's in the back, through the double doors."

His face didn't look so bad after he washed it. His left cheek had long pink welts though the skin had only been broken in a few places. The eye was red, a blood vessel broken under his bottom eyelid. He rubbed it with his clean hands. It would be fine. He poured alcohol onto a paper towel and scrubbed his cheek. He had hit her too hard. He should have left her alone. There was nothing he could do to help her, not even in the smallest ways. The Movement, the pamphlets, the endless muttering—nothing had reached her. His bottom lip quivered.

"What are you going to do?" he said to himself. His face wrinkled; crying made him look ridiculous—an old man, lips bent into a cartoon frown. He stopped crying and laughed a little. "What are you going to do?" He reached to touch his face but his mirror self blocked his hand, palm to palm, quick, defensive. "Get the room. Take a shower. Call

Jesse. Sleep in a bed. Just that." He tossed the alcohol back into the bag and saw that he had forgotten to use the cotton swabs. Wasted money.

Buddha had begged, Christ had wandered the streets: this would be temporary. Nothing more could be taken from him. He was begging, lost. Lost as any fairy-tale child with the wilderness looming, the wolves and demons circling in. But even lost like this and sad—okay, yes, he was sad; his every step felt like a species of weeping. And scared, yes scared too. *Enough!* Even lost and sad and scared and begging he was just August. Just August leaning against the Mull buildings. It couldn't get much worse. If it did, he would still have himself.

By mid-afternoon he had thirty-eight dollars and twenty-three cents, enough for the room. He decided to wait until the last movie was over and the laughing people burst forth, buzzing with illusion and spare change. As he waited, a woman in a blue suit walked quickly toward him, smiled a toothpaste-commercial smile, and shook his hand. White stockings, manicured nails, a black leather bag swinging deftly behind her left arm, eyes sparkling. There was a little boy standing shyly behind her, also in a little suit.

"My name is Mary. This is Teddy, and you are?"

"William." His middle name.

"Hi, William! May I sit?"

She settled herself cozily next to him on the bench, swinging the bag around to the other side so her hip was touching his. The child, playing with weeds near the gutter, had acquired a long black smudge on his sleeve.

She kept smiling as she spoke, her face now very close. "Have you ever wondered why the government doesn't provide for all its citizens?"

August tried to hold still. Who was she recruiting for? The Witnesses? Scientology? Just plain old-fashioned Christ?

She continued, "What if I told you that soon we wouldn't need a government anymore, that everyone everywhere would have food and housing. That war would end completely and forever?" August shook his head. It couldn't be; she was dressed too expensively. Maybe they had updated their strategies.

"We're traveling across America," she said, "to share this good news that has been revealed to us by the living prophet, Papa Narshima."

August stared at the pamphlet she'd handed him. It was a recent one, and he opened the flap to read the dedication inside. He had written it himself just last month. She was still talking, trying to reel him in: "…Papa shows us that all human beings are one true family. The different religions are actually one religion, just seen from different angles, like the facets of a diamond." If she was going to recognize him, she would have done so by now; still he kept his tattoo against his thigh.

"How long have you been on the street, William?"

"Not long."

"Well, we have a place for you to stay at the Movement house in Phoenix. You can get cleaned up. We have a rehab program as well. There are also free meals on Wednesdays and Saturdays. How does that sound? Best of all is that you'll get to hear more about Papa and his revelations. Too good to be true, right? I know. I can personally promise you that Papa's words will change your life. Papa was sent to bring the world to a higher plane of consciousness. That's why there has been so much turmoil recently—the final changes are coming."

Meredith slumped like a dead fish on the floor, Melody smiling at the crowd. He faked a smile, nodding, "Okay."

"Good! I knew you were smart when I saw you. I said, now *he's* going to know what I'm talking about! All you have to do is get to Phoenix. Do you think you can get enough money for a bus there? The address is on the pamphlet. If you lose it just look up 'The Movement House' in a phone book and one of our people will direct you." She leaned closer and he could smell her perfume. "Do you think you could be there by next week?" she asked.

"Maybe."

She touched his hand, sending a chill across his shoulders. Who had condoned this? Years ago, when he was fishing the streets for recruits himself, flirting was unheard of. "I'd really like to see you there next week, William. I have a good feeling about you. I know you have a big, good heart. I can see it. Papa's teachings allow us to see things other people can't, so I know you are a good person who's just a little lost. You just need someone to answer a few questions for you. To know which way to go. Am I right? Of course. I can see your glow. It's going to be alright, William. Get to the Movement house. We'll take care of the rest. Will you do that? I'm so glad. It was a pleasure to meet you. I'll see you in Phoenix. One week. Understanding and Peace are waiting for you. If I don't see you there I'll send someone out here, and don't let me catch you on this bench, right?" That brilliant smile again, the luster of pleasure glistening in her mouth. "Promise me."

"Okay. Thank you."

"No, thank *you*, William. Thank *you*." Then she winked as if they had shared a sexy secret. It was something he had seen in movies years ago but had never seen a real woman do. She took the child by the hand and strolled jauntily down the street.

August flipped the pamphlet over, knowing what would be on the back cover. The picture of Papa was small and outdated, a much younger version. The eyes pierced into August: *I see you!* He slapped the pamphlet against the bench, trying to ignore the irritation of the envelope against his thigh. Enough. Just get the room, shower, sleep. Goodbye fish bench. It was time to open the envelope. He knew he wouldn't be able to handle it on the street. He couldn't put it off any longer; he needed shelter, a bed to crawl into in case Papa's wrath burst from the envelope like a plague of beetles.

He counted the money again as he walked, passing the bridge and the bus stop, looking for the flamingo motel he had spotted on his way in. A dark man in a cowboy hat was selling fruit from a cart on wheels and August paused to buy another orange, thirty-two cents.

As he peeled it he realized that he no longer felt particularly congested, that his shoulder was feeling better all the time. The money in his pocket, the smell of the orange, and the shower he would soon be taking made his footsteps light. The sugars burst on his tongue, far better than anything he had eaten at the Center. He kissed the last wedge of citrus like a small beloved pet before chewing it. Right or wrong, path or no path, he was doing the best he could. He was a little crazy maybe, but he had earned it. No one, knowing his history, could blame him.

14

The flamingo was a blotch of pink against cinderblock, poorly drawn and wearing sunglasses.

"Sorry, we're full." The mousy child behind the counter looked too young to be in charge. His head was big and he didn't make eye contact with August. Instead he peered at something on a computer screen.

"Wait. Are you sure?" August asked. Was he being turned away because he looked homeless?

"Sorry," the kid repeated as he tapped a button on the keyboard, trying to wake the computer up. "We can put you in a double for forty-eight."

"I don't have forty-eight." It was just a child. August could reach over and shake the key from him. "I have thirty. Like the sign outside says. That's all I have."

"We have one vacant single but it's being repaired. The shower doesn't work. We could give—"

"No. Look at me. I need a shower."

The child peered at August through the corners of his eyes without turning his head, then looked at the computer again.

"That's all we have."

August moaned, leaned on the counter, and put his head in his hands, feeling his energy dropping through his feet. There was a little stack of postcards near his elbow: a beach with palm trees, a woman in a bikini giving the camera the same knowing look that Mary had just given him. He felt feverish. This was his life. Homeless. He had shunned his Mull family, given all his possessions to Papa, and then washed out, a slow-motion explosion.

"There's the Traveler's Inn."

"What?"

"Down on Piccolo."

"A motel? Which way?" August pointed, waiting for the child to look at him.

They gave him a plastic card instead of a key and he trudged upstairs looking for the number. A cart of cleaning supplies and towels was abandoned just outside his room. He opened the door to find a bear's den—brown, dark, and musty, a wide bed with a vomit-colored cover, an obsidian-faced television. As he stood in the doorway a cockroach crawled between his feet into the room as if invited. "Unbelievable." Grabbing the broom from the cleaning cart, he swatted the cockroach out. No one was around so he kept the broom, tossing it to the floor under the draped window, then slammed the door and collapsed on the bed. The rough polyester smelled like cigarettes and sweat; even so, it was such a relief to lie down that he felt his body preparing to cry.

Instead he stood to take his clothes off. There was a mirror on the open bathroom door and in it he saw a primitive cousin to Homo sapiens—filthy and thin. There were silver blisters along the top of the mirror, some kind of creeping disease. Also, something was wrong with the reflection: he could not really be that gaunt. Jutting cheekbones and shoulders, dirt streaked along his neck.

He plugged the sink, letting the water run into it while he

put the envelope, the key card, and the remaining money on the counter next to the phone. Then he wadded his clothes into the sink, trying to submerge them. Brown water poured over the counter onto the dingy bath mat. Thinking better of it he lifted the muddy mass and threw it into the shower; he would wash everything at the same time.

The shower was a bludgeoning torrent, dragging his lips away from his face, stinging his nipples and back. It felt so good he kept surprising himself with obscene, involuntary groans. He wanted to be washed out, completely flushed. It coursed down his body, making a little fountain leaping from his penis like an endless stream of urine.

August lifted his deafened face, letting his mouth fill with water. With the warmth gagging him, he shaped the words: *What have you done to us, Papa?*

He stamped on his clothes like wine grapes, soaping and rinsing them again and again until the water running through them was clear. There was no bell. The hot water was endless, the motel was like a god, infinitely producing the nectar within itself. Though it was a waste, he stood under the downpour for half an hour. Then he turned his back to it and took himself in his hand but he was as soft as wet bread.

When his fingers had bloated into prunes, he turned the water off and opened the curtain to a world of steam. The long mirror was fogged, a ghost door. He tried to smear a clear spot and saw, for an instant, something animal: diamond eyes glittering in fists of darkness, shifting masses of silver fur. Then it fogged over again. "Boo!" His laugh was high pitched and childish.

After wringing them out he draped his shirt and pants

over the heater in the corner. Naked, with the air beginning
to clear, he stretched, then slapped his chest like a gorilla and
crossed to the phone.

*Desk 0. Local *0. Long Distance *00 credit card or
collect.*

It was a long shot. She could have moved. For all he knew
she could be married. He imagined a man's voice sounding
jealous, which made him smile. He had always had a good
head for numbers; still, he had to look at the keypad for a
minute before he dialed. The operator took his name and he
heard a female voice on the other end accept the collect call.
It wasn't Jesse.

"Hello?"

"I'm looking for Jesse Russ. This is August, her brother."

"Oh. I'm really sorry. Hold on, she gave me the number
in case you called." He heard the phone rattle.

He memorized the new number and dialed again.

A different voice took his name. He could hang up now.
It wasn't too late. Then he heard Jesse say, "Oh my God! Yes.
I'll accept the charges. Hello?"

"Jesse. It's me."

"August! Oh my God, August? Hello?" Her voice
sounded older, frayed.

"It's me."

"I didn't think you were going to call. I can't believe it.
You got my letter. Are you coming?"

He looked at the envelope on the counter. "Coming
where?"

She was sobbing. There were other voices in the background. "Did you get the letter?"

"I haven't opened it."

"Oh my God."

"I just wanted to say hello, and tell you I'm alright."

"Why didn't you open it? Goddamn it, August."

"Wait a minute. I'm just, I don't know, I just thought I could tell you I'm still alive. Things are changing. I'm a little confused. Really confused. I've been thinking a lot. Too much probably—"

"Stop it. Stop talking about YOURSELF!" Her voice broke as she screamed, then became a boiling whisper. "You have no idea, do you? I love you August, I do, but for one second of your life... can't you see it's not about you? I thought you were calling about—" She made a sound like a bark as she cried. "You hurt her so much. Being confused doesn't make you special. People don't just run away and *disappear*." Then her voice melted into tired sweetness. "Oh, August, honey. ... What's going to happen to you?"

He held the phone a little away from his ear, looking at it as if he might be able to catch a glimpse of her. "Jesse?"

"Mom's dead. The funeral was last week."

It was already a memory; August felt himself watching it from much later on. He could hear someone saying his name, trying to get him to answer, but he couldn't hold on. Jesse pushed the merry-go-round too fast, he slipped off, floated out, and couldn't breathe. Nothing to hold on to. All decisions had already been made.

The phone was back in its cradle. August was on the floor, slumped against the bed. Ego had crept through the mirror and stood hunched and panting a few feet away. A slavering wolf's head on a starved human body, looking sideways at August with sunken eyes. The parched tongue hung like a piece of unswallowed meat with a jagged tooth piercing through it. A blood red cock bobbed in front of the emaciated belly. Below the swollen knees, the crooked angles of dog legs branched into dozens of clawed pads, enough for a whole pack of wolves, like bouquets of dried roses hung upside down, skittering on the bathroom floor.

Run. There was nowhere to run and August couldn't stand. He curled away, trying to protect his face, and it was on him, digging, chewing into his stomach. The room was filled with roaring wind. He rolled, trying to crawl toward the broom with the wolf tearing at him. It slid its tongue between his ribs. Its teeth clicked together in the rivers of blood inside his neck.

When he felt the broom in his hand he swung blindly and heard a lamp shatter against the wall. The beast was behind him, slipping between his legs, then flapping above his head like a vulture. He managed to get to a corner and kept swinging. He hit something hard, breaking the straw head from the handle. He screamed and screamed again. Someone in the next room yelled, "Shut the fuck up! Jesus Christ!" August fell to the floor, still gripping the broom with the wolf humping and thrusting over him, its tongue shoved deep into his throat.

Now the attack slowed. August managed to get to his knees, swaying and coughing. How long would it last? The television was on, sending shudders of light against the walls. He pulled himself into bed and wrapped the covers around him. Then Ego found him again. August wept and held his head.

It came in waves. When the rolling and moaning stopped, the room was quiet for a few minutes. August sat up slowly, trying not to look at Ego, who was creeping just behind the edges of his vision, waiting to pounce again. An audience laughed hysterically. On the screen was a huge white kitchen with dozens of mixers churning different pastes and a man running back and forth between them. He shouted something over the noise of the machines. The audience laughed again.

The images shuffled themselves: a news report of some kind, a war-torn country where rebels were going from village to village, terrorizing. Thatched houses and a dark woman carrying something on her head. A little boy with his mouth covered by a black cloth, holding an enormous gun. Jesse's white face, his mother's moldering corpse, Meredith's legs turning purple under the ropes.

When Ego tore into him again he groaned, scrambled for the broom, couldn't find it, and tried to crawl under the blankets. When he peeked out again the White House was surrounded by picketers. Then there were gorgeous, half-naked women dancing in a club, shaking their breasts. Music like a fire alarm. They were rolling their hips, trying to fuck the camera, gazing out at August with half-closed lids. His penis stiffened and he covered it with both hands. Ego backed into the shifting shadows while August rubbed himself, watching the women move. Chafing and raw, he pumped harder. There were people being chased on speedboats, palm trees, beaches. The boats slapped the water with their broad white chests. Then the women dancing again, their clothes tied fiercely around their soft bodies.

He thought he was coming but the top of his head opened like a box and he moved up, looking down at the bad son, the washout, churning the sheets. The music screamed, the women pulsed, and Ego pressed close, waiting to lap him up completely.

"God."

It gagged up out of him, wet against his stomach. When he opened his eyes Ego was gone and the television was dead. August touched his navel, the puddle of sperm cold and drying already. Everything was quiet. He could hear his own pulse gasping in his ears, evidence of his heart somewhere deep below still quivering with life. How had she died? Cancer. Heart attack. It didn't matter. She had gone thinking he hated her.

He wanted to see Jesse badly now, her older face, how she would look at him. He had been a coward, running away from everything. If he could see a glimmer of forgiveness in Jesse's face, or if he could look at her anger without running again, he would have something to hold on to.

August woke up sweating in a soupy black heat. He rose, slammed into something, and found his clothes. They had molded solid as plaster casts over the searing metal. He peeled them away, threw them near the door, and turned the heater off before falling back into bed. The room was empty. Ego was gone. The battle had not been romantic; Ego had been vanquished with a dumb endurance, the kind of weathering a blade of grass manages through a hurricane. He felt victorious nonetheless.

The curtains began to glow. Morning. Mucus ran from his nose. He was hungry and sore as he got up. He shuddered once and peeked through the curtains at the sleeping city, the trees, and the distant highway. How many hours had he slept? Not enough. Still, he was happy to see the light. The idea of setting off to find Jesse lit something bright in him, though even as that hope grew, he knew it would have to wait. She would see it on his face: Meredith was still tied and gagged in his mind. She would see Melody in her wedding clothes and, he was sure, the smear of Papa's come across his lips. Jesse would be kind, hugging him and letting him stay with her, but she would know, as soon as she saw him, that after six years of unrelenting certainty, he had nothing to show for it besides a deep and abiding humiliation. He could not go back crippled by confusion. He had to know if Meredith was okay, had to find out what Papa had known, and what he was doing with Melody. He needed to confess to Meredith that he had seen her and left her there.

The mirror was clear again; August looked terrible. It was like seeing a relative he had forgotten, a child who had grown up too quickly. A spotty beard clustered around his chin like mold, and near his forehead were several graying hairs. August laughed. A quarter century of struggle.

The Center was pulling him back. He felt resigned to it, almost grateful not to have to run anymore. The growing sense of inevitability felt like a kind of strength, a decision so firm that it was making itself.

He showered again thinking about Jesse's letter and put on his stiff clothes. They stood out in ridiculous angles, making him look like he was smuggling fruit. He balanced the pieces of the lamp precariously back into place on the bedside table. It would collapse again as soon as someone touched it. By then he would be long gone, sneaking away like a thief before the cleaning staff came. Another shame, another debt on his karma, though he felt that this wreckage was a small price to pay for the sense of direction he had now. He was near the end of wreckage. He would not run anymore.

Sitting on the edge of the bed he took the envelope in his

lap and tore it open before he could change his mind. There was a smaller legal-size envelope inside with his full name on it and, in the upper-left corner, the Center logo stamped in bright blue, smeared a little from the rain. August stared. It wasn't from Jesse. It must be a dismissal. It didn't matter.

He ripped the seal and unfolded the cream stationery to reveal Papa's handwriting:

> A,
> *The troublation is different. Emergency. Emergence. Standunder stand. When you will coming back. Brokenseals, KaliYuga. Final Mother ever will. We will coming back. All Medicine Meredith. Harmony Melody Mother. You must ever. prescribedescribeit. The it. kingDemonHell. Youmustaaron. Until. Your task is do task. DO TASK DO TASK DO TASK DO TASK. Forme promise.*
> Papa

Beneath that in Mother Li's careful script:

> *Urgent that you return at once. All is forgiven.*

He folded the letter, then unfolded and read it again. Papa's mind had broken; it was undeniable now. The thought settled like a dirty cat curling on his lap. How could he have believed otherwise? There would be no new language, Papa was simply losing control. He scanned it again, lingering on *Medicine Meredith*. There was no way to interpret this. In his imagination he saw Meredith bleeding, dying, dumped in the desert. If he had been unsure a few moments ago, he no longer had any choice. He had to find out what had happened.

He wanted to stay in the room a little longer, but he didn't know when the cleaning staff made their rounds so he gathered the envelopes and remaining money, kicked the broken head of the broom under the bed, grabbed the wooden handle, and stepped out into the humming morning. As he hustled to put distance between the motel and himself, he scraped the jagged end of the broom against the sidewalk until it was less spear and more walking stick. The black paint was worn to blond wood at the top and middle where the hands would normally grip it. It felt good to hold something so solid, something that he had already used to fight the devil.

A dog in the shadows behind a trash bin peered at him. Was it Ego? He lifted his stick and the dog scrambled away. August's stomach cramped with hunger.

Going back. It was not so much a decision as it was the shape of his life, the bent fabric of space sloping toward the Center. What could Papa say to make it all right? By knowing or by ignorance Papa had been corrupted. August was separate now, awake, watching Papa from a distance. He imagined sinking his teeth into Papa's throat. He wanted to tell Papa that, out here, nothing had changed: no news of unexplained spontaneous healings, no miraculous crop growths in the starving countries. The muttering, the revelations, the Chapters hadn't made a dent in Mull consciousness. No sign of the Great Days, not a glimmer. It was war, confusion, and gluttony, as it had always been.

If they were expecting the prodigal son, they would be disappointed. He gripped the stick like a weapon as he walked toward the bus stop. He was not going home for forgiveness.

August tried to sleep on the bus. His arms and legs were sweltering, but the metallic draft of cold air blowing on his face didn't help. His remaining eight dollars had bought him a bagel and a bus trip that would take him only a third of the way back. It would be hitchhiking the rest of the way. Then, perhaps after more begging, he would buy himself a bottle of water, maybe another orange, then head down into the desert on foot. He realized with disappointment that he would have to spend the night somewhere outside again, probably curled on a bench in Silkweed, worried about the police.

It was a full bus this time; a sunburned man with a base-ball cap sat snoring softly in the seat next to him. August's neck ached and he felt drugged. There would be no sleep. Eyes burning, he watched the passing landscape. A herd of something in the distance, neither cows nor sheep: something with a long neck. August squinted. They looked like enormous birds—ostriches? It didn't have the buzz of a vision, no intensity, just his eyes telling him that there was a flock of ostriches in a field in northern Arizona. The world felt like a joke he had missed the first part of, a party he had stumbled upon. He hadn't been invited.

15

Right away something was different: in the late afternoon light, two new trailers were just outside the gate. Not trailers but mobile homes. Initiates moving to and fro, carrying boxes. Was this what the letter had been about? From the subtle slope where August was standing a quarter mile away, he could see the figures moving though he could not identify them. Dizzy from the day's hike, he crouched near a bush hoping they hadn't seen him.

Perhaps they were making preparations for the Great Days. At the last minute he had missed it. Papa's final revelation had come, the changes were under way without him! He pressed his hands against his eyes and tried to remember the independence he had when he left the motel. Instead he found himself craving the forgiveness of Papa's gaze.

The sun slid on its greased heat toward the mountains and more figures amassed in a hoard near the gates, a few of them still carrying boxes to the trailers from somewhere in the middle of the compound. He watched until his eyes were sore and the compound disappeared, erased by sand and shrub, his mind covering the burnt patches on his retina. His stomach lurched; a sour taste rose in his throat. He had spent a restless night on a park bench in Silkweed, listening for approaching police cars. The old Native American woman who had driven him halfway into the desert had given him a dry corn tamale to eat with his last orange; now, with his stomach cramping, he wondered if it had been cooked with lard. His shadow stretched insect-like beside him, a long blank face, somewhere in its abdomen the shadow of the orange and tamale.

He found a pile of warm boulders and hunched against one, waiting for the courage to walk through the gates. A pewter stain nearby raised itself on lizard arms, performing military push-ups. Would they throw stones? Mother Li had said, *All is forgiven*. Maybe he would wait until sunset and sneak in like a feral cat. The sun touched the rim of earth and he let his eyes close.

There was movement behind him, something massive, breathing like a horse. He found his stick and swung around looking for Ego. Matheson grabbed his arm, lifted him to his feet, and began slapping at his back, brushing off the dust. Then he let go, grimacing with disgust. "How long were you going to sulk out here?" he said.

August gripped the broomstick, sensing a hidden wound in Matheson, as if his swollen body had been punctured and he was deflating slowly. August tried to keep the panic from his voice. "Where is she?" he said. "What did you do to her?"

Matheson shook his head. "Whatever you think you saw, Ego was in that trailer."

"Don't do that. I saw you."

"She was going to ruin the wedding," Matheson said.

"You could have just kept her confined. You didn't have to torture her." He paused. "Where is she now?"

Matheson began to grow again, his anger lifting him above August, his face wide as a jack-o-lantern. "I *saved* her, you arrogant shit. She was washing out. You know how badly Ego wants a toehold here. The *mother* of the final Mother washing out, in front of the Chapter delegates. How would that be? *I* pulled her back. What did you do? Tell me one thing you've done?" He smiled now. "Nothing. You're an errand boy. A parrot. You have no right to even think about what I do, what I face, for the Movement. I don't care what they're saying about you; I saw you run."

"There are other ways," August insisted. "You didn't have to hurt her. Tell me what happened to her."

Matheson's fingers flicked the air near his hip and he looked tired again, his eyes slipping away. "You don't have any idea what you're talking about. I answer to Papa. Anyway, she's back to her old self. Centered again. Because of me. That's what I do. What no one else is willing to." Matheson looked over August's head toward the crowd gathered at the gates. He lifted his massive arms and began to wave, like someone needing to be rescued from a desert island. The initiates poured out of the gates and headed toward them.

She was alive; the relief made August want to collapse. Instead he scowled at Matheson. "Does Papa really know?"

"You're shaking! Look at you. What's with the stick?"

"Has he been in z-trailer? Has he seen how you do it?" August said.

"Papa knows."

"Has he *seen?*"

"Papa knows everything."

August felt his legs shaking now and planted one end of the stick in the sand, trying to brace himself. "You can't admit to doing it alone. You have to say Papa knows."

When Matheson looked at August again, his eyes were almost kind. "The one thing I don't understand—" The initiates crashed around them like an ocean wave nearly knocking August off his feet. "—is why he loves you so much."

There were shouts and August heard his name being chanted. Hands were all over him, pressing. He couldn't see Meredith. *Back to her old self.* He tried to pull away but it was impossible. All he could do was hold his stick above his head as they hugged him from all sides and kissed his cheeks. Then someone had his feet and he was lifted, carried above them, under the sunset sky, bright washes of violent pink, clouds like viscera hanging above him. August squirmed to see their faces: not a glimmer of anger or betrayal. They were as joyous as if they had caught and killed Ego himself. He floated on their hands as they sang celebration songs.

"Where is Meredith?" he rasped. Their chanting was too loud. They carried him past the mobile homes, dark and closed now, through the gates, setting him down near the main-hall under the floodlight next to the new foot basins. The three NewFaces stood in an eager row with towels and smiles. A stool was offered and he sat down, a cloud of moths quivering in the teal light above him. When NewFace Rebecca removed his sandals, there were gasps at the blood from the blisters on his heel. Someone shouted, "Give him room, let him breathe!"

"I want to see Meredith," he said. But they had turned their attention to someone coming through the crowd. Everyone hushed as Mother Li appeared.

It was silent enough to hear the moths smacking into the

light as she knelt before him, took his foot from Rebecca, and dipped it in the water. "While we were celebrating and feasting," Mother Li said, "August set out alone to clear a path for Papa in the wastelands. He could have been killed by Ego, or worse, but he didn't hesitate. He is a harbinger of the Great Days! Like Hanuman, like Michael, he was a lone scout among enemies!"

Someone began wailing in ecstasy, then they were singing again, filling the darkened sky with their voices. He wanted to pull his foot away—a Mother washing his feet! "Mother, I'm confused—"

"Hush, child. Let us show our gratitude."

When his blisters had been bandaged and new sandals brought for him, Mother Li began to lead him to Papa's trailer, the crowd following close behind. He stopped, whispering to her, "Where is Meredith?"

"How will it look, greeting her before Papa?" Then she sighed, "In the kitchen. Hurry, Papa has been waiting for you." As he ran for the door of the main-hall he heard her gathering the others around for more singing.

Meredith was standing near the enormous sink with two other Sisters grating carrots into an orange froth. Upright, not bleeding or weeping. When she saw him she lit up and nodded as if he had asked her a question. She spread her arms wide, still holding the ruddy stump of a carrot. "Welcome back, Brother."

As she embraced him, he felt her back, warm and rounding toward him. Alive and smiling! Had he imagined the whole thing?

"Are you okay?" August asked as they stepped apart to look at each other. He didn't want to let go and held her wrist while she transferred the carrot to the other hand. The Sisters stood back and averted their eyes, giving them privacy.

She put her wet hand on his cheek. "Of course, I'm fine. But what about you? How was the journey? A secret mission for Papa, August! So glad to see you in one piece." He felt his head rocking and saw by her suddenly careful expression that he was crying. She pulled him in again. "You made it, you're safe now. Welcome back. Have you seen Papa yet?"

He hovered near her as she continued to grate carrots, terrified at everything he didn't understand. He knew that his homecoming would be strange, he had been prepared for awkwardness and difficulty; still, he had not expected this. His questions had become tangled together in his mind. He no longer had words for them. Like a child, he stared and kept asking her, "You're okay?" She laughed, patted his arm, and tried to get him to sift flour. Was he dreaming?

"They think I'm a hero," he said.

"Because you are." The answer came from behind him and August turned to see Mother Li's stern face.

"Mother, what is going on?"

"It's rude to keep Papa waiting, August." The initiates crowded in behind her and filled the hall with a festive bustle, tuning guitars, pushing tables arounds. Though he was scared to let Meredith out of his sight, he allowed himself to be taken by the elbow and led, like an old man, toward Papa's trailer. He tried to feel the comfort of the Center, but his heart had seized up. He felt nothing but bewilderment. They stopped in the wide dusty trail just outside the penumbra of the main-hall lights.

"He never doubted you, August. He knew you'd be

back."

"You lied to them about me."

She glanced up into the sky where the stars were beginning to cluster. "He said, 'Wait for August,' and hasn't spoken since. I'm not very good at interpreting. They prefer you. We all do."

"Did you know what Matheson does in there?" he asked.

"He told me you tried to interrupt her redirection. Why would you do that?"

"He was torturing her with a car battery."

"August, enough drama. Please. Have you been eating at all? You look so thin, child." She put her hand on his arm.

He shook it off. "A *car battery*."

"You'll calm down now. You don't seem to appreciate how generous Papa is being with you."

"Did you *know*?" August asked.

"She's *fine*, August. Have you been worrying all this time? Having your visions? Didn't you see her in there? Where's your center? Matheson can be stubborn but he would never hurt an initiate. You know that."

She began walking again, pulling him along. Had he hallucinated some part of it? August saw himself in the motel's blighted mirror, a wolf's head, a crown of cold fire. Maybe Ego was deep in him, a parasite confusing his memory. What had really happened when he fought Ego in the motel room? Maybe he was a Trojan horse: when he got close enough, Ego would erupt from him and rip Papa in half.

They moved into the ring of trailers; across the courtyard he could see the other Mothers gathered like pale moths. Identifying Melody by her height, he felt his outrage unfurling inside him again. He placed his hand on the door of

Papa's trailer, but Mother Li tugged at his shirt so he hesitated.

"Where *did* you go?" she asked him. The bridge, the aluminum cans bursting out of the homeless woman's cart.
"Anyway, try to get him to say something. We need to know
if he's ready."

"Ready for what?" August asked.

"Just ask him. Don't pester him with all your panic. Just
try to get him to nod."

Papa looked small sitting with his back to the door, books
open on the desk in front of him. He was shirtless, his broad
back speckled with old-man spots. His hair made a furious
silver storm spinning around the calm bald spot.

He looked up without any surprise, as if August was just
arriving for their usual reading. Yet there was something
exhausted around his eyes.

"Papa—"

Papa raised his finger. August shut his mouth. The finger
curled and August stepped closer. He felt a tremor of fear at
the base of his skull, trying to find the bitter strength that
had carried him back through the desert. He could smell talcum. Papa pointed at one of the books. August shook his
head. "I'm not here to read to you, Papa."

Papa stood and for a moment his face sagged; he looked
like a poor imitation, some imposter in a Papa suit. He had
lost weight. Then something shifted and the light behind the
desk caught Papa's face. August stepped back, bumping into
the bookshelf. The eyes were moist. The whites surged like
milk around the slate stones. Leaning toward August, his
mouth spread into an O, then a dark slot. A hot lungful of

air came hissing out and August tried not to blink. Papa pointed again. August shook his head.

Papa seized August's wrist, pulling him toward the desk. August tried to resist but his thigh hit the edge of the desk and he fell forward, scrambling over the papers. He felt Papa's hand on his neck pressing him against the desk like a schoolboy about to receive a whipping. A thick finger tapped a book in front of August's nose.

"I won't read." Papa lifted a page, holding it in front of August's face. August closed his eyes. "No, Papa."

Papa let go and August straightened. They were both breathing hard and Papa's eyes wandered off of August for a moment. Then, like bread falling out of the sky, he smiled. He stepped back and sat on the chair.

They watched each other for what felt like a long time. Papa seemed to have lost all anger. August was shaking again; where had he left his stick? He could hear the distant singing coming from the main-hall, then the soft laughter of the Mothers from the nearby trailer. Papa scratched his chin and crossed his arms, waiting, bemused.

"I came back to ask you questions," August finally said. "Mother Li is telling them. ... Do you know what Matheson does in z-trailer?" Papa sighed. August's hands balled into fists, released, and balled up again. Papa's gaze was beginning to bore into his head, like a heavy hum just below the threshold of hearing. Could Papa even understand English anymore? "Matheson tied her up. He gagged her and there was electricity... nod your head, did you know? Or point to the books—I'll interpret your answer."

Papa closed his eyes. Then he rose and pointed at the book he had pushed August into. August took it reluctantly and scanned silently: ...*when enlightenment is near, even the bright light of truth becomes a distraction and a temptation, one must proceed in its glare, not ignoring it yet not mesmerized. Even the jewels of attainment must be let go. ...*

"No, Papa. This doesn't answer my question. I want you to say it. Answer me yes or no. Just nod. Did you know?"

Papa reached to tap the pages again but August slapped his hand away. "Yes or no!" For a moment they both stood there stunned. Papa began chuckling and August felt reality slipping away. The memory of what they did in this trailer, August on his knees, Papa grunting into him, lit his body with adrenaline. He threw the book across the trailer where it slammed into the wall.

Still smiling, Papa sat back down. Looking into his eyes was like staring at the surface of deep water. Maybe Papa was down below, shouting, explaining everything. Nothing made it to the surface, not a bubble.

August was scared now. This was going nowhere, and Papa was the only one who could help him understand. August kneeled next to the chair, softening his voice, "Please, Papa. I need to know. Just nod your head. You knew. You let it happen." Papa put his hand over August's and shook his head. Was he saying "no" or just showing his disappointment? August felt himself beginning to melt into Papa's heat. Maybe it didn't matter. Meredith was fine now; he had seen her. If she was okay, why was August holding on to his rage? Wasn't everyone okay? If Papa said something, even a single word, August felt he would let go. The voice would put everything in its place. Just one word would be enough, just his own name, *August,* and he would let go of everything he had seen. Let the whole world go up in flames.

"Please, Papa. I'm completely gone. I can't interpret, I'm so lost. Explain it. Point to a book that explains it. Make it make sense." Tears welled in his eyes as his head sank against Papa's arm. "Oh, God. Please." He felt Papa stroking the back of his neck and wept harder. Papa was there, under all of it, the love, wisdom, and strength waiting under the silence.

When he opened his eyes he saw the bulge rising under Papa's robes and August stood up, horrified. The founder's cock filling with blood, the Harbinger of the Great Days, the Comforter.

"You poisoned me, Papa."

He opened the door and turned back to look. Papa was smiling again, holding his finger to his mouth, hissing, "Shhhh."

16

Someone was playing guitar in the main-hall, but when August entered the music stopped. Several initiates rushed in to hug him again. An enormous platter of sweet cakes had been made in his honor: carrots, walnuts, honey, flour, and raisins.

They seemed to be waiting for him to make an address. August told them to keep singing. They let him sit quietly with Meredith at one of the back tables while they sang late into the night.

He alternated between watching the rocking crowd and Meredith's tanned cheek, waiting for something to make sense. She looked a little tired though her face was clean. She joined the songs occasionally and smiled at him when she caught him staring. He ached to stop thinking; instead he whispered, *"Sister, I know what he did to you."*

She looked toward the guitar players and he could only see the high shelf of her cheekbone. "I just have to stay out of the sun," she said.

"The sun?"

"It makes me faint. I'm fine working in the kitchen."

"You were gagged—"

She waved as if there were a mosquito singing by her ear.

"I'm past it. It can happen to anyone."

"I saw you tied up—"

"Please, August."

"The electricity—"

"Don't." She was looking at him now and her face made him stop. "Why would you do that? I have nothing to be ashamed of."

"I'm trying to say—"

"You have no right to test me. I'm past it. I'm back on the path, Brother." She hissed the last word and made him flinch. She stood, then sat down again. "Please, August. It feels like a long time ago. I'm glad you're back. Don't... rattle me." She patted him lamely on the back. "Maybe being outside rattled *you*. But you're back now. Get centered, take deep breaths."

She let her knee touch his and he dropped his head onto his crossed arms, feeling perversely fatigued. He had begun to nod off when the music stopped. There were more shouts of greeting. Little Melody walked into the hall wearing Mother robes, her head a ridiculous burst of new hair. August felt Meredith go rigid, as if a ghost had walked in. Melody was carrying a necklace of tiny pink desert flowers. For a moment August thought she would bestow it on Meredith. Instead she hung it on him and said, "Welcome back, child." She smiled at him, ignoring her mother.

There was a cloud of silence while everyone waited for him to say something. Sitting, he was eye level with her. Had Papa fucked her yet? Was he supposed to call her Mother? In the corner of his vision, August saw Meredith reach out under the table and pinch her daughter's robe, rubbing the cotton between her fingers, a slow guilty movement.

August coughed. When people saw tears in his eyes they cooed and surrounded him again, saying, "You're safe now.

You made it back, you're home." Melody wandered over to the platter of cakes.

In the morning he sat at the small table in his own trailer staring at the photo of his sister. There was a knock. Before he could rise Mother Li ducked in, pulling her robes through the door and closing it gracefully behind her. "I asked Papa this morning if he still thought you were the one to do it and he nodded. Papa knows what Papa knows." She sat softly next to him and tossed her braid over her shoulder.

"The one to do what?" August asked.

"Just keep an eye on things. Keep things in order. Stay and give the addresses until we get back."

"Where are you going?"

"There are some tests. The changes in Papa are happening quickly. It's easy for me to be worried, I'm his wife. Really it's just to get a clearer picture of where things are going."

"Tests," August repeated.

"These are Movement doctors, August. Just to give us a better picture of how the transformation is progressing, how the revelations are manifesting in his physical form."

"All of the Mothers are going?"

"He wants us to go. That's why we need you to do this for us."

August shook his head. "Maybe Brother Thomas or Sister Chavez, she's good. She's smart."

Mother Li sighed. "They trust *you*, child. You're Papa's voice. This will be difficult for them. It's a strange time. They need you to comfort them, to keep them at ease until we get back. Of course—" Her face became very serious. "—you would not tell them about the tests. It would only confuse them."

"Doesn't he care that I washed out?"

She took the photo of Jesse from him and looked at it before putting it facedown on the table and gripping his hand. Her fingers were soft and slightly cold. "You know he's seen all of this. Some of us… we're special. We serve God and Papa at all times, even when we sleep. Even when we think we've fallen off the path, almost in spite of ourselves, we are so *guided* by his grace. If you had washed out, Ego would have destroyed you right away. Papa's light protected you. If you had washed out, why would you be here, just in time to do this for him? He forgave you for leaving before you were born. He's already forgiven you for the mistakes you are going to make while we are gone. It won't be long, just until we get back. Why do you think he's been grooming you these last two years? Don't fight your dharma. Without Papa there is no August. He makes you and remakes you. Relax! Papa has taken care of everything. Again." She stroked his fingers like a lover. August heard voices nearby.

"Is that what the letter was? Mother, I don't think I can."

"My dear child, if we had a choice, if there was someone else who could do it. … Papa said you're the one, and I can't think of anyone else who could really pull it off." She squeezed his fingers, whispering, "You know he thinks of you like a true son? None of the Mothers has ever gotten pregnant. You are the only son he'll ever have. Don't look so worried. It's temporary. Just until we get back."

"When?"

"That's not clear yet."

"I only came back for—"

"True understanding is a lifelong practice. You can't see the big picture when you are focused on yourself. This is not about you at all, August. Your worry and confusion don't matter at all. Trust Papa."

August took his hand away and could see that her patience was evaporating. He heard muffled banter just outside the door. Who was out there?

She said, "Do you think you're the first to try to leave?"

"The other washouts—"

She shook her head, making him feel dim-witted. "I'm not talking about them. I'm talking about those of us close to him. Us. Those who have his grace."

"*You left?*"

"Even if you left again, you'd be back, because Papa loves you and when Papa wants you, you come. *He* won't leave *you*. You can't wash him out. How to live *with* him, that's the task, the real work. Papa will never give up on you. Things get foggy, that's human experience, we get confused—you aren't the first. You have to keep going even if you think you might be totally lost. This is exactly what you've been training so hard for. This very moment."

She had begun to smile again. August wanted to see these events arranged in a beautiful predictable pattern, as she seemed to. She continued, "See beyond yourself. Your doubts are like flies buzzing around your head, they can't hurt you, so don't panic." His silence erased her smile again. Her eyes became a deeper brown. "So you've changed, things change!" she said. "That's good. Change, grow up.

But don't run in circles. Get yourself together. Help us move forward, stop lagging."

"Don't say 'lagging.' I'm not a child."

She stood quickly. "We're all children to him! Papa is Papa!" He could smell the musk of her breath now, the moist, grassy wind from her lungs. "You can't know what he knows. You can't go where he's been."

He felt himself wobbling, nodding, then shaking his head, then nodding again. "I need some time to decide," he said.

"Of course we don't *have* time." She turned, opened the door, and ushered the NewFaces in. Smiling and happy to see him, they each bowed low to touch his feet, then stood again, shuffling awkwardly around each other in the suddenly crowded trailer. Rebecca handed him his broomstick; they must have found it near the main-hall. Mother Li spoke to August as if the Faces were not in the room: "You will do this for them."

"This isn't fair."

"Because they need you. Because it's your task."

Their smiles faded as they watched August. August wanted to hug and hush them. He wanted to chase them out into the sand.

Chris asked, "What's happening?"

August needed to stand but there was no room. "Nothing—everything is all right—Mother and I are just talking."

"Are you leaving again?" They all watched him.

"There is a lot you don't understand. ..."

Luke said, "Did we do something wrong?"

"No, of course not."

"We'll train harder."

Mother Li patted Luke on the back, saying, "They *have* been working very hard. None of them has needed redirection yet."

August stared at her, stunned by her threat.

Mother Li spread her wings out behind them. "It isn't about you at all. You have perspective now."

Rebecca asked again, "Are you leaving?"

Mother Li smiled at something she saw on August's face, then turned to the NewFaces, ushering them out again. "No, of course not," she said. "Where would he go? He just wanted to see if you were keeping to your tasks." She closed the door and they were alone again.

August felt fragile. His head balanced precariously on his neck; the slightest touch would make him crash to the floor. He drew breath to speak again but she interrupted him with a dismissive wave. "Your hunger for drama is killing you," she said. "It's poison. Everything you think is tainted with it. Papa sees through this world like a dream. Sin can't touch him. You're shivering? August, honey, it's all right!" She hugged his head against her belly. He could hear the dark eddies of fluid in her gut. "We're leaving you to babysit, that's all. A few weeks. Maybe a month. Then, when we return, if you're still… upset we can talk again."

Her eyes were the color of rain-soaked clay. She squeezed his head against her breasts and despite himself, despite his rage, he needed it.

"The Chapters have already been informed that you'll be in charge," she said.

The certainty of it entered him: he could not leave them with Matheson. He stopped shaking. It had been taken out of his hands; he felt disgusted and relieved. He forced himself to stand and said, "No redirection while I'm in charge."

She patted his cheek. "We'll see."

"No. I can't. ..." He wanted to go back to sleep. He felt his body looking for a place to fall. "If I do this," he said, "Matheson can't touch anyone."

"Fine. That wasn't so hard, was it? Just let Papa steer." She laughed. "Remember how easy that is?" She hugged him again, her silk robes wrapping around his arms.

August and Papa stood behind Mother Li as she addressed the initiates: "He has prepared Papa's path to the outside. Now he will be your light until Papa returns. Listen for Papa's voice inside him, speaking directly through him."

Out of habit, he scanned the corners of the room for Ego. A day ago, he had expected to be spit upon. Now, looking across the crowd, August saw adoration. He could feel the heat from Papa's body warming his left side. He was blinking too frequently. The hall was just as it had always been. He felt suspended in formaldehyde, a dreamlike listing that made him want to shake himself awake. If he was going to stay he had to try to keep centered. He rubbed the back of his head. His hair had grown too much and instead of the reassuring scratch against his palm there was only soft fuzz.

Then Mother Li turned to him and the initiates swamped him with stares, their pupils a net of black holes. As he stepped up to the podium he felt Papa's heavy hand on his back, moving with him. What could he possibly say? Shaking again, he held on to the podium to steady himself. Papa pushed him slightly: *Go on.* Meredith was there in the middle of the crowd; he was comforted to see the NewFaces sitting near her.

Without knowing what would come out, he opened his mouth. "It's a mess," he announced. He swallowed. The initiates were perfectly silent. Papa's finger tapped on his spine. "When I speak, I try to say what Papa wants me to say. My own experience is too confusing, too... maddening. So we give ourselves to Papa, like we give everything else to him. Ego is real. I know that. It's brutal, vicious. ... I think about war sometimes. ..." The initiates were being compassionate, nodding even though he wasn't making sense. "Well, it's a confusing time. Life is confusing. What can we do? We don't want to fight alone, we see the teeth, we're afraid. Papa gives us things to do to occupy our minds. He gives us purpose. I lost my father when I was nine. My Mull mother is dead now." How long would they let him ramble? "They call us a cult. We come here, we say, 'This is my family,' we weed the crops, we dig a well, and call it home. When God incarnated himself as Rama, his wife was kidnapped. You know this story. He nearly went insane with worry. He tried to destroy the ocean in frustration and panic. What can we do? Even Christ ended up begging for mercy. I mean..." The initiates nodded, their grunts of agreement rose toward him, and he paused, confused. What were they agreeing to? "I don't have an answer. I thought it was just me but I think everyone is like this, maybe that's what life is: lack-of-answer. It's astonishing, this poverty, so what Papa gives me, that looks like a lot. It's all I have."

Hands rose shaking into the air—like sunflowers facing the light. Initiates closed their eyes, rocking. Someone shouted in the back, the yelp of a person electrocuted by ecstasy. Moans rippled toward him. Some of them were crying. He gripped the podium, alarmed. Papa and Mother Li had retreated to the back of the stage, beaming at him approvingly, as if it was the best speech he had ever given. "I'm saying, if we trust Papa, it's because we have no choice." The shouts rose up, folded into singing, and soon the entire hall was quaking with music. What had they heard him say? The singing got louder. It was clear that the lecture, whatever it had meant, was over. It was ridiculous; the ship was sinking fast and he had just become captain. There was nothing to be done; the initiates interpreted for themselves. He raised his arms and let the chanting fill his mouth. He was laughing, the hall blurring behind his tears.

A hot wind shook the sheds as Papa and the Mothers left. Work-practice stopped spontaneously when the initiates gathered along the fence to watch the parade of bags, Mothers, and, finally, Papa holding on to Mother Li's arm, his head wrapped with cloth against the biting sand. Wraiths of dust churned in his wake, obliterating his footprints. A droning wail rose from the initiates, who shielded their eyes to watch Papa's slow progression.

When the mobile homes had disappeared in a haze of dust, the wind stopped abruptly and silence settled across the compound. August watched the initiates move quietly back into the fields. Everyone seemed dazed. The awe and respect they showed him earlier seemed to have evaporated. As they moped past him, he itched for a fire hose to blast them with.

While the others resumed their duties, he paced the perimeter of the compound, letting it all sink in. He had been lied to and manipulated, though somehow that still felt beside the point, as if the worst traumas had not been recognized yet. He stood facing the mountains, wishing for something catastrophic to put it all in perspective. If a mushroom cloud suddenly rose in the distance, if a meteor was racing toward the earth—would he be able to walk away?

Papa was sick. It felt like a sin to think it at the Center but it was obvious. Even the initiates knew it. If Papa died, would they drift out to try to make lives for themselves? Would the Chapters dissolve, turning back into churches, yoga studios, and YMCAs, the spell suddenly broken and the entire kingdom waking up?

As he came around the back of the compound nearing the fields, he heard a shuffling behind him and knew what it was before he turned to look. Ego had shrunk into something shriveled and jackal-like. It loped behind him pathetically, scuttling away when he glared at it. He spit and watched it creep up to lap at the brown spot. No matter what happened, he had to keep Matheson from hurting anyone else. Melody had gone off with Papa—there was no way to protect her— still he could keep an eye on Meredith and all the rest. Ego scrubbed its flaking neck against his pants. He spat again and the creature caught it on its white tongue, adoring.

17

In the afternoon he sat in the gloom of the study trailer, staring at the letters he had written: *DESK*. The object bearing its own name, as if the trailer were Eden and God Himself had labeled things for His children. For two weeks he had been delivering dry lectures on mythology instead of real addresses, though the initiates didn't seem to care. They had entered into a mass depression, shuffling off to bed every night with little talking. He was glad they left him alone to his own brooding. Meredith was aloof. She worked hard, doing twice as much as the other kitchen Sisters.

He remembered that she was okay; the relief spread over him again and he felt himself sinking. But he was tired of crying and simply stopped. He found the thick pen and was about to cross out *DESK* when something moved softly against the door. He waited, wanting to remain alone, insulated. Then someone knocked timidly.

Meredith stood on the second step, looking up at him with her chin nearly against his chest. He was startled by her gaze and something else that caused him to bring his arms up against the jamb to make a little closed door of himself: her smell, the iron soup of her blood, her organs in their dark bath. Her body, which never left her, which had been there for everything. He felt his center break from its foundation and begin to roll.

"Sister, are you okay?"

"I miss my daughter," she said simply. Her gaze didn't waver.

"Of course... we all do," he answered. "She'll be back. Breathe into patience." It was Papa's aphorism and August felt like an ass saying it. When she lowered her eyes, he felt worse. Then the crown of her head settled against his chest, warm, bristling against the fabric of his shirt. He touched the sides of her head, the stubble behind her ears tickling the crotches of his fingers, and lifted her chin to look at her. She was weeping.

He stepped back. As she made her way up the steps, her face rose and then they were kissing, not like lovers, but like lost family who had thought each other dead: lips planted hard against the forehead and cheek, closed mouths pressed together as if trying to seal a wound, fingers squeezing each other's shoulders and skulls. Their faces were wet, and when he kissed her neck it rose to him, textured with goose bumps.

He whispered, "Your skin."

"What?"

He shook his head and pulled her tumbling onto the couch. For a moment she was on top of him, like the sky itself coming finally to press its cool weight against the earth. Then Meredith scrambled to sit up.

"This is Papa's couch," she said, blinking.

August tried to keep his hand on her back but she stood, wrapping her arms around herself. She looked like a thin leafless tree shuddering there. He felt he had gone years without really craving anything and now, with her so close, his appetite was frightening. They were antidotes for each other, exactly what each was missing. With each beat his heart doubled itself, shedding its skin, revealing desire after desire: *hold me, sex her, heal her, leave, disappear together, kill me, climb inside her, protect her, look at me again.*

"We could go to one of the other trailers, but he sleeps in all of them," August offered. As soon as he said it he wanted to take it back; of course she was thinking about her daughter. Where had Papa taken Melody on the wedding night, when Meredith was in z-trailer? August's erection was obscene, a creature that had crawled into his pants. He could see the child under Papa, her breastless body not fitting right, arms too long, torso too short, Papa grunting over her. Then August saw himself kneeling mouth open to Papa, the acts filled the trailer like dead bodies. There was nowhere they could go.

She was sobbing hard now, beginning to make low, wounded noises. Hadn't she been fine? He had wanted it so badly that he had let her pretend. Now he didn't want to see this. She sounded like she was suffocating. When he touched her back she jumped and turned, leaning into him. She brought her fingers up to the side of his face and he remembered his scar, how self-conscious he had been when he first met her. He touched her hand and ran his fingers along his own cheek.

"What happened to the dog that did this?" Meredith asked, as if the dog had planned his face.

To keep her from crying again, he tried to think of something light, some happy twist on the story, then gave up. "They killed it, I think. I think I remember they killed it."

She nodded, seeming to remember it herself. He felt angry and giddy. He saw Ego, a smoldering monkey, its ashy face peering out from under the desk. August glared and shook his head, and it hunkered back out of sight.

She wiped her snot into a dark patch on his shoulder.

"Are you okay?" It was a ridiculous thing to say. He wanted to tear the roof off the trailer and scream away from the earth. She said something into his shirt, pressing closer to him.

She looked like a bird trying to sleep, her head crooked under his arm. "You don't take chances," she said. "When you have a child, you want everything to be perfect. You want to give her... surround her with perfect love. You want her to be safe, no matter what. Absolutely safe."

He thought he could smell the inside of her elbows. By now, the tears had made a course onto her neck. Her pulse jumped there like an insect under silk.

He kissed the saline next to her collarbone; the taste of the skin reminded him of Papa but this was different, this would cure that. They would start over. Everyone was hurt and scarred, but now they knew what to watch out for. He drew his tongue all the way up to her cheek and stopped.

Why was she looking at him like that? Unmoved, impenetrable. She was watching him as coolly as if he were eating soup. "When are they coming back?" she asked.

He let her go, stepping back. "I don't know."

"I want to call her."

"Melody? We don't know where they are. No one does." He wanted her to stop looking at him. "Sister, I'm sorry so much... has gone wrong."

"It's not your fault I can't keep my center. I was asking for it." Her face was still cold. Was she testing him? "Now I'm desperate again. I think if I just hear her voice, just for a minute. Just tell me where she is."

"Sister, if I knew I would tell you."

"Call the Chapters."

"The Chapters don't know. They aren't staying with the Chapters."

"When are they coming back?"

"I'm sorry, Meredith."

"How could you NOT KNOW?" Her voice rose like a siren heating up into a scream. "Papa sent you out, and as soon as you came back, he left! You know something!"

August took a step back, pressing his palms together. "Papa didn't send me out. I washed out."

"What?"

"I ran away."

"I don't understand."

"I lost my center when I saw... you. I opened the door. I saw you there. You were gagged. I washed out. I told you: the battery. I saw." August watched her body tightening with the memory.

"You're confusing me." Meredith stepped backward toward the door, a veil coming over her face, the neutral mask she had been wearing since he returned. He wanted to rip it off.

"What exactly happened in there? What did he do?" August held her shoulder. "I need to know."

She shook her head, reaching for the door handle. "Don't," she said. The blood had left her face.

"Just tell me this," he said. "Do you think Papa knows?"

She was silent, clutching herself like a straightjacket. Out of the corner of his eye he saw a shadow slinking out from under the desk. "Do you think he knows?" He tried to pet her shoulder but found himself gripping too hard. "Just say yes or no."

Her eyes closed as she nodded.

"Yes? What makes you think so? Why yes?" He was rocking her shoulder, trying, absurdly, to keep her awake.

"That hurts."

"Why yes?" he repeated.

"Oh, God."

"Just tell me. How do you know Papa knows?"

"He was there."

August let her go. "Where?" he demanded.

"He was watching. I can't remember… when I woke up they were both there and Matheson was burning my tongue and my feet and my…"

The floor came rushing up and August sat hard against the wall. "You mean *his voice*. Matheson was playing his voice on the stereo. You thought Papa was there. You were confused. Did you actually see him?"

The door opened and Meredith was gone. He threw up, the gray fluid pattering against the linoleum. How many opportunities had he missed to keep her from that trailer? How many initiates had he suggested redirection for? Papa watching Matheson burning her tongue! Then going to bed with her daughter. Ego crept forward to lap at the puddle of vomit. August watched it shimmer, a rustling pile of beetles.

Then he was standing over the desk holding a pen in his left hand. The word *DESK* had been crossed out and replaced with something else. Something his vision was too blurry to make out.

August approached the podium to deliver the evening address. He scanned the sullen initiates, looking for

Meredith. Brothers Matheson, Jeremy, Mark, and Jerome sat in the back, each with his eyebrows pinched together, sour curls of flesh where their third eyes should be. They looked like children pouting.

The initiates watched August with apprehension, noses in the air like animals smelling smoke in the distance. Things had gone wrong somewhere; it was up to him to retrace the steps. Strip things down, start over, get back to the clean love, the joy and awe he had felt as a NewFace.

"We can't go on like this—" he said and then stopped abruptly. They were already nodding. He could say anything and they would think it was inspired, truer than their own impulses. "Papa left me in charge. I tried to tell them it wasn't a good idea." They smiled, thinking he was being humble again. His mind blurred like a bell struck hard, and he had an urge to slam his head against the podium. The ringing grew into a metallic halo sawing around his skull. He wanted to show them something terrible, enough to scare them awake, to send them running into the desert. Where would they go? They had no money, no houses, they'd forsaken their families. They were completely dependent, not just on Papa, but on the teachings. If he took that from them, what would he replace it with? He imagined them all pressed together shuddering under the bridge in a hailstorm, wandering the streets of a hostile town with Ego running between their legs. The red-faced man who gave him the letter in Overwill, his expression, the way his body froze when August told him it was over. That wasn't the way to do it. It was too brutal. Just get back to basics, find the original virtue. Start over.

"We have to get ready for some sort of change," he

announced.

There was clapping: the Great Days again. Matheson coughed impatiently. August saw him hunched over Meredith in the heat of the trailer, huge over her limp body.

He tried to find his favorite icons in the row but it was just shelf after shelf of trinkets, blocks of wood, flower vases. Meanwhile the initiates waited. What could he do for them? He had let Papa put his cock in his mouth.

August stepped off the stage, pushed through the crowd, and headed for the door. There was a ripple of confused murmurs behind him. He walked faster until he came to the generator shed. When he opened it something touched his back and made him jump. Brother Thomas was standing there looking nervous, as if in the presence of a madman. "Brother August?" he said.

The initiates had gathered at the door of the main-hall, watching him. Yes, perhaps he had gone a little mad, yet something had to be done. He had drifted out too far. They all had. It would take something brave to reel them all back in. He found the red tank and pulled it sloshing out of the shed.

Brother Thomas looked back at the initiates, then asked again, "Brother, what are you doing?" August ignored him, hefting the gas can a few feet, then dragging it in the sand behind him. "Brother—"

"Do you trust me?" August asked.

"Of course, August."

"Get matches. From the kitchen."

"What are you going to do?"

"What are these petty questions?" August's voice was louder than he had intended. The initiates heard him, flinching as a group. He lowered his voice and kept pulling the can. "You think this is a game? You haven't wrestled with Ego. I have. Go. *Now*." Thomas paused, then ran toward the main-hall.

August stumbled backward as he pulled. It would take this kind of action to set things right. The initiates watched him like a flock of chickens.

He tripped, found himself in the dirt next to the bamboo fence, and remembered Matheson choking him. Then Brother Thomas was back, breathing hard.

The tank was too heavy to slosh at z-trailer so he unscrewed the cap, tipped it into his hands, and tossed the gasoline at the white plastic walls. The solvent stench sank into his skin. He kicked at the bamboo fence, trying to knock it down so the initiates could see what he was doing. It was planted too deeply in the soil, so he doused it too. The smell was suffocating, a volatile wind peeling the surface of things, threatening to lift the props of reality into the air. Maybe Matheson would come to pummel him again.

Thomas shifted nervously from foot to foot, holding the matches flat in his palm as if he didn't know what they were. "Brother, please explain this," he said.

"You can see."

"But why?"

"We don't need it anymore." August kicked the tank over and watched the gas roll out in a slow puddle along the base of the trailer. The ground soaked it in. Fine, burn the sand too. Burn the whole desert.

"I don't understand."

"I'm trying to salvage your mind, Brother." He screamed into the sky so they could hear: "*All of your minds!*" Then

he lit a match and tossed it toward the trailer. The wall fluttered yellow like a sheet in the wind. "Call them over."

The initiates arrived, flocking nervously together; when
they saw the smoke lifting above z-trailer there were gasps.
As they watched the fire grow August looked at each scared
face. He thought: *Okay, then, the Great Days.*

He was afraid too, but fear couldn't hurt him anymore.
He felt the heat grow behind him and thought: *If you wait
for things to make sense it will be too late.*

The initiates stood silently until Sister Chavez shouted,
"Brother is giving us a lesson!" They looked at each other
and then a few of them began clapping. Was Meredith
watching? The walls warped, pieces of paint curling and
popping off, trailing smoke behind them. When he looked at
the crowd again the initiates were smiling at him, rocking,
muttering, bowing. He heard someone shout, "The Great
Days are so near, we don't need z-trailer anymore!" He
watched them dance. The fire laughed behind him.

Had Papa foreseen this? As the trailer blackened, sending
a slanted trail of smoke into the sky, August slipped into
ecstasy. His guilt for having made Papa's fantasies so seductive, for having let redirection go on for so long, was giving
way to inevitability and invincibility. Everything he did
would provoke awe. He would help them push through this
crisis until they found something better, blazing a path for
them as a revolutionary saboteur, an angel with a flaming
sword.

There were screams and the faces of the initiates near him
changed. A few rushed at him. When he lifted his arms to
keep them away his left arm was creeping with flame. As
reality slowed he saw the hair of his arm curl and disappear.

Someone was slapping him. He tried to shake it out. The flame held on, rippling, sticky. As he hit the ground the initiates beat him and threw dirt until his arm was only smoldering.

A gust of wind blew the smoke across them and the whole crowd moved back suddenly. He stood, yelling over the sound of the fire, "Keep dancing. I'm alright. It's okay to celebrate this! This is, itself, a revelation!" His hand felt icy. "Congratulate yourselves! You have all passed a test. This is tonight's lesson. Don't hold on to things because you are comfortable. We must continue to change."

He spotted Matheson farther behind the main group of initiates. He was watching the burning with half-closed eyes.

The tingle became a fluttering pain. A bad burn.

As the smoke gushed upward in a dark torrent, he walked toward Papa's trailers. The fingers were bright red with a splotch of frightening white curling near the knuckles.

He turned and saw the others dancing, making a ring around the conflagration. The pillar of smoke was like the cloud Jehovah came to the Israelites in, thick and poisonous, yet they were singing.

What had he done? The siren in his mind had stopped. Beyond the dancing crowd he saw a figure lift itself from between the rows of purple cabbage, look into the sky where the smoke was making a celestial whorl, then lie back down again. So that's where she hid. He crept into the trailer and found his way to the bed, where gasoline and burnt hair mingled with the sweat, talc, and sweet oil of Papa's skin.

18

He had been awake for hours and looked out to see the morning sun sitting like a marble in the sooty haze that still rose from the other side of the compound. Though his hand burned fiercely now, he didn't look at it. Instead he stepped out into the bright circle of trailers. The bathtub sat planted in the ground like an enormous molar. Papa's throne. He pulled the hose from the spigot under the book trailer and began filling it. If he didn't look directly, he could see the sun on the surface of the water. He brought the hose over the reflection. The sun exploded into crescent shards that bounced off the white edges and swarmed together again, rocking back into a single burning fist.

When the tub was full he turned the spigot off and removed his clothes. The Mothers would have poured boiling water in for Papa. He braced himself, sliding all the way into the chill, a continental shelf crumbling into the sea.

"Okay. Yes."

A plane was leaving a silver scar in the sky.

"Yes. Yes, yes." He sank lower and let his body float. He listened for sounds of the initiates chanting but could only hear the plane, a distant ripping. He chuckled at the thought of getting a book to read to himself and the water rolled from his neck to his feet.

The knuckles of his left hand were puffed with gems of

liquid, the blisters bulging like buds of new fingers. He washed it gently, looking for other marks. His forearm was as hairless as a child's. The tattoo looked like a bruise. Questions had done nothing for him.

Somewhere a strange bird began to chirp with an urgent rhythm. He washed his face, cupping some of the water into his mouth. He had burnt z-trailer. Shiva dancing on the corpses of the earth, Jesus tearing the market down—these were not good or bad, they were beyond mind. Unquestionable. If he kept moving like this no one would be able to rattle him again. When things wanted to happen, August would be their agent.

The chirping was the phone in Papa's trailer. August tried to sink himself underwater. No more redirection, no more torture. He had already begun freeing them. "Okay, yes," he sighed. He threw water against his neck and when he rubbed his eyes he saw Brother Thomas just outside the ring, looking in.

"Should we just go on with the schedule?" he asked, speaking to the ground to avoid looking at August's nakedness.

"Of course. Just like always."

"Is your arm okay?"

August hid his hand under his thigh. "Don't worry about me." There was a pause. "What else?"

"Matheson is lagging. He won't work-practice. He's saying…"

"Yes?"

"…that Ego has you."

"What about the others?" August asked.

"Most of them are ignoring him."

"Most?"

"There are three, maybe four who are with him. We should just continue as always?"

"As always."

The Brother left and August tried to let the water soothe him again. His body had warmed it to a soup of sweat. Maybe it would all fall apart now. Would it be a showdown? Maybe August would be thrown out after all.

He stood. His clothes were full of sand and still smelled like petroleum smoke so he jogged to the trailer naked, leaving them by the tub.

Inside the phone was ringing again. There were no clothes in closet. A sandy puddle was growing at his feet. Ego crouched in the corner, an emaciated hare, one of its long ears tattered and bloody.

He picked up the phone and heard a man's voice. "Papa?" the voice asked.

August leaned against the desk letting water dribble from his ass onto the varnished wood. "He's not here," he said. "Who is this?"

"Can I speak to him?" The voice bounced; the man was walking quickly as he talked.

"He's not at the Center at all."

"When can I speak to Papa?" the man asked.

August thought he heard a car honking in the background. "I need to know who this is," he said firmly.

"Who are *you*?"

"This is Brother August."

"Oh! Can you talk now? Is someone around?"

August looked at his penis, leaning shyly from its nest of hair. "No one is around."

"It's an honor to be talking to you. We actually met, I don't know if you remember—Seattle Chapter—at the retreat. Lloyd Peters."

"Yes?"

"Anyway, I was wondering when you guys wanted another run. I have to schedule ahead a couple of days. Or should I wait for Papa?"

"A run?" August asked.

"With the chopper. Are you doing drills anymore?"

"The helicopter?" Warmth spread itself up his neck.

"Maybe I should wait to talk to Papa. Usually he calls me …I just thought I'd check in because it had been a while."

August set the phone down on the desk. He felt much too light and tried to call himself back by rubbing his face. Then he picked it up again. "Listen to me," he said more forcefully now.

"Can you hear me now?" The man was yelling over the sound of traffic.

"Listen."

"Go ahead."

"No more drills," August said.

There was a muffled commotion, August heard a car honking. "Maybe—"

"We won't be doing it anymore. We are done with that."

"I should talk to Papa."

"I speak for Papa now."

The man cleared his throat. "I had been counting on at least two more runs this year. And I never saw the money for the last one—"

"How did he pay you?"

"I got a check from Phoenix Chapter. I didn't want to call

them because I'm not supposed to talk to anyone about it."

"How much?" August asked.

"I mean, of course it was for the Movement, for training. I'd do it for free if Papa asked me to."

"How much?"

"Five hundred a run."

"I'll have them send you two thousand, then it's over. Does Phoenix have your address? Don't ever speak about this."

"I never would. I've never told anyone. I'm Papa's servant."

August hung up. He covered his mouth with both hands.

In the main-hall a large cauldron of onion soup carried a rank steam to those waiting in line with their bowls. August stood with them, bracing himself against their stares. They seemed unnerved by his proximity. Matheson had been taking his meals in b-trailer with three other Brothers, and the entire compound was skittish.

He joined the NewFaces at their table and found he had nothing to say to them; they ate in silence. They were still shy but they weren't the timid children who had arrived months ago. What if Papa wasn't back by the time they were due for initiation? He felt eyes on him and looked up occasionally to nod reassuringly at whoever was staring. He waited for signs of dissent, scowls, or whispers; there were only smiles and bows. Still the air felt volatile. Was Matheson plotting some sort of coup? The initiates seemed galvanized for the time being, though he knew the situation was precarious. It was essential to maintain the momentum and awe. If he faltered he was sure they would see it. They would smell his weakness, lose their faith in him, and turn to Brother Matheson.

He scratched at the sores on his knuckles, trying not to think about the helicopter. He had ended that too. No more redirection. No more lies. He would clean up the entire mess.

To clear his head, he looked for Meredith. He hadn't noticed her for days. He wanted to see her neck muscles relaxed with the knowledge that she would never have to endure redirection again. She was not among the kitchen staff still ladling soup for the endless queue of initiates. He took one sip, stirred the urine-colored broth, and decided he was not hungry. The others ate quickly, grabbing handfuls of dried oats from the heaping bowls set along the tables.

When he stood the entire room stared at him as if their heads were tied with invisible threads that he had accidentally tripped over. He had intended to look quietly around the room for her. Now they all expected something from him, some wise, encouraging word, some note of hope and benevolence. He lifted his hands and asked, "How is the soup?"

"Delicious!" they shouted, as August smiled, waved, and walked outside, leaving his coagulating bowl for the Faces to divide amongst themselves. He passed b-trailer and listened for whispering; he couldn't hear anything. The soup's sour oil crept up his throat. With everyone crammed into the main-hall the Center had a pleasant, deserted quality. He walked around the perimeter toward the fields. There she was, in the carrots, close to the fence. She was wearing a wide straw hat, the green shoots like a thousand silent fountains around her. As he approached he saw that she was ankle-deep in the soil, hypnotized, staring out toward the mountains where the mobile homes had disappeared. This far away she looked like an old woman, her right hand gripping her left shoulder.

When she saw him approach, she lurched in the other direction, then stumbled, planting one hand in the mud. She scrambled up again and August found himself chasing her.

Though he could leap two rows at a time, they were plowed unevenly in places and he had to stop periodically, teetering on a mound to keep from pitching forward. "Meredith!" he hollered. She changed direction and began to run parallel to the rows, arms out for balance, crushing sprouts as she went. One of her sandals slid out from under her in a spray of mud. She kept running. He kicked it aside, calling, "Meredith!"

She glanced back once and tripped again. For a moment she was flying, her arms reaching for the horizon, her hat hung in the air behind her; then she landed, rolling into a muddy ball.

When he knelt beside her, holding her hat, she gazed at the sky with a disturbing serenity as if she had chosen the spot for a short nap. She flinched when he reached for her, slicing an angry glance toward him without meeting his eyes.

Rubbing the dirt off the hat, he said, "No, it's okay. I'm just trying to... I wanted to apologize for upsetting you before. In the trailer."

"I'm not crazy anymore, I just miss her. It's not Ego, missing my own daughter. I don't need anything, August. Just leave me alone."

He winced at the way she said his name. "I feel responsible," he said. "Partly responsible—"

"I won't talk about redirection anymore. You have to let

me forget it."

"Okay."

"Don't try to help me," she said. "I was fine before you came back. I was doing fine. Now Matheson will think I wanted you to burn it."

"Don't worry about him."

"You're just confusing everything. You won't let me center myself. I'm falling and falling."

"You're not falling," he assured her. "There's nothing to worry about now. I'm fixing things. You have to trust me."

"Oh God, August."

"Just say you trust me."

She covered her ears, her eyes pinched shut, and he saw her again in the trailer; the electricity must have made her face look like this. He wanted to cover it now with the hat. She was muttering: "Blessed is the Eye of the Lord. May we be granted true-sight, you didn't have to burn it. You're undoing all the work I've done. I just wanted to talk to Melody, true-voice, true-heart, true-mind that we might serve the will of the Lord. Oh God."

August stood, dropping the hat. He wanted to run. Instead he forced himself to kneel again. He bent to kiss her brow. She shook her head, continuing the mutter. How had it gotten this bad? "Meredith." He touched her shoulder and she grabbed his wrist hard as if to say *don't*. She held it and stopped muttering. Her eyes were still closed.

They were both filthy. Unearthed nearby, the pale finger of an immature carrot pointed at something behind him. Then she was looking at him, begging with her eyes. "Don't make me crazy. Don't confuse me. I can't take it."

He shook his head, trying to wriggle from her grasp. "I'm

going to fix it. I'm taking care of everything." She had closed her eyes again.

When she stood she looked disoriented, waking from a bad dream. "I want you to go ahead and shower," August said. "If someone asks, tell them I allowed it. Trust me, Meredith. Say you trust me."

"I'm so tired."

"Have you eaten yet? Sister, you need to eat."

19

Their meetings were a secret they could not even tell each other. By the time August could no longer smell Papa in the trailers, Meredith had become two people. One came to his trailer a few nights a week, opening the door quietly and slipping under the sheet with her back to him, like an old woman bored with her husband. In the dark, she let him caress her face, rub her taut shoulders and rasping scalp. If he tried to speak she would stand quickly and leave. They never kissed and she was always clothed next to his nakedness. Stiff and unable to sleep because of the pressure in his groin, he would point his body away so she would not bump into it. She was a fugitive, silent and in danger, only tentatively alive. She allowed him to place his arm around her rib cage, holding on under her breast. He was grateful for the mute comfort they managed, like a strange childhood dream he could have again and again. He understood that she slept better next to him, that it was a kind of surrogate lovemaking, and that it was her gift to him. She was being generous by letting him soothe her into sleep. Though he wanted more—wanted to press his body deeply into hers, wanted to fight off some attacker and spirit her away—her body next to his was more than he had earned. She always left before sunrise.

The Meredith of the day did not speak to him, either. She worked hard in the kitchen and refused to have anything to do with him, responding to his questions as if harboring a deep grudge, her face a frustrating blank. There she was, he could see her clearly among the things of the world though he had no idea how to call her back, like a balloon that had slipped from his grasp and fell gracefully, silently upward. He sought her out every day, trying to find ways to reach her: "Sister, the beans are delicious. How are you?"

She would reply, "I'm fine. The beans are fine too." Her smiles were disturbing. She rocked and wept with devotion during mutter, sometimes staying to do three more cycles after the others had left for breakfast.

Once he had tried to force an acknowledgement from her. Leaning close in the kitchen, he said, "You were sweating in your sleep last night—" She pivoted quickly, a pot of boiling water, and he had to jump back to avoid being scalded. Sometimes he wondered if she knew she came to him in the night. Perhaps every morning a quick black curtain was pulled modestly across half of her mind.

Three weeks after the burning, during evening meal, a crowd gathered at the bulletin board. When he approached the initiates scattered. Only Brother Monkey remained, reading the handwritten note tacked over the schedule:

We must be true to Papa. August has been lost to Ego. He is leading us astray. Do not attend morning address. Meet in the fields after morning mutter.

Monkey clicked his tongue and said, "Look at that."

"Who put this up?" August demanded.

Monkey put his arm across August's shoulder. "Well, I guess we all know the answer to that question, don't we? Easter Bunny, no two ways about it. That fuzzy son of a bitch has been sneaking around for years. Only solution is traps. Traps everywhere until we catch him."

August shrugged him off and glared at the initiates who had seated themselves at the tables. As he walked away Brother Monkey said, "What do you want me to do with it?"

"Leave it," August said, loud enough for the tables near him to hear. "It's a good test. We'll see who falls for it."

In the morning the hall was crowded with silent initiates waiting for August's address and the poster had been taken down. Even Meredith was sitting primly near the front of the crowd.

August pointed at Sister Chavez. "Go to the field and tell me how many are there," he ordered.

"The fields are empty. They're in b-trailer," she said.

"Then there can't be more than five of them!" he said. Laughter. "My friends, when you feel someone pushing you, don't push back. Step aside and let them fall. When they play tug-of-war, let go of the rope. Don't punish them; if any of the confused souls in b-trailer right now want to rejoin us, be kind. Give them room at your table." He scratched at his head; his beard had grown, rounding out his face, and his hair was long enough to get matted.

"It's true that Ego attacked me outside. Viciously. There was a battle. I thought he would destroy me. But Ego is essentially a coward. It feeds on fear and cannot do anything once we decide to fight back. I beat the beast," he announced, swinging the broomstick in the air for effect.

He felt full and glowing, speaking from a script written for him by God. Like Christ he had surrendered himself to the drama. Buddha, knowing that the truth was unteach-able, had delivered sermon after sermon anyway. Krishna had driven a war chariot. Even for avatars, life was full of mystery. What could August do but fill the role he had been given?

A motor roared in the middle of the night, and for a half-dreamed moment August thought it was the helicopter, ris-ing like an undead bird. He lay still to keep from disturbing Meredith and eventually the sound faded into her quiet breathing. Then he heard footsteps nearby and an anxious knock on the door. He felt her body freeze next to him in a spasm of panic, kissed her shoulder, and stood to gather his clothes.

When he opened the door Brother Thomas was breath-less. "They left," he reported. "They took the Jeeps."

August tried to peer out toward the gates, but the trailers obscured his view. "Why didn't you tell me this was happen-ing?"

Brother Thomas peered into the darkness behind August. Of course they knew where Meredith slept. He remembered the trailer rocking when Papa was fucking one of the Mothers. August pulled his clothes on and stepped outside. "How many went with him?" he asked.

"Eight. And they disabled the satellite dish."

"Disabled?"

"Well, it's gone. Broken off. No phone."

"Both Jeeps?"

"Yes."

The adrenaline made standing still difficult. They were stranded. The phone was their umbilical connection to

Phoenix and food. August had a nonsensical impulse to call Phoenix and have them come repair the phone.

"Don't panic," August said, stepping around the trailer. He could see the blue box of the main-hall hunkered under the night sky, and imagined Matheson like King Kong on the roof tearing the dish apart. "What about the well?" he asked.

"What about it?"

"Check the pump," August said.

"You don't think he would—"

"Just check it," he ordered. "What time is it? Try to keep the gossiping to a minimum, get them to mutter as soon as possible."

Thomas touched August's arm. "Maybe we could skip mutter. You could talk to them now. They're awake."

The thought of Matheson hulking around the quarters, turning the lights on, trying to weed out the scared ones, the ambivalent ones, made August furious. "I said, do mutter. It's important. Tell them I'll talk to them afterward. We have to keep our rhythm; we can't let him disrupt things more than he has."

"He said he was going to find Papa."

"No. He washed out. Papa won't receive him. Keep everyone calm. Tell them I've got it under control. He washed out. We all saw it coming, he cracked."

"What if we need supplies?"

"Pay attention! We have weeks of food. We also have the crops. Where is your center?" August softened his voice; he needed Thomas on his side. "I have it figured out already. Check the well, check the pH, smell it—in fact bring me a bucket, not from a hose. From the source. Do that right now.

Go ahead."

"Yes, Uncle."

August turned in a circle and sat in the dirt. Then he stood again holding his head with his hands. Things would get bad if they couldn't reach Phoenix. He imagined they could stretch their supplies if they had to, though it would be another month before anything was really ready for harvest. Even so, under all of the worries he began to feel light.

In the trailer, Meredith was waiting beside the bed with her arms wrapped tightly around herself. August said, "Matheson left. He's gone. I came out on top." Her shoulders shifted; was it relief? Then she edged by him coldly.

"Meredith, why do you come here?" he asked, holding the door so she couldn't open it.

"I'll stop."

"No. Please, don't. You know I want you here."

"What do you want me to say?"

"Just something small if you want, just one thing you're thinking."

Her voice was monotone. "The mutters don't help. I don't know where Melody is or even how far away she is." She covered her face. "I can't tell what's Ego and what isn't. I don't trust my mind. All of these changes. I can't sleep in the main-hall without her. I feel like they're watching me. Like they know I'm a fake and they're just waiting for me to make another mistake. I'm sorry, I know I don't make any sense."

"It's okay. Thank you." He took his hand from the door and she opened it. She hadn't said that she loved him, yet she slept well near him. Maybe she was afraid to say it.

She paused halfway out the door. "August?"

"Yes?" he said.

"No more questions. I can't do this if you ask me questions." She shut the door quietly.

He picked up the phone expecting a hiss of static; instead there was complete silence, the phone had reverted to its inanimate components, just a lump of plastic. Then with a delayed jolt he heard what Thomas had called him. *Uncle.*

The dish was completely destroyed; they found parts of it scattered in the Jeeps' tracks. The well hadn't been tampered with. As he got closer to the main-hall, he could hear the commotion; the initiates were scared. August smiled. The compound was completely his now. He would rally them, give them tasks. Their urgency would be easily dispersed with hard work. He would point out that because their supplies were jeopardized, the crops were crucial. They would have to rally around him now. They would need August more than ever, and he had a bright well of light in his chest to share with them.

While the initiates sang prayers in the fields to ensure bountiful crops, the NewFaces were sent out laden with water and with a note to read to Phoenix Chapter from a pay phone in Silkweed. August instructed them on how to hike to the dirt road and to follow it to the highway that snaked along the base of the mountain. "Hitchhike. Don't mention the Center. Say you've been camping." He warned them to avoid policemen and gave them money to buy water for the return trip. "If you see Ego, just say the mutters, and he won't touch you."

A van arrived two days later to repair the satellite dish and the NewFaces were welcomed back, exhausted and glowing with pride. Their feet were washed as they rested in the freshly cleaned b-trailer.

With the phone working again August sent orders to all Chapters to turn Matheson away as a washout. Matheson had not tried to contact Phoenix but had visited other Chapters looking for Papa.

A week later August officiated the NewFace initiation himself, following the ritual as it had always been conducted, though with one alteration: he had their Center spirals tattooed on his own arm, stacked above the fading one. "I will bear your marks for you. What is inside you is inside me. I will interpret and shepherd you toward healing." The hair on his arm had grown back and the burn scars were just pale glazes over his knuckles.

Reality had proven malleable, more deferent to his will than he had ever expected. He was hurtling out, broken free, headed for unknown regions—yet he was winning. One evening after watching Ego skitter around the floor of the book trailer he picked up the phone and called Phoenix himself. Sister Chavez had already made the regular orders of flour and oats for the month but August wanted more: "Dried fruit. Any kind. Avocados. And milk. And sugar." *We'll make cookies.* "Tofu. Miso, enough for all of us. Spaghetti. Tortillas. Can they be frozen? A thousand." He saw the feast piling in front of him like a new holiday, an adornment on their lives. He was hungry, and he let the hunger speak. "Nuts. Almonds and cashews. Vitamins for the boys, the chewable kind. Cheese. Ha! And chocolate, and juice. Grape juice, apple…" Then it hit him. "Oranges. Tangerines. A lot of oranges. Any kind of citrus."

Just months ago there had been the special food for the

wedding. This was already far more extravagant. August imagined it would take two trucks and in those trucks not a single box of oats. He had expected some resistance but the voice on the other end said, "Anything else?"

"Vanilla ice cream," he said.

The initiates were quiet. The chatter that usually filled the hall was absent; everyone cupped their bowls in front of them with the pale mounds melting quickly. They no longer remembered how to desire food like this. They were flustered, just having finished a three-course meal of butternut squash soup, salad with goat cheese, and grilled tofu with roasted-red-pepper pesto over rice.

The ice cream reminded August of his mother and he took small bites, letting it melt on his tongue. Even with the cold numbing his palate and the cream clogging his taste buds, he could still find the bright note of the vanilla.

Now August stood, saying, "It's okay! Nothing bad will happen if you eat this. You have already earned joy. It can't hurt you, it's ice cream!" There were nervous chuckles. Someone coughed, spitting white foam. "Okay, it *can* hurt you if you choke—don't choke!" More laughter. He wanted to make them laugh forever and wished for Brother Monkey's cleverness. "Maybe you are thinking this is a test. Sister Chavez, do you think this is a test?"

"No, Uncle."

"Well it is. You are all being tested." They froze mid-chew. "To see if you are ready to be really free or if your mind is still imprisoned. Congratulations, you pass. Eat the ice cream, be free, let yourself enjoy it. You must be ready to let go of the old ways. How long has Papa been asking us to leap out? So leap. Vanilla Ice Cream. That's your lesson for today."

There was a rustle of relief, spoons clinking. Somewhere near the back a table of initiates began talking quietly. Soon the whole room relaxed, laughing and scraping at the bottoms of their bowls.

Brother Monkey approached bowing, then sat across from August. The two initiates who had been sharing the table sensed something in his demeanor and relocated. Brother Monkey looked at the foamy remains in August's bowl as if something fascinating was happening there, and whispered, "Brother August, please slow down."

"Monkey, did you know what happened in z-trailer?"

"I'm talking about the food."

"I burned it for a reason."

"Papa said to trust you. I'm just saying, as an elder, don't shake them up too much. You're asking a lot. Making big changes. Papa's gone, they're... impressionable."

"I've never heard you so serious."

"I've never seen ice cream served at Movement Center."

"Don't you like ice cream?"

Brother Monkey scratched his shiny head and August saw that he would be bald even if he weren't shaved regularly. "Brother—"

"I thought you, of all of them, would understand."

"Ego feeds on gluttony," Monkey said.

August reached across the table, hooking the back of Monkey's sweaty neck. "I'm not going to let anything happen to you. I have Ego in my pocket right now." Brother Monkey blinked. Then August whispered, "Wake up, these *are* the Great Days."

ugust began to praise God in his heart again, and his joy was infectious; initiates bowed low and rose up beaming to be near him, jockeying for the right to wash his feet. When Sister Karen came to him with a crippling headache, he healed her in front of all of the others by touching her with his left hand.

Ego, the malevolent god, the devil itself, had become his simpering pet—a pet he tolerated as a reminder of the other life when he was rolling about the motel room, suffocating. Anyway, he wasn't sure how to send it away completely. It seemed devoted to him, and no amount of stomping or shouting could make it flee for long.

He watched his own body, thrilled at the new padding around his waist. The tattoo machine was brought to the study trailer and after some tutelage from Brother Ken, August began to elaborate on his spirals himself, spreading the blue eddies across the back of his hand where he had been burned, wiping the excess blood and ink on his pants.

He wanted a sign of the changes he was feeling, something to remind himself of this clarity in case he fell backward. He ordered a stereo and had one of the Brothers install speakers in the main-hall so they could listen to classical music as they ate.

In the kitchen the initiates sometimes deferred to Meredith as if she were a Mother, though she declined any responsibility, saying, "I don't know, ask August." She slept with him every night now.

Years before, Papa had come to visit Monterey Chapter and for the potluck after the lecture Meredith had made a large pitcher of carrot-apple-ginger juice. After Papa drank three glasses of it, he asked who made it and the whole room had pointed to Meredith. She blushed and found a table to wipe up. Later that night, as Melody slept wrapped in a blanket on the floor, Meredith and August stacked chairs alone. She threw her arms around him, pressing her face into his chest and shivered. She said, "When he *looked* at me!" rubbing her cheek against him in a way that felt so sexual he was afraid Melody would wake up and see them. Then she went back to tying garbage bags.

Now, the blue bled from his fingernails to his elbow. He'd left his palm unmarked. The dark border made it shine with its own light as Vishnu's palms had. He found symbols in the swirls he didn't remember making, little characters from a language he felt he knew intuitively. Sometimes he drew pictographs in the air with his blue hand. They hung there like smoke rings until Ego lapped them away.

He walked slowly through the quarters at night letting his fingers trace the bones along the initiates' shoulders, across their rough scalps; they lifted their heads like cats, purring. He ordered kites for the little boys who missed Melody almost as much as Meredith did, and they ran happily with the diamonds of color laboring behind them.

Only one thing made him hesitate: the memory of his sister, Jesse. Her shining hair pulled back with a pink butterfly, holding his lunch pail as she walked him home from school. He could feel her disappointment and confusion like a lacquer over his life. If she came for a visit he could show her all the changes he was making, how he had taken the dark things and strangled them, making them gag up light and singing and feasts. He would tell her, *I'm here for them. They need me. I am mature fruit—misshapen, perhaps, with a worm inside. God will have to eat Uncle as is.* She would see the adoration in their eyes.

Sometimes he had an apocalyptic sensation, like he was looting the world, or perhaps looting himself, his windows all broken, the ruins smoking after a great revolution. He positioned a chair and a large shade umbrella atop the trailer so he could look out across the compound to see everything that was happening. Sometimes smoke came from the door of the main-hall where some experimental new food had gone wrong.

After dinners he would drive them into a frenzy of devotion, calling them up, one at a time, to confess, then, like turning water into wine, forgiving them while they trembled under his hands.

The original tattoo had now become a faded husk of itself, like the casting of a seed after the plant has grown. At night his hand sometimes glowed as he waved it in front of himself like a warning flare with Meredith deeply asleep next to him, her skin emitting a smell like wet soil. When it was too much, he would go to one of the Mothers' trailers to masturbate, leaving gobs of semen on the bare mattresses, and return to curl up next to her.

The summer sun went to war. Light adhered to all surfaces. The crops wilted at noon, barely recovering in the amnesty of night. Still, the refrigerators, pantries, and freezers overflowed with August's generosity. His own hair, darker than he remembered, collected the heat but he refused to shave it. Seeping out of him like tar, it hung near his eyes, oily and almost too hot to touch. He turned up the classical music during the meals to drown out the cicadas' screech. He filled a wheelbarrow with popsicles and trucked around the fields, hand-delivering bright red smiles.

And for Pepper, the last chicken in the old coop, he showed similar mercy. She was hunkered on the shade side of her coop, pecking her thanks at the blue worms on his wrist before he grabbed her by the head and snapped her like a wet towel. No undignified chasing. "Rest now, Sister," he whispered. He carried the body to the kitchen where he held her on his upturned palms, saying, "Pepper finally left us. I will honor her."

The women stared, then Meredith began pulling her dusty feathers off as if she had always wanted to. The other Sisters joined in, grabbing the flaccid animal's legs. That night August ate chicken roasted with almonds and orange peel. He expected to get sick, but even his body seemed unable to question him and digested the stringy meat without objection.

In the study trailer, he blacked out the words Papa had written—*bed, light, wall*—replacing them with symbols and characters, his own unspeakable language. Some of the symbols were playful, some of them thick and ominous, scrawled in broad black ink above the bed, or on the pages of the books. Ego, now the size of a humming bird, smacked into the walls leaving scratches that August traced. He had broken through. His true-mind blazed. Papa had been the catalyst, now August was the reaction.

The crops came up well and the initiates, when they saw him, would run to offer him a yam or a squash, as proud as if they were handing him their own livers. August ordered new pillows and mosquito netting for every bed.

Initiates came to his private sessions in b-trailer wanting instruction about mutter or cures for distraction during meditation. They were still so lost they didn't know what to complain about: "Uncle, I've had trouble sleeping. I just lie awake thinking, 'I have to sleep, I have to sleep.'"

"You are asleep now," he would say. "You got your wish. Congratulations, welcome to your dream. Come back when you want to wake up."

He did his best to break them, offering what he could to tear their illusions away.

"Uncle, I still have headaches."

"Yes?"

"They are really unbearable sometimes, especially after work-practice. It's so hard to concentrate at evening mutter."

"If you didn't have headaches, what would you complain about?"

"Nothing. Everything else is okay."

"Good, keep the headaches then, like a growling dog in your yard that keeps the thieves away. You think you don't like the dog. However, if you shot it you'd hear a knocking at your door. When you don't need the dog anymore, it'll go away by itself."

At night, he and Meredith fit together like form and emptiness. He held her when she jerked in her sleep, when she called out her daughter's name. Or if he was the one rolling in a fever of inspiration, she would stroke his thickening hair and shush him. Once, she sang a Mull song, something sweet about a boy and a girl and a fast car. The words were ridiculous, foreign and soothing.

He no longer worried about her. Her suffering had woken him up. Her torture had been the fire that burned away his ignorance. It had been a gift. He understood: there was nothing confusing about anything anymore. She was living directly, just as he was. They had come from the same place, they spoke the same language, and had been stranded on this strange planet together. They were demonstrating, for the initiates, what enlightenment looked like.

The door of b-trailer rattled and Rebecca, an initiate two months already, came in blushing and bowing as she always did. Of the three former NewFaces she was the most adoring. She always had trouble reading, her eyes lingering instead on his cheek or his aubergine fist. She was desperate for communion; he knew that she would happily do anything he asked.

Leaning over her to point to a passage, he could smell her breath, which was as delicate as the scent of the fennel that the kitchen Sisters had begun to use in soup. He could have her here, now, and regularly, filling the great sex-starved basin of himself with the salt from her ears and lips. He could say simply, *undress*. And she would not hesitate. But every time he got close enough to smell the tang of her scalp, to feel the cushion of her shoulder, he was met with Meredith's besieged body; with his mother's grief lumped under blankets, moldering in a coffin; with the bag lady's pale, unloved calf; with Melody's willowing legs running after moths in the floodlight; with Jesse's sprint from the dog; with his own genuflected shadow pulling like an oil derrick to draw from Papa the precious promised gift. And he could not touch her.

Here she was again, her ache for an unequivocal gesture filling the air like the thrumming of crickets. He leaned close to her neck, felt her stop breathing, and said, "Wake up. You're in danger."

She smiled, the long, curved beach of her neck waiting for his touch. "Ego can't reach me here, not with you so close," she said.

"Child, I have Ego in my pocket. Wake up. Wake up. Wake up. Open your eyes, and ask yourself, 'What am I doing here?'"

She squinted, "Is this a test?"

August laughed, "God, yes. Yes! It's all a test." Even this sounded mystical so he roared to try to break the spell. "We are all, all of us being tested!"

Her eyes closed tightly and her head tilted back mesmerized, her lips moving close enough to kiss him. "Uncle, show me how to pass the test," she said. She was a house; every single door, window, and shutter had been thrown open, waiting for him to enter.

He left her standing there, kicked the trailer door open, and marched to the main-hall where the initiates were just beginning to line up for evening meal. They saw his anger at a distance and began to cluster together. By the time he made it to the podium, the desert was absolutely silent.

"You are stubborn! Stubborn as any Mull ever was!" August shouted. Some were already crying. Those nearest him dropped and the wave spread back like slow-motion footage of an earthquake, until the entire room was on the floor, even Brother Monkey, even Meredith, rocking like children. He clutched at the air near his head to keep his hands from shaking. "Do you want me to send you out there? Into the Mull world of clutter and greed?" He waded among them and they scuttled to let him pass. "Do you want me to tell you that Papa lied? Where would you go? You sold your houses!" Something like a laugh made his voice break. "What can I do for you? Look at you, where would you go?"

In the kitchen, a pot boiled over, hissing. No one moved. Then Rebecca hunched into the room, red faced. She dropped to the floor and yelled, "I'm sorry Uncle! Don't punish them for my mistake!"

"It's not just you, child. You all think you can just hand yourselves over; it won't buy you peace. I'm telling you, Uncle is telling you not to sell your houses anymore. How did it happen—your face on the floor? Me screaming at you? Someone here has the courage to answer me." He pointed at a male initiate near him. "You, look at me. What are you doing?"

"To be close to Papa. To practice truth. To follow him and to follow you, Uncle."

"You will obey me?"

"Without hesitation."

"Then wash out. *Now.* I'm ordering you to get up and leave."

"I'm pitiful. I'm weak willed, Uncle, I have petty urges all day, but I know you are testing me. Papa is life and you are the light. There is nothing outside the perimeter except pain and confusion."

"You see? I try to make it easier for you..." The room held its breath. The metal roof pinged as the evening air began to cool it. "I give everything to you!"

A sound came from behind him. He swung around to stop the source of the singing. Too late. It had already spread from one weeping face to another. He shouted over their voices, "How does it come to this?" They were already muttering, the hoard around him pushing through the words, some of them lifting their heads and hugging themselves, some of them kissing his feet as he kicked through them.

21

Warm rain pattered down intermittently for four hours and the desert bloomed in pastel violet and yellow. Sitting on his makeshift throne atop the trailer August was looking at the long streamers of chalky color woven at the base of the Harquahala Mountains. He saw the dust flag long before the initiates did. It was just a single Jeep, he reassured himself, so it couldn't be Papa. Who would come unannounced?

As the vehicle got closer, he saw it was driven by a broad-shouldered man. Though her head was wrapped thickly in a silk scarf, August recognized Mother Li sitting in the back. By the time the Jeep pulled up to the gate, the initiates had pooled against the fence, wailing and waving.

August remained in his chair as the gates were opened and Mother Li was ushered through the cheering crowd. Buckets and a stool were brought for her feet. She waved them away, peering around the compound. The elders huddled around her—what were they saying? Then she was nodding, walking with them, the horde a respectful distance behind. The driver waited in the Jeep.

They skirted the main-hall, moving toward the crater of ash that had been z-trailer. Mother Li stopped a hundred yards away as if she were afraid of contamination. Then she must have asked something because, all at once, they pointed at August. Mother Li cupped her hand over her eyes to see him better, took one more look at the heap of ash, then began walking toward him.

As she neared, she didn't look up. Her robed body fore-shortened, showing him only the sleek top of her head as she came around the trailer to the ladder. He had been waiting for something like this and stayed seated as she climbed.

"Aren't you afraid it's going to fall through?" she asked as she approached him from behind. He turned and saw her royal face: more wrinkles than he remembered, the corners of her mouth branching out. She was still awe inspiring, like the weathered wooden figure on the front of a ship. There was a creak and they both glanced down at the aluminum roof bowing under their combined weight.

"I never thought about it," August replied.

"No?" The sun was behind her. With the glare he couldn't see her eyes well. Was she angry? It wasn't possible to stand fully upright under the umbrella so he was stuck in an artificial bow. They stared at each other. He could smell her grassy lotions, and swallowed an impulse to offer his seat to her.

"Mother, how was your trip?" he said at last. "Would you like some water?"

"Child, what were you thinking?"

"Did you come back to scold me?"

"I came back to see if it was true. We couldn't believe what we heard." She was staring at his blue hand.

"Did Matheson find you?" he asked.

"What exactly are you trying to prove by muddling their heads?"

He tried to straighten up again but the umbrella kept him bent. "I want Papa to see this."

"Have you lost your mind?"

His guts kicked against his heart and when he opened his mouth he was nearly shouting again. "I'm cleaning up after you!" He knew he sounded like a child having a tantrum, his voice crusted with emotion. Still her condescension enraged him. "I'm bringing it back to what it was. Something simpler. Something good."

His outburst seemed to calm her. She threaded her fingers in front of her belly. "Z-trailer doesn't matter. Papa has their hearts."

"I'm just trying to do it right." He felt his legs shaking but refused to sit down. Stepping out from under the umbrella, he groped, hoping to hold on to the rim of cloth near his head. The sun sat like a demon on her shoulder, and he felt outnumbered. "I'm trying to fix my part in all of this," August said. "My Mull mother died six months ago. Did you know that? I have to get this right." Suddenly, he could open his eyes; her head had eclipsed the light. Had she done it on purpose, a small kindness?

"Is that where you went when you left? To find your Mull mother?"

"NeverMind."

"An initiate telling a Mother to NeverMind!" She moved past him in small, careful steps, touching him lightly on the shoulder for balance, then looked out at the Center. "This will break his heart, child. What am I going to tell him?" She pulled her robes under her to protect her legs from the hot metal and sat directly on the trailer roof. After a moment August sat down next to her, trying to imagine what she was seeing. There was noise on the ladder: Sister Chavez bringing iced tea in a precarious feat. She pushed the tray toward them and hurried back down. Mother Li and August sat in silence watching the initiates moving back to the fields.

As they drank their tea he tried to see her as a younger woman, marrying an army officer, her future growing like a sickness inside her. She said, "What are we going to do?"

"Is it cancer?"

"Benign neoplasm. I don't really understand the difference. Benign, but it's killing him." He saw her fatigue; she had been on the road for six months, mobile homes, hospitals. Papa was her husband. They had been a young couple. She had stayed loyal while the Army accused him of crimes and insanity, while he preached a new way of thinking. She had fled with him to the desert, helped him build his own world.

"Has he spoken?" August asked.

"You know." She imitated Papa pointing at a page in a book.

"With his voice. What is the last thing he said?"

"That was before we left, before you came back. He said 'Wait for August.' Maybe he meant the month."

Their smiles were like a sudden pair of birds lighting on a bare tree. She peered at him, interested. "I don't think I've ever seen you laugh," she said.

"I'm a serious person."

"Really?" They were both chuckling now. August felt light, *benign*. "So, August, the protégé, 'the one who understands,' you tell *me*."

He didn't know what to say. The sun began to set behind them, pulling darkness across the sky. The initiates moved toward the sheds, hanging up their tools and gloves. As the blue failed, the light in the high windows of the main-hall got brighter and the distant generator sent its lonely hum into the desert.

Mother Li's foot knocked her glass over the edge. It seemed to take too long to land, plenty of time to think, *the glass is falling.* Then they heard the shattering cough. They both watched the spot where the glass had disappeared, as if they expected it to climb back up.

August waved his hand. "Don't worry about it. They're down there trying to eavesdrop anyway." They heard whispers, someone moving around the trailer, then the sound of an initiate setting out for the main-hall.

Even in the failing light, August recognized Meredith racing across the sand. He felt his ease evaporate, but Mother Li's voice was still bemused. "A strange way you're running things," she said.

Meredith had to walk back to keep from spilling the fresh tea and with every step she took, August felt his breath leaving him. He wanted Mother Li to leave again. He wanted everyone to disappear so he could watch the sun set and wait for it to rise again in peace.

They heard her taking the ladder slowly, impaired by the glass that clinked against the rails.

When she stepped up behind them, the roof groaned and they froze. Mother Li took the glass carefully, then said, "Oh, Meredith! How are you?" August started to greet her but Meredith's face stopped him: she was ashen, her smile grotesque.

"Mother, Uncle. I'm fine, thank you."

"Good. It's good to see you. Now, before we all fall to our deaths—"

"How is Melody?"

Mother Li turned her back on Meredith and took a long swallow of the tea. "Of course, Mother Melody is fine, she's with the others. She says hello. She misses you."

"She said that? Did she say that?"

"Please, child, before this roof collapses—"

"When can I see her?" She was half-kneeling, hands knotted together in a double fist.

Mother Li glanced at August, rolling her eyes, then said, "When Papa comes back, of course."

Meredith opened her mouth but nothing else came out. There was a long silence as they all waited for Meredith's next question, then Mother Li said, "Child, please, Melody is fine. The other Mothers would never let anything happen to her. Have patience."

August didn't want to be sitting near her, didn't want Meredith to see them together like old friends. He stood and the roof gave a metallic yelp. Mother Li held one palm up to Meredith: the *do not fear* mudra and also, August saw for the first time, the Mull sign for *get out of my face*. She said, "Child, the roof. Please."

Meredith crept down the ladder. The ice clicked in the glass. August struggled to center himself as he heard Meredith running out toward the darkened fields.

"*Uncle?* You allow them to call you that? When did it start?"

"When is Papa coming back?"

"Z-trailer burnt. And your arm." She pulled a black and yellow cellular phone from her robes and held it out to him. "It's a direct connection. All decisions go through us from now on." He didn't take it. Her voice became pitying: "Okay, child. This is my fault. We shouldn't have burdened

you with this. Take the phone. It won't be too much longer."
She held it between them, waiting. He shook his head.

When the last of the western light was gone they
descended the ladder, bowed to the elders who were waiting
nearby, and entered the book trailer. Mother Li turned in a
circle. "Oh my…" The symbols had gotten so thick in places
that they overlapped into black briars with bright bits of the
original wall breaking through like moonlight. August
thought that if she saw what he was working on, she would
concede that he was on to something. She would have to tell
Papa, *He's outgrown you.*

She examined the walls closely. When her eyes fell on his
face again she looked sad. "It was too much for you," she
said. He shouldn't have let her in. She continued: "Where
has your mind gone? Ice cream? *That's* your plan? It doesn't
matter now." She put the phone in his blue hand. "It won't
be long."

He should have ordered the gates locked. His fingers tin-
gled and he felt himself getting closer to her without moving,
as if the room were shrinking. Meredith hadn't done anything wrong. Gagged and electrocuted. Papa's cum. Little
Melody. He squeezed the phone, trying to reduce it to ash.
They were face to face now. She was breathing quickly, eyes
wide. She touched his arm, trying to keep him from getting
closer, and he gripped her wrist hard.

"That hurts." She blinked quickly.

Close enough to bite her now, August thought he might
vomit.

He had pressed her against the wall. She looked at the
door, expecting help, then tried to assume the authoritative
voice: "Child, get *off* me."

If she saw how wrong it had all gotten, she would understand the changes he was making. She was being intentionally blind. He lifted the phone into her chin. She winced and turned her head away, trying to slide past him. They grappled and fell into the corner of the room, her hair spreading up behind her like fresh ink on the symbols.

She refused to look into his eyes, her chest heaving under his. Tears, gasps.

He whispered, "Tell him I've changed it."

She was weeping harder, maybe starting to understand. He tried to find her ear beneath her perfect hair to whisper, to explain it all again gently. She made a pathetic mewling sound and he stood up, wanting to die, wishing for an explosion.

She got up quickly, brushing off her robes, trying to seem nonchalant. When she went for the door he tossed the phone at her. "Tell him I'm changing everything." As she stepped out he realized he had forgotten to ask her if she knew about the helicopters; at the same time he understood that it had never mattered who had known what. He sat in the trailer watching the marks scintillate until he heard the Jeep engine rattle to life and draw away.

Papa,
The garlic is coming up well. No one has asked about you for months. They are beginning to suspect the truth.

You can come back. I think you know things won't go back to the way they were. I am atoning for my part. Even Ego sleeps at the foot of my bed.

Mother Li and I had a miscommunication. You

*might be the only one who really understands what
I'm doing. All sins will be atoned for.*

*Maybe Meredith wants to kill you. Will your
voice return if you apologize? It might be enough just
to give Melody back.*

*Have you noticed the mutters don't work out
there? They don't do a thing.*

August

P.S. I know that you never really escaped the war.

22

Two days after Mother Li left, Phoenix stopped answering the phone. Three weeks later the monthly shipment didn't arrive. August tried to get information from the other Chapters but none of the Movement phones were being answered.

August took inventory in the kitchen, deciding that if they went back to the old way of eating they could have two months of food. As he stood in the freezer counting the foil packages and slabs of tofu, he wondered for a moment if Papa had died. Would they be stranded in the desert like soldiers who didn't know the war was over? No, he was sure it was Mother Li's doing. He had no idea how long her punishment would last. He ordered the elders to keep quiet about the phones and left a note for the kitchen Sisters: "Shipment delayed—don't waste salt or flour. Or oil. Don't waste anything."

In the book trailer he placed a call to a Mull company. They bickered with him, insisting they couldn't deliver food to the middle of nowhere. He offered to pay twice as much and listened to "Für Elise" while a distribution manager was consulted. Another voice got on the phone, offering to take the account numbers. It took two hours to confirm that all three bank accounts had been frozen.

During morning mutter August took Brother Monkey aside and said, "Brother, I need you to distract them until I can figure something out. Make your jokes."

Monkey was stoic. "This wouldn't have happened—"

"We are not going back to the old ways."

"What choice do we have?"

As the simple mush was ladled into their bowls the initiates eyed August with a mix of confusion and disappointment. When they had all found their seats he stood behind the podium, raising his hands. "You must not cling to. ... The universe changes quickly. Papa wants us to eat like we used to for a little while." He knew what they needed to hear, the magic words that would make it all right: *This is a sign that the Great Days are near.* They would tolerate any insult for that lie. He couldn't make himself say it. Rebecca raised her hand. August ignored her. He said, "Go ahead and eat now, your soul must be flexible," and lifted his own bowl above his head to show them that it was full of something precious.

He wanted Meredith to sit with him on the roof of his trailer, hoping her company would ease his growing panic. She had left halfway through morning meal. Heading for the fields he spotted Brother Monkey and another initiate leaning in the shadow of b-trailer; as he got closer he saw it was Meredith. They were both startled. Monkey shuffled awkwardly away.

He could feel his eyes bugging. Had they been kissing?

Then he saw that she had hidden something pinned between her shoulder and the trailer. He had to push to grab it: the black and yellow phone Mother Li had offered him. *Direct connection.* He rolled it over, thumbing the rubber studs. "What have you told her?" he asked.

"August, I just needed to hear Melody's voice."

"When are they coming back?" he pressed her.

"She won't tell me."

"You know she's doing this. She's trying to starve me out. Why didn't you tell me?"

Meredith began to cry and August tried to hug her. She slapped his hand away, saying, "What am I supposed to do?"

Noon meal was beets over unseasoned couscous. August found Brother Monkey moving like a shadow against the main-hall. He was whistling while he coiled loop after loop of the hose, its tail snaking between the foot basins. When Monkey saw August staring he stopped whistling but continued to coil the hose, leaving a dark track on the soil.

August stepped on the hose. "What's the plan?" he asked.

"Do you mind?" Monkey tugged on the hose as if August had stopped his progress accidentally.

"How often do you call her?"

Monkey sighed, holding the bundled coils heavily under one arm. His thick eyelids drooped and August hated him for his composure.

"Every day? Twice a day?" August wanted him to drop the hose, wanted him to have to start all over again. "I thought you would understand. I thought you would like the changes." It made everything sound petty, as cosmetic as a new couch for an apartment.

Monkey stood still, ready to continue his chore as soon as August stepped away. "Brother, it's not *personal*."

"Personal? Who said personal? I never said that."

"You've just fallen off the path."

"Maybe I need redirection?" August said. "When they get back they'll bring Matheson and clear everything up?"

"You just took it too far."

"I did?" August grabbed the hose, jerking Monkey toward him. Monkey's back straightened, a museum model of human alarm, eyes lacquered in their sockets with a rim of white around the color. "I thought you liked ice cream. You're always talking about how you miss real food. What about Meredith? And Melody? Tell me this—" He pulled the hose again and Monkey took a reluctant step toward him, refusing to let go of the hose. "Did Papa ever take you into the trailer to give you his special gift? Did you ever see Matheson do his work?"

"You're just sick, Brother. Something was too much for you. Ego is opportunistic. He's been poisoning you."

"I just told you what was too much for me."

"The Great Days are bigger than all of this. How could you be interpreter and not understand that? It's bigger than your confusion and fear. Papa sees beyond all this. If we follow him we have to leave everything else behind."

"Don't preach to me."

"You're lost."

"Papa is *dying*," August said. "It's a tumor. *That's* the revelation." August kicked one of the foot basins. It didn't go far. He let go of the hose and Monkey began reeling it in, keeping his eyes on August.

August overturned the tub and sat on it. "When are they coming back? At least tell me that."

Monkey pulled the final length toward him and hung it on the hook. Its little surprised mouth vomited the last of its water and he stood, looking useless. "I don't know," he answered.

August couldn't tell if he was lying. The whites of

Monkey's eyes were too wet. August kept pushing: "Something. How is Melody? Tell me something."

"She doesn't tell me those things. I just report," Monkey said, turning toward the door.

August whispered, "Do you know about the helicopters?" He crooked his finger trying to get Monkey to come closer. "They were a hoax."

Monkey looked at his feet, saying, "She said to tell you, if you keep the initiates centered she'll be lenient when they come back."

Monkey went inside and August spotted a distant flock of birds coming over the mountains. He watched them moving closer and when they crossed over his head he listened for the sound of flapping but heard nothing. He knew Meredith would not come to his bed again.

Picking up the phone in the study trailer he was relieved to hear the dial tone still humming. He dialed the numbers before he could change his mind and listened to a distant ring. Then Jesse picked up.

"August! Where are you?"

"I'm here. Still here."

"My therapist asked what I would do if you called again."

"Therapist? What happened?"

"People go to therapy." She sounded shaky.

"Okay."

"I dreamt this last night, you calling again. Just like this."

"What did you say?"

"I don't really remember what we said, just that you called."

"No. I mean to your therapist."

"I told her I'd hang up."

August felt the door of his life closing and tried to stall it.

"You wouldn't believe the things… I thought I'd call my big sister."

"You can't do this. You don't understand what it does to me. I can't live like this, thinking every time it rings it might be you." Something shuffled and he thought she was covering the receiver.

"I wanted to say I'm sorry about missing the funeral. Things have been strange."

"You have no right. You just call expecting me to be here?"

"Where *would* you be?"

"That's not what I mean! You can't say you're sorry until you stop doing the things you're sorry for."

He pressed the phone tightly to his head with both hands. He imagined saying, *They call me Uncle*. Instead he pushed the desk chair against the door of the trailer with his foot. He wanted to lock himself in and listen to her talk. "Do you have a boyfriend?" he asked.

"You can't ask me questions! Don't you understand? I had to let you go. I have no family left." Something thumped and then he heard her weeping, a rhythmic explosion of air.

"Things are changing quickly—"

"I can't do this. Don't call again."

"Jesse, do you know what ever happened—"

"I love you, August."

"—to the bear suit?"

Crouched between the desk and the wall, August thought, *The onions will be ready to harvest soon*. They could do onion soup for a week. He went through the refrigerators in his mind again, trying to make the food stretch. There was no way around it. They had less than a month left.

It could have been contaminated fertilizer from the onion fields or perhaps someone on the kitchen staff didn't wash their hands thoroughly after using the toilet. The dysentery hit everyone at once. The toilet sheds were constantly occupied and the initiates resorted to using the foot basins, which quickly filled with soupy excrement. The tubs were tied with rope and dragged, sloshing, a hundred feet outside the gate where they were dumped in a growing marsh. Those who were well enough to walk were organized into teams, carrying water to the bedridden and sterilizing the kitchen.

On the second day of cramps and shitting, August lay on a cot near the bathtub, stumbling to Papa's private toilet every half hour. He kept the trailer phone nearby, ready to call a hospital helicopter if anyone drifted too close to death, checking the dial tone periodically to make sure it hadn't been disconnected. He was grateful that the little boys seemed to have only mild cases. It was horrifying to see how thin the initiates had become; after months of real food they had been reduced to their old wooden frames overnight.

When his bowels were wrung completely empty he rose and stumbled slowly toward the main quarters, his vision shimmering green near the edges. His body felt as ravaged as it had in the desert, yet Ego was not chasing him. It had been getting smaller, from a jackal to a hare to a rat; perhaps it had taken the form of a microscopic pathogen and caused this plague. He shook the idea from his mind.

He had seen films of ramshackle hospitals filled with

moaning soldiers. The smell and heat in the quarters had made it real: some initiates were on the floor, unable to crawl to the upper bunks. Many lay side by side, just within the shade near the door, to be closer to the basins. A heap of soiled sheets sat like a fetid monster in the corner.

Those who noticed him raised their hands as he passed, hoping for relief. He knew he couldn't cure them and didn't bother trying. Meredith was on her bunk wrapped in a wet sheet, shivering. He kissed her forehead. When she opened her eyes she smiled so widely that August was afraid the fever had hurt her mind. Then she said, "Well this is... interesting. Want some of my sheet?" He laughed and clutched his belly. Her smile drifted and he let her rest.

Brother Monkey was under his bed, pressing his face against the cool concrete. August tried to lean down to see him but felt too dizzy; he tried to crouch but that was too risky. Finally, he slumped on his ass next to Monkey's bed. "Does Mother Li know?" Monkey nodded. "If the shipments hadn't stopped coming this wouldn't have happened."

Monkey said, "You know that's not true."

August closed his eyes, leaning back against the bunk frame. He fell asleep for a few moments and was woken by a torrential urgency. He poked Monkey on the arm to be sure he was awake and said, "If it gets worse we'll need money for medicine and water. You'll have to... I'll need their cooperation."

Monkey nodded again and August lurched out into the sun looking for a place to shit. It was too far to Papa's toilet and there was a line of people waiting for the toilet sheds. The side of the basin was caked with feces and dust. A cloud of flies knocked against his face as he pulled his pants down. Three paces away another initiate grunted as fluid spattered out of him.

Swooning, August nearly fell into the basin and had to brace himself against the side. He winced, trying to ignore the human mud between his fingers. Reaching for one of the dusty rolls of toilet paper that lay in heaps between the basins, August heard a groaning in the distance. He wiped himself quickly and half-jogged to wash his hands at the hose near b-trailer. From there he could see it coming.

Some of the others had already spotted it and began shouting as the helicopter tore the air toward them. August pushed through the initiates who were clustering around him. He shouted: "Just get inside! Don't panic, close the doors! Help them up. Where are the boys? Hurry."

Once inside he waved them away and kicked Monkey in the arm hard, roaring, "What is this?" Monkey yelped, rolling deeper under his bed. The initiates nearby were aghast at this outburst. August ignored them and stomped on the metal frame. "Get up!" he barked.

The helicopter was right overhead now, buffeting the walls and sending sand through the upper windows, which hadn't been closed in time. The door kept opening to a sand-storm as sick initiates stumbled in while pulling their pants up. August kicked the bed frame.

From under the bed Monkey said, "Ego is stronger. You brought this upon us."

"Come out from there!" August roared. His stomach cramped again and he had to brace himself against the upper bunk. By the time the last of the initiates had made their way inside, the helicopter was already churning away. August turned in a circle to look at the coughing, wretched masses.

The stench was awful. August shouted, "Wash your hands! It's leaving now, everyone go wash off!" Then he sank to the floor.

Close to the ground he could see Brother Monkey's head in the shadow and said, "Did she tell you *that* was coming, you son of a bitch?"

23

When the color at the base of the mountain had begun to fade to rust, a nervous depression settled throughout the compound. The last of the sick were recovering. Food supplies had run so low that they had been eating increasingly bland bowls of carrot soup. A tiny pot of grain was cooked for the little boys at every meal though that stash was quickly running out as well.

August sat on the roof in the heat, holding the broom handle in his indigo hand, wondering if there were any desert plants that could be added to the soups—whether coyote could be hunted.

Then, finally, he spotted them in the distance, the plume from their vehicles obscuring the mountains. The initiates in the fields had not seen the dust flag. Their limbs rose and fell in a jerking peristalsis as they turned the soil.

The mobile homes rushed toward them flanked by food trucks with a Movement flag flapping above like a war banner. Then a cheer rose from the fields and August felt himself melting. He tapped the stick against the roof trying to gather his rage. But he felt only a pathetic relief. As the initiates swarmed toward the gates August longed to see his Mull mother alive, microwaving some prepackaged cheese meal, squeezing ketchup from a plastic bottle. He wanted to sit next to her on the couch, under the same blanket, while the television spread light against their faces forever.

The initiates were hushed as Papa was carried through the perimeter gate on a stretcher. August watched the scene as if from heaven. Mother Li followed, surrounded by an entourage of large, stern-looking men, Matheson among them. Then came Mother Jessica, Mother Star, Mother Monica—all of them, a parade of returning majesty. And there: Melody running with outstretched arms toward Meredith. Now, certainly, there was not a single thing August could do for any of them.

Even from this distance August could see that Papa was changed. He looked like a whittled effigy. If he hadn't been placing his shaking hands over the heads of the silent throng as he was carried past, August would have thought he was dead.

Then the doors of the food trucks opened. Slapping each other on the back, the initiates rushed to carry sacks of grain, beans, and salt.

Papa was carried directly to his trailers. From his rooftop perch, August listened as furniture was dragged around beneath him to accommodate the Founder. He sat in his chair watching the jubilant crowd dancing. "This is it, stand up," he said to himself. But he sat there until Mother Li herself clambered up to tap him on the shoulder. She said, "You'll be gone by morning. Pack your things quietly."

"I don't have any things," August said.

"I won't turn them against you, August. You've hurt them enough. Come to evening address and we'll send you off like a hero."

"I need to say goodbye to some people."

"Quietly."

"And I need to see Papa."

"You don't deserve it, but he would want to see you one more time."

She left and August stayed in his chair until the sun set. Papa was silent beneath him.

There was clapping as August walked into the main-hall. Mother Li stopped whatever she was saying to beam at him. He spotted Meredith in the back with Melody sitting on her lap. She was rocking her child, the girl ridiculously large in her arms. Had anyone ever looked so happy? Melody seemed to have regressed to an infant state, four fingers in her mouth. Meredith stroked her daughter's face, whispered, and kissed her forehead. If August stole a mobile home he could take them with him.

"Papa's transformation is nearly complete," Mother Li told the crowd. "Brother August was preparing you for the final push. Distracting you from missing Papa. He has been a loyal servant. Thank you, Brother August!

"Now we will begin the real work. August will head out again to begin seeding the good news outside. We might not see him again until the world is a paradise, so thank him now! Wish him luck out there in the vicious Mull world. Ego will set his sights on him and make him a special target—he might die. He is very brave. Our thoughts are with him."

Then they were singing for him. That was it. She had done it quickly, taken the reins without trouble. He thought about rushing back up to the podium to tell them that she was lying but the guards were there, Matheson was there, and what good would it do? She was being merciful, letting him just walk away.

He stepped out of the hall before the initiates could surround him. The western sky was muddy where the sun had dropped, the mass of the earth rolling between August and the light. *He might die.* If August began to make waves outside, she would simply tell the initiates that they had lost him in the battle, that he was dead or had become a puppet. Simple.

As he approached Papa's trailer, he spotted Mother Jessica sitting on the steps of the study trailer shaking her head. "What happened here?" she said.

August didn't know what to say to her. He was overwhelmed by the uncanny fact that Papa was in the bed where August had woken that morning. He wanted to burn the trailer with Papa in it. Mother Jessica watched him closely.

He said, "NeverMind," then opened the door.

It already smelled differently, stuffy and wet with Papa's breath as well as new hospital odors. The body seemed inert, long and thin under the single sheet. Even in sleep the right side of his face sagged against his skull as if gravity were pulling it from a slightly different angle. He looked like a potato left too long on a shelf. Something stirred his sleep and his mouth gaped open; the space where light and warmth and love used to be was now simply a black hole pinching open to suck air.

August touched the bony shoulder tentatively. Then more vigorously. Papa's eyes blinked blindly at the ceiling, then roamed until they fell on August.

"Papa, it's me. Do you know me?" The eyes closed for a moment and August thought Papa had fallen asleep; then they were fixed on him again. "I'm leaving. Can you hear me?" August squeezed Papa's shoulder. "You're being punished. If you ask for forgiveness, if you aren't stubborn, maybe God will let you live to make it right again." Papa's eyes rolled back toward the ceiling and closed; a wet rasping snore began to roll in his throat. August leaned closer. "Why did you order the helicopter on your wedding day?" August asked.

A voice came from behind, making August jump. Mother Jessica entered with a bowl of steaming water and a white towel thrown over her shoulder. She said, "When the delegates and visitors went back to their Chapters with a story about how the Center was attacked by the Army, donations tripled." Placing the bowl on the floor next to the bed, she whispered, "It's time for his bath. I'll give you five more minutes. I'm sorry you didn't make it, August. If it's any consolation I don't think it's entirely your fault. I think you were... misused. I should tell you that Mother Li won't be gentle anymore—she can find you outside. Please don't give her reason to."

"How long have you known about the helicopters?"

"The abrasive sand makes the pearl. The pressure makes the diamond. The polish makes the jewel. Papa does what's best for the Movement."

"How can you live like that?"

"If you really believed in what we do here, August, even for one day, you wouldn't have to ask that." She shook her hay-colored hair over her shoulder.

"What do we do here?"

"We share, poor August. We cooperate. No greed. No theft. We take care of each other. We're setting an example for the world. I'm sorry you are so lost." She turned around and shut the door behind her.

The sheet had fallen off of Papa's white fingers and

August looked at them, the wide bones still trying to show strength under the puckering skin. August had held Meredith where Papa now moldered.

"Papa, wake up." August tapped his shoulder again. Papa didn't open his eyes. Something moved near his hand and August watched an Ego beetle crawl from somewhere behind the bed onto the pillow. It lifted a slow leg and began a deliberate ascent up Papa's cheek. It clambered out onto the upper lip, its antenna waving over the crater of the mouth. It turned in a slow circle, its obsidian head looking across a great distance.

The trailer swam with unbearable currents. Suddenly August wanted Papa whole, healthy and strong again, to rise and make everything all right. The beetle took a single dancing step toward Papa's eye and, sensing August for the first time, raised its ass in defense. Then in a quick dash it dropped over the rim of the lips into the mouth.

August felt the strange course of his life moving in him as hot and inescapable as his own blood and he took a step back. The insect struggled out again and perched on the mottled cheek. August felt the door touch his back and groped for the handle. As the beetle tapped around the face, August saw a dark circle of urine spread over Papa's hips. He stepped out, ready to run, and forced himself to shut the door slowly in case Mother Jessica was watching.

The initiates were headed out toward the fields. August hid behind the main-hall until he saw Meredith and Melody walking out holding hands. He tugged on their shirts and they both turned, regarding him with expressions he couldn't interpret. Melody shook her mother's hand off and offered it to August. "Good luck on the outside, Brother. You have my blessing."

Meredith smiled weakly at him as if to say, *Kids!* Then, seeing something in his face, she began to shake her head.

He said, "We can take a vehicle. Right now. All three of us."

Melody turned to her mother, asking, "What does he mean?"

August stepped closer and took Meredith's hand. She was still shaking her head. "I think you needed out a long time ago. This is my life here. You know that. I'm not like you. I have to make this work."

"They'll start redirection again."

"I'll be careful."

"I can't leave you here. Please, Meredith."

"This is what I want. To be close to my daughter and my Brothers and Sisters here. I have you in my heart. Thank you for helping me sleep."

"For her sake."

"Don't you dare do that. Besides, he never touched her."

Melody groaned, "I'm right *here*. I know you're talking about me."

"She's my daughter, I can tell. Didn't you see him? Papa can't do that anymore. She'll never be redirected. She's a Mother. I appreciate what you tried to do for me, but Melody's back now, Papa's back, things are going to start rolling again. I know you have to leave—you've outgrown us. This is my home."

"I haven't outgrown you," August said.

"Don't be mad, I know I'm hopeless. I'm not like you. There's hope for Melody. She's young. She still has a fresh mind."

"Please—"

"Don't make this harder, August—I'm trying to be strong."

Melody shook Meredith's arm. "What are you guys talking about? Tell me right now."

Meredith pulled her in, hugged her, and whispered, "I have to see it through."

Melody regarded August from the safety of her mother's arms, then smiled again. "I saw X-rays," she said. "When he has a new body you won't have to be sad anymore." Then both of their faces changed and he felt a hand on his shoulder.

Mother Li held out a small canvas bag. "Water and food," she said. "You can't waste any more time here, Brother!"

He hugged Meredith fiercely while Melody tried to pull them apart. As he pressed his nose into her neck he thought, *This is it—we never had anything to give each other.* He was flooded with a mourning love, the kind of generous warmth that he hadn't felt since he was a NewFace. This sympathy spread to include Mother Li, so anxious nearby, who was only trying to keep things together, and out toward the whole struggling lot of them.

Meredith kissed him slowly on the cheek and at the same time slipped the black and yellow phone into his bag, then walked toward the fields holding Melody's hand. Mother Li began to say something. He shrugged her off and headed toward the perimeter.

As he passed through the gate he held his broom walking stick with his blue hand and slung the bag over his shoulder with the other. It was going to be a hot day. The keys would probably still be in the ignition of the mobile home. No, he was looking forward to the solitary walk, to being outside with nothing above him but the evaporating sky. Rising on a cracked slope, he stopped to look behind him at the Center, still looming, not far enough away yet to see with any perspective. They were in the fields, their limbs pinwheeling. Were they watching him go? They had begun singing one of the field songs. As he wondered if he'd miss those sounds, he heard Brother Monkey's voice mixing the prayer with a Mull jingle: *Tidex shines a light! Gets your family's clothes so bright!*

He decided not to look back again, though he paused to check if Ego was crawling after him. Nothing. It would be easy to find Jesse. He tried to imagine her face but could only see her as a little girl, running terrified toward the house. Even if she locked the door he would knock and take his time and she would hear the assurance in his voice: *The dog is dead. It's just me. It's just August.*